Dead Line

Brandy Walsh

Mansion on Main Publishing

Iowa

Copyright © 2017 by Brandy Walsh
ISBN 978-0-9987977-0-0
Mansion On Main Publishing, Iowa

To my family

ACKNOWLEDMENTS

To begin, I want to thank my editors, Cate Williamson and Emily Browning, two very brilliant individuals who were able to take a stack of papers off my desk and turn it into what it is today.

To my cover designer, Josie Clarke, who has this amazing ability to know what my visions are even before I do. I admire your creativity.

To my cousin and dear friend, Mike. Thank you for listening to me as this story unfolded, for letting me bounce ideas off of you, and for reminding me that the quickest way to fix my computer is to "reboot... reboot... reboot."

To my brothers, for being exactly who you are. I love you both. Now you're going to have to keep the boats docked long enough to pick up a book. Can you guys handle that?

To my mother, a beautiful woman who has always believed I could do anything I put my mind to. Thank you for being the practical voice in my life, even though I rarely ever do things that are practical. For being one of this book's first critics and enlightening me that it is perfect for the big screen. I know you're a bit biased, but I absolutely love you for it! And to Ken, for reminding me, often, to follow my dreams.

To my wonderful father, for also believing in me, for supporting all the choices I make in life, and reminding me to take the time to enjoy the dance. And to Sandy, for your added encouragement and support (and the extra push to get this book published) by ensuring me that you know you will absolutely love the book when you get the opportunity to read it.

A special thank you to my husband, for being so accepting of my obsession for writing and being happy with late suppers and tapping keyboards.

And to my children, for being somewhat patient throughout the writing process, for being the beautiful children I had always known you would be, and for making me proud each and every day.

To my beautiful daughter, my first critic, and the only person I know who has read *The Iliad & The Odyssey* in elementary school.

Thank you to my friends and extended family, for your valuable input. You have waited so patiently for this story to finally come out in print. I hope you enjoy the story as much as I have enjoyed creating it. If not, please be a great friend and lie to me.

Dead Line

The prison walls are soft pink, the same color for the last eighteen years. They are decorated with shelves, pictures, and academic awards. There is a window, a large rectangular bay window, with imaginary bars that trap me inside and a comfortable bed that helps me to dream of the world outside. Conservative clothing that disguises me instead of what I really want to wear; things that would make me feel beautiful. This prison has two wardens, successful people who say they love me, who say they only want what is best for me. Do they really know what is best for me? Do they think about what I want? If they only knew that these walls are closing in on me…suffocating me.

Chapter 1

Graduation

I could feel the frustration boiling inside; it was working its way though my body, burning my throat, and threatening to escape through the tears that welled in my eyes. I held the plane ticket in my hands. A plane ticket to Paris. I wanted to scream, to run. I wanted... anything but this. It was my graduation and this was their gift to me, to whisk me away to another country.

My parents watched from across the table with their tight controlled smiles. "We both have twelve weeks of vacation," Mom began, "and we thought this would be the perfect trip before you start college in the fall." She seemed so pleased with herself, which frustrated me even more.

I swallowed hard, trying to find the voice that had been lost somewhere at the breakfast table. "But—Jess is having a graduation party and—"

"Courtney," Dad interrupted, "you know we don't approve of parties."

I lowered my head and chewed at my bottom lip, as if that could deter the tear from falling. There wasn't any point in arguing with them; they were always right and I was still just a kid that didn't know any better, even though I was eighteen. I wanted to stay, just this one time, when all of my friends were having fun.

The untouched eggs on my plate grew cold and hard. I

picked at them with my fork, but I knew I wouldn't be able to swallow even one bite.

"May I be excused?" I asked.

Dad laid his fork on the table and eyed my plate.

"It's graduation," I said, "and I'm a little nervous about my speech."

"Yes, dear. Why don't you go upstairs and pack," Mom said. "We'll be leaving for the airport after the ceremony."

After scraping the eggs into the garbage disposal, I rinsed the plate and placed it in the dishwasher. I made my way up the wooden staircase towards my room, stopping briefly to listen in on the muffled conversation coming from the kitchen.

"We can't keep her from everything," Mom said.

"Well, for now, she's still not old enough, or mature enough, to make decisions on her own," Dad replied.

"She's a straight A student—valedictorian. I think she would make the right choices when it comes to—"

"When it comes to what? Parties? Drinking? Her friends? I don't trust any one of them—especially that Jordan. He's never going to amount to anything, yet she still insists on talking to him. And the girls she's friends with are—"

"Keep your voice down," Mom said.

I heard a chair scoot across the floor and I tip-toed the rest of the way up the stairs. They don't know Jordan like I do; they've never given him a chance. He's been my best friend since the second grade. He's not like other guys who are into cars and sports and girls. Jordan's different. He doesn't date or party. He doesn't drive his car up and down Main Street at night or hang out at the skate park. He works and reads and he paints the most beautiful pictures I have ever seen. They just don't like him because he's a guy. They just don't know him; they don't know any of my friends.

I walked to the vanity mirror and pulled the photo from it, leaving the scotch tape clinging to the mirror. It was taken at the beginning of our senior year; the five of us stood smiling, an image frozen in time, in front of our small high school. Our arms were intertwined like a chain link fence with me in the middle, Jessica and Kari on one side while Jordan and Bethany stood on the other. They were like a force field, protecting me from the elements.

I flopped down on my pink canopy bed and gazed at the red graduation gown that now hung like a fiery ghost from my closet door. Just last night I imagined it was the gown of a princess and I would be wearing it to the ball where I would meet my handsome prince. Now it is just another cover to shield the pain I feel, to trap the emotions, to hide me away from the rest of the world like my parents had done for the last eighteen years.

They were too old to understand.

I thought back through all of the times they've insisted on traveling somewhere. It was always when something important in my life, in any teenager's life, came up. During freshman year, the cute guy in my algebra class smiled at me every day, eventually asking me to the homecoming dance. Instead, I had to go to the city to some boring banquet my dad's company was putting on. And my sixteenth birthday…no sweet sixteen party, just a trip to the Botanical Gardens in Oklahoma City. My junior prom, a trip to Chicago to visit the grave of a relative I'd never even met. I remember staring at the small headstone, wondering why this person, who had never existed in my life before that day, was suddenly more important than me. My frustration created a tidal wave of emotions.

"Why do we have to be here?" I exclaimed with the same irritation I had in my voice through the entire trip.

Dad glared at me with scornful eyes. "We did not raise you to be disrespectful. It is not always about you," Dad said sternly.

"Maybe you should have had more than one kid then," I snapped back. I had never really spoken that way to them and I immediately regretted it when Mom started crying softly and hardly spoke two words to me the rest of the day.

That same weekend, we stopped at a house in the suburb of Chicago, to a home with a well manicured lawn, where the inside had never seen a speck of dust. The old, extremely religious woman that lived there had been so cold towards my mother, wondering aloud how my mother could set foot in that house. I felt extremely uneasy as this old woman glared at me during our short fifteen minute stay, as if I were an evil thing that had been spawned from Satan himself. The ride home was deathly quiet.

Even last month, the weekend of my senior prom, they insisted I spend it with them visiting college campuses. I've never had any birthday parties where my friends were invited, never been on a date. The cute guy from my Algebra class never spoke to me again. It's not that I'm even remotely attracted to any of the guys at our school. Most of them have very little ambition, avoiding any class that ends with the letters *"try"*.

Mom appeared in my bedroom doorway. "Have you started packing yet?"

"Couldn't we go tomorrow?" I asked. "Or next week?"

"Courtney, the plane tickets are non-refundable. You need to start packing your things or you're going to be late to your graduation."

I swung my legs over the side of the bed and sighed.

"Most people your age never get an opportunity like this, to visit such a beautiful city. You should feel fortunate," she said before she turned and walked away. The clacking of her heels upon the wooden floor echoed throughout the house.

Fortunate? Yeah…so fortunate to NOT have much of a life. So fortunate to NEVER experience a first date, a first kiss, to never do anything everyone else my age gets to do. My head was screaming with my unfortunate good fortune! I grabbed my pillow and threw it at the closet door, which made the graduation gown sway as if it was dancing…as if it was mocking me.

I stared at the digital clock beside my bed, watching the

numbers change. When the clock finally read 11:11, I made a wish. *I wish this vacation would go by quickly so I can move away to college and not have to deal with these people on a day to day basis.*

I pulled the two red suitcases from the back of my closet and laid them on my bed. I had no idea what to pack. I sifted through the bottom dresser drawer, grabbing mostly shorts, sweatpants, and a couple pairs of jeans. I opened the middle drawer, and without looking, pulled out several shirts. I did the same with the top drawer. I didn't have name brand stylish clothing like the other girls wore at school. It's not that I didn't want them; my parents said they were an unnecessary waste of money. I didn't think that was it, though. Once I borrowed one of Jess's sheer, plaid tops that she bought from Abercrombie & Fitch. It fit perfectly and looked really good on me. Mom, being the prude she is, gave me some lecture about looking modest, and Dad refused to allow me to leave the house in it.

I grabbed a few cotton dresses from my closet, folded them, unfolded them, rolled them up, unrolled them, then, finally, wadded them in a ball and shoved them in the corners of the suitcase. I picked up the stuffed green frog that Jordan had given me for my sixteenth birthday and placed it on top of the clothes. I turned and scanned the room, searching for anything I might have missed. I picked the frog up again, kissed it softly, which I did often, hoping some day a handsome prince would appear. *Childish? Maybe.*

Jess's ringtone chimed from the bottom of my purse, and as soon as I flipped open the phone, I could hear the excitement. "Courtney! Jeez girl, where are you? Everyone who's anyone is already here."

"I'm packing," I said, as I hugged the frog to my chest.

"No way! Where are they taking you now? I told you—last night. Didn't I tell you?"

"Yeah." I had hoped she would have been wrong, but my friends were onto my parents as well.

"So, where are you off to? I mean, Heaven forbid you go to a graduation party where there will be umpteen adults and no alcohol," she said.

"Paris," I replied.

"Paris?!"

I could hear the others echoing her in the background.

"Wow, Court—for how long?"

"Twelve weeks." I could feel the lump forming in the back of my throat again.

"Twelve weeks?! That's the entire summer! Well, that should be fun. Maybe you'll meet some drop-dead gorgeous French guy with black curls and mysterious bedroom eyes."

I laughed a little as I laid the frog back inside my suitcase. When I turned around, Dad was standing in the doorway, dressed in his stiff suit and tie.

"I'll meet you at the school, Jess. I've got to go," I said.

"Pack your camera!" she yelled into the phone before I flipped it shut.

Dad looked uneasy standing there. I could tell he felt uncomfortable coming into my room, like it was forbidden ground.

"Are you finished packing?" he asked.

I quickly zipped the suitcase closed. "Yes," I said, as I opened the desk drawer, pulled out my camera, and dropped it inside my purse, along with the photo of me and my friends.

He grabbed both of the suitcases and proceeded down the stairs. I slid the red gown over my head, letting it fall on top of my white cotton dress, and I stood, figureless, in front of the full length mirror. I used bobby pins to fasten the oversized cap atop my head, knowing that every time I turned, it would threaten to fall. In just three months I will be living in a dorm at Kansas State University where my parents won't be able to control my every movement.

I stopped at my door, turned and sighed. Twelve weeks. I had never been away that long. I had never been away half that long. Maybe this wouldn't be such a bad thing. I gripped my purse tighter, as if the picture inside was calling out my name. *I would miss my friends*, I thought, as a salty tear fell from my eye, resting in the crease of my lips. I wiped it away with the back of my hand and flipped off the light switch.

Dad locked the house up behind me and I slid into the backseat of the Cadillac.

Without turning around, Mom asked if I had my valedictorian speech.

"Yeah," I replied.

****

As we pulled into the parking lot of the school, I could see the entire graduating class all gathered into their various cliques. The jocks were all high-fiving or doing their testosterone induced chest slams with one another, a macho thing that made some girls laugh and giggle, while others, like Jess, Kari, Beth, and I, would stand back and roll our eyes. I had heard rumors on the last day of school that they were planning on wearing their birthday suites underneath their gowns and, from the looks of their bare legs, they might just follow through.

The cheerleaders, who were never very far from the jocks, had enough hairspray in their hair that I wondered how they would ever remove their caps. The Goth kids, with their black hair and various facial piercings, stood as far from the jocks as possible. The rockers were grouped together in the middle of the lot. There was a group of kids wearing military boots and I realized, after looking closer, that they were the ones who always wore the army coats and smoked cigarettes behind the school every morning. I could see the drama kids, one being the cute guy from freshman Algebra, were all wearing loosely knotted neckties.

I wondered if any of my classmates realized that it wouldn't matter in life where you fit in while you were in high school. Once

11

high school was over, the cliques would disappear. I imagine college would have some cliques but probably nothing like it is here. Where you fit in here could either make or break you. I'm not sure what clique my friends and I belonged to, if we even belonged in one. We all had something different about us. Beth was athletic, Jess was musically inclined, Kari, although very pretty and this years prom queen, could knock about anyone out with one punch thanks to growing up with three brothers, and Jordan was... artistic. I guess I was good at academics; what else was there for me to do?

I spotted the four of them. It was hard to miss Jordan towering so tall above everyone else. I pulled my speech from my purse and reached for the door handle.

"Courtney," Mom said before I could escape, "make sure you meet us at the front doors immediately afterwards. We don't want to be late for our flight."

"Yeah, okay," I said as I slid out of the car and began walking quickly towards my friends.

As I drew closer to the crowd; Jess, Jordan, Kari, and Beth came running towards me.

"Are you really going to Paris?" Jordan asked as he grabbed me around the waist, twirling me two feet off of the ground.

"I guess so," I said, feeling a little lightheaded once my feet touched solid pavement again. I looked back at my parents who were still standing, watching scornfully, by the car.

"Ya know, Court, you turned eighteen last September," Kari said. "If you don't want to go, just tell them."

I pictured Kari batting her long eyelashes and showing her dimpled smile to her parents and getting anything she wanted.

"I'll be back in August. It'll be different when college starts," I said as I looked at each one of their skeptical faces.

"We'll just have to throw you a secret party when you get back," Jordan said.

"Yeah!" Beth said as she bounced on the balls of her feet. "What do you think, Jess? It'll be perfect, a secret welcome back party!"

I could tell by the look on Jess's face that she was already making plans in her mind.

"You guys are really the best," I told them. Before I could say another word, the tears began to flow.

Jordan wrapped his arms tightly around me and I buried my face in his chest. I could feel the others huddling around, holding me close.

"We could kidnap you, ya know," Jordan said.

I let out a small laugh. "Would you really do that for me?" I asked after I had composed myself.

"Yep, that's just how I roll," he said.

I knew, and my friends knew, that I would board that plane and go to Paris.

****

13

Since it was a beautiful spring day with only a slight breeze, our graduation ceremony was to take place outside on the football field. We gathered just inside the back doors as Miss Cobberstone instructed everyone where to stand, like we hadn't learned the alphabet by now. Since Jess's last name was Nash, she stood directly behind me.

"Oh, look—the twins," one of the pom-pom wielding cheerleaders said as she passed by Jess and me.

We both sneered at her. It's not that we didn't like looking so similar with our blonde hair and slightly under average height. In fact, there was only one characteristic that was so different between the two of us; she had beautiful, emerald green eyes whereas mine were blue...not even a pretty blue, just blue.

My nerves were causing my stomach to ache as I clutched my speech in my hand. I looked back towards the S's where Jordan stood. He smiled and waved and I felt a little more at ease. Kari and Beth were towards the front of the line. Our class song, *'We Weren't Born To Follow'* played over the stadium speakers and, when the song ended, that was our cue to file out onto the football field.

I could see my parents smiling in the front row as we passed. They looked terribly out of place sitting between Mr. Edwards, the proprietor of the local tavern who drinks most of his profits, and Mrs. Smythe, the eccentric flower shop owner. They never really associated with anyone from town. Mom is too prim and proper and Dad is, well...hard to explain. Sometimes I think he would have made a good politician instead of a CEO of an insurance company. You never see him in anything other than a suit and tie and he's extremely meticulous. I swear, if he could plan his own death, he would, right down to the very last detail.

Our graduating class took their seats in the chairs that had been arranged on the field, everyone but me, valedictorian. I took my place up on stage with the superintendent, principle, and various other staff members. I tried desperately to smile, to appear as though I was paying attention to every dull word the principal was uttering into the microphone. As I scanned the crowd, I realized that none of my classmates were paying attention either. This was good because I could get through my speech without feeling scrutinized. As each name was being called, I counted the rows of chairs on the field. Six rows of twenty one. I watched as people fidgeted with their diplomas, whispered to one another, and football players kicked the seats in front of them. I listened to babies cry and siblings fuss from boredom in the stadium bleachers. And I knew, once it was all over, the town would be filled with excitement and I would be nowhere around…again.

When it was my turn to speak, I stepped slowly up to the microphone. Even though I had read my speech aloud a hundred times the night before, I couldn't remember the first word. I unfolded the paper, took a deep breath, and lifted my eyes…and realized everyone was waiting, staring, quietly wondering what the only daughter of two of the most successful people in town would have to say. I looked towards my parents, much older than everyone else's parents, sitting straighter and taller, and happy to keep me from the fun that would take place in our small town afterwards.

"Fate and destiny," I began, "Have you ever really considered the meaning behind these two words? Fate happens and you have absolutely no control, it's predetermined. Maybe it's fate when you fall in love. But what we do in life determines our destiny. When we make the choice to go to college, we are paving the way to our own future... where we will end up in life. We are the creators of our destiny. High school," I said, "is just the beginning of our journey. It's where we make friends—lifelong friends." I smiled at Jess, Jordan, Kari, and Beth. "Today we make decisions. Decisions about college, careers, life. Some of you will decide to stay in our community, while others will move on. Maybe there's more out there—outside of this small little town—more jobs, more opportunities. Some of you will follow the path through the woods that others have traveled, while others will cut down the underbrush and create a new path. But you must remember, it's not about how much money you make or how successful you are in life, it's how you live your life that matters most of all. And, although some of us may not see each other again until our twenty year class reunion, where half of the football team may have grown bald and half of the cheerleaders will have gained twenty or more pounds, we'll look back on our high school days and wonder, why all the drama? We are free to make our own choices, our own mistakes; we are free to follow our dreams, to—live. Our destiny awaits us. Congratulations, we finally made it!"

I fought the lump in my throat as everyone cheered and removed their caps, letting them soar as high as they could…everyone but me.

I made my way down through the crowd of people on the field, relieved to see the jocks in their shorts. Kari's boyfriend had his arms wrapped around her and Beth was scribbling her number on a piece of paper to give to the older brother of one of our classmates…and I suddenly realized that I might just be the only person here that is graduating a virgin, with the exception of maybe Jordan.

I felt my feet lift off the ground again as Jordan came up behind me. "Take plenty of pictures," he whispered into my ear before setting me down again. He draped one of his muscular arms over my shoulders and gave me a tight squeeze.

"I wish you could stay," Beth said.

Jess cut in before I could go all emotional on them again. "We'll see you soon," she said as she gave me a tight hug.

Soon. Soon would be in a few days, or maybe a week. Soon was NOT twelve weeks. This was an eternity. I embraced the rest of them before I left to meet up with my parents. My heart felt heavy as I was already missing my friends.

****

The car ride seemed to take forever and the lines at the airport took even longer. Every minute of idle time that passed made me dread this trip even more. I would miss Jess's gossip, Bethany's high-pitched laugh, and Kari's drama about her current boyfriend, Sam. Knowing her, she'd have a new boyfriend by the time I returned home. I'm going to miss Jordan most of all. He's so intellectual and deep; always talking about beauty and being a free spirit, something I wished I was. Instead, I was a puppet on a string.

Our first flight, which had been long and uneventful, took us to Atlanta, where, once we arrived, we sat for nearly an hour. At ten o'clock in the evening, once I was positive my friends were thoroughly enjoying themselves, we stepped aboard the second flight that would take us directly to Paris. Mom and Dad tried to talk about college and career plans with me but I either pretended to be so engrossed in my IPod or faked being asleep. They expected me to follow in their footsteps. Go to college, major in business, work my way to the top. They didn't know it but, I planned to take every literature class available, hoping some day to be a writer or journalist. The hours ticked by slowly and, because all I could see was darkness out of the small window, I found myself drifting in and out of sleep.

I startled awake, feeling as though I was falling into a black pit of nothingness. By now we had flown into daylight somewhere above the ocean. I gazed out the window, through the cloudless sky, and could see nothing but the brilliant blue below. The urge to open the escape door and jump overwhelmed me a time or two. I looked over at my parents as Dad read a *Money* magazine and Mom watched a young child in the other aisle climb all over his mother like a baby monkey would do.

By the time our plane touched down in Paris, it was one o'clock in the afternoon. I trailed behind my parents, much like the prisoner I was, as we retrieved our luggage. The jet lag was not helping my mood any. A tall man, probably in his late twenties, held up a sign with our last name. NACOAL. He was a quiet guy, with dark, wavy brown hair and a smile that would turn Kari's eye in a second. We followed him to the waiting limousine where he held the door for me like a gentleman. Of course I knew it was his job to be as polite as he could possibly be but I hoped, some day, I would find a man who would treat me like this…a queen.

As the limo made its way towards the condo that my parents had reserved for eternity, the driver, who spoke with the most sensuous French accent, pointed out several landmarks. Both he and my dad were deep in conversation about the sights we should visit during our stay. Although my dad appeared interested, I knew he already had our itinerary planned out down to the very last minute. I was sure he had spent months researching museums, art shows, operas, and whatever else that could fill every day of the next twelve…never ending…weeks.

I pulled the picture of my friends from my purse. I bet Jordan would love this trip more than I would. He's always talked about Paris and the beautiful architecture and how some of the best artists are French. He would fit in here, perfectly. I, on the other hand, couldn't stop thinking about being back in Kansas with my friends. My mind was off in another country, my own country, and how I should be having fun.

My parents seemed a million miles away, their voices too faint for me to make out their words as I knew I was drifting off to sleep in the back of this limo. Dreaming of being home would pass the time quickly, so I let the blanket of sleep wash over me.

Fate and destiny. Some believe they're one in the same. Is it fate when someone looks into your eyes and you just know that person is your soul mate?

Chapter 2

The Accident

"Wake up," a soft spoken voice said.

I felt an excruciating pain shoot through my leg as if it were being burned with a red-hot branding iron. My head had a freight train roar and it felt as though someone was crushing the inside of my skull with a claw hammer. My eyelids were too heavy to lift, no matter how hard I tried to see what was causing my body to scream out in agony. Maybe I didn't want to see. Maybe I didn't want to wake up. *Let the pain stop! Please...please just let me die.*

"Wake up."

I heard the soft voice again. Could it be my own sub-conscious trying to prepare me for what was obviously a horrific surrounding? I could hear people around me crying out for help while others were screaming in agony. There were sirens far off in the distance and a thump-thump sound overhead. I tried desperately to remember where I was. Why was I hearing a helicopter? Pain was pulsating through my body right down to the nerve endings in my toes.

"You need to wake up."

It was a male voice. I struggled to find the person who was talking so softly, so calmly, in the chaos that was obviously surrounding me on all sides. I could barely open one eye. My lid parted just slightly, enough to see him just a few inches from me. His hair was golden with a slight curl. His eyes were as clear blue as the vast ocean. As he came into focus, he smiled at me. I had never seen such a beautiful smile before in my entire life. He was gorgeous. My heart began to race as I tried desperately to open my other eye. And then he was gone…everything was gone.

****

As I struggled to open my eyes once again, I could tell I was somewhere else. The terrifying sounds had vanished, replaced with an annoying beeping rhythm and the strong smell of disinfectant. The more I strained to regain consciousness, the more the pain pulsed through my body. As my heavy eyelids opened, I could feel an enormous weight against my chest, crushing me. I needed to breathe but it was too difficult. My heart began to pound loudly, uncontrollably, as panic set in. I frantically scanned the room for someone, anyone, who could help me. My mother rushed to my bedside as my father ran for the door, shouting for a doctor.

The room began to spin. Pain was now soaring through my body and the annoying beeping rhythm increased its pace nearby. There was a lot of commotion as people moved quickly around the room; alarms emitted from machines beside me while doctors barked orders.

"Courtney, stay with us," Mom pleaded.

I tried to speak but nothing came out.

The images of my mother, the doctors, everyone began to

fade. A steady constant buzzing sound replaced the beeping noise in the distance.

"No!" My mother screamed.

A husky male voice shouted, "Clear!"

The room went black, the noise was gone, and the pain was gone as I felt myself drifting away again. Somewhere from a distance, I could hear the steady beeping sound.

The soft voice from earlier spoke into my ear, "You're going to be alright."

How calm he sounded. I could picture him in my mind again. He sounded like an angel. He looked like an angel. I didn't know why I was here. I didn't even know where I was. My body began to feel heavy, like a blanket of lead lay over me…and I slept.

****

The daylight seeped though the slight opening in the blinds as I opened my eyes. It seemed like a peaceful tranquility compared to the last time I had been awake. A whiteboard hung beside the door; Claire LPN was written with marker across it. Above the nurse's name, the date read August 9. *August ninth?* Graduation was May fifteenth. Nearly three months had passed and I had no idea where the time had gone. I reached for my throat, which burned terribly, feeling as though someone had rubbed it raw with very course sandpaper. I slowly turned my head to scour the room for any other occupants - my parents, doctors, nurses…him. Who was he?

There was no one around. The only sounds I could hear were

the machines beside my bed monitoring the rhythm of my heart. I lay there as I carefully tried to move each finger, toe, and limb. I found the more I moved, the worse the pain felt but…at least I could move.

When I tried to move my leg, a pain shot through it so profoundly that my back arched in agony. This triggered another dull pain that began in my temple and crawled across my forehead. I felt my forehead with the tips of my fingers. My head had been wrapped in gauze but, when I pulled my hand away, the tips of my fingers were smeared with blood. I twisted my body just a little to see if a mirror was in sight. The pain was excruciating so I lay back against the hospital bed and attempted to steady my breathing as much as possible. I tried desperately to remember the recent events that put me here, wherever here was, but the further I reached into my mind, the foggier the images were. What was the last thing I did? Graduation? Obviously I had some sort of accident, and memory loss, which I prayed would be temporary. Mom and Dad could fill in the blanks for me until I regained my memory.

I looked up as the door began to open. I was hoping it was the soft-spoken guy from earlier. My parents and an older gentleman walked in. I could tell he was the doctor by the stethoscope draped around his neck and a clipboard in his hand.

"I'm Doctor Andrews, Courtney." He smiled a broad, friendly smile before he looked down at the clipboard. "Can you tell me where you feel pain right now?"

I tried to talk but my throat would not let any noise escape. My lips felt dry and cracked. I wanted to yell at him that I felt pain everywhere; in every limb, in every joint, in every cell that seemed to exist in my body, but I couldn't seem to find my voice. My parents noticed me struggling and both were at my side, caressing my arm. Mom reached for the Styrofoam cup that sat on a wheeled stand beside the bed. She pulled out a long stick with a blue sponge attached to the end from the center of the cup. Water dripped from the sponge as she reached over and wiped it across my lips. It was going to take a lot more than one swipe with a tiny sponge to quench the dryness that had invaded my throat.

The doctor explained that my body had been through a great deal of trauma, but it was quite possible I would make a full recovery.

Quite possible...not definitely...? I thought.

"There will be some scarring. You're very lucky, young lady," he said with a smile. "You stared death in the face and he backed down." He said this as though it should comfort me in some way but instead, my stomach tightened like a knot. "You have a cast on your right leg, a knee brace on your left. There are many cuts and some extensive bruising. Your head—well—there will be quite a scar but it will be mostly hidden behind your hairline." He shook his head in disbelief. "You're just so extremely fortunate."

I felt like laughing aloud but I knew the result would be pain coming at me from all areas of my mangled body. How could he say I was lucky? I was in so much agony; death would come as a relief right now.

He turned to my parents and reassured them that I would be able to talk soon. In the meantime, he would have a nurse bring in a small whiteboard that I could use to communicate with until my throat healed.

"It's a combination of the injury she's sustained and the breathing tube. Just try to keep her mouth moist and I'll come in to evaluate her a little later."

At that cue, Mom brushed my lips again with the wet sponge swab. My throat was so dry; it felt as if I had been walking in the desert for months. A wheezing sound escaped as I tried to tell Mom I needed more water.

Once the doctor disappeared through the doorway, Dad returned to my bedside and stood directly behind Mom. Both of them looked so tired, as though they hadn't slept in weeks. Dark circles outlined their eyes as they stared down at me with weak attempts at a smile. I could see the worry in their eyes mixed in with lack of sleep. Mom leaned over me, lightly brushing the side of her face next to mine…an extremely careful attempt at a hug. Dad just stood there, staring. I felt a sudden need to know how bad I looked. What had caused me to lose months from my life?

I lay in silence, trying not to move; afraid any movement I made would give away the pain I felt. I could read it in their eyes, though. They knew…they knew how bad things were. Was the doctor serious? Would I live through this? Or, was he just trying to give me hope? Would I die here? I thought about my friends; when was the last time I saw them? It was graduation day. Would I ever see them again? I could feel a tear fall from the corner of my eye.

The door opened again and a beautiful petite woman in her late twenties walked in carrying a small whiteboard. Her smile was genuine. She had deep-set dimples in her cheeks and auburn hair that reached her jaw line. She seemed to have a bubbly personality, and her smile never left her dimpled face. Yet, her energy seemed out of place in the somber atmosphere.

"My name is Claire. I'm your nurse, but you can think of me as your best friend," she said as she leaned closer. "We've had a lot of time to get to know each other. Well, I've been telling you all about me," she said with a laugh. "I've just been waiting patiently for you to wake up so you can tell me all about you." Her smile and enthusiasm seemed contagious as I tried to smile back at her. It hurt to smile.

"Dr. Andrews says you might like to try to say something soon." She stopped next to the bed, opposite my parents, and slid the whiteboard between the mattress and bedrail. I followed her movements with my eyes as she turned to the recliner, grabbed a thick white pillow, and fluffed it up even though it looked like there could be no possible way to make that pillow any fluffier. Why did nurses always think pillows needed to be fluffed? She carefully laid the pillow across my legs, pulled the whiteboard out, and set it on top of the pillow. Clipped to the bottom of the board was a black dry-erase marker. She pushed a button on a control that gently raised the back of my bed, slowly enough that the pain was not too intense. She reached out and pulled the marker from the board, placing it in my open palm.

"Okay, Courtney, what's the first thing you would like to say to the world?" She smiled down at me.

There were so many things I needed to know, so many things I needed to tell them; the pain was intense, my mouth was too dry, and why was I here? As my hand shook, I began to write.

WHERE IS HE?

All three wore puzzled expressions on their faces. They looked at one another hoping someone would know to whom I was referring.

"Who, honey," Mom asked, "the doctor?"

I shook my head slightly and thought for a minute. His golden wavy hair, his flawless skin, the brilliant blue eyes. I remembered his calm voice. I didn't know what to write. I had no idea who he was. Silence filled the room as they stared at me in confusion.

I DON'T KNOW

"Maybe if you describe him, I might be able to tell you who he was," Claire said. "There are many attendants and residents here at the hospital."

How could I describe him, especially with my parents standing so close? He was breathtaking. I wrote the first thing I could think of that could even come close to describing him.

AN ANGEL

I waited in silence, looking from one to another, hoping someone had seen him.

Claire laughed. "Well, I'm not sure who you mean, although it wouldn't surprise me if you were talking to angels. Maybe it was one of the paramedics that brought you in. What a close call you had but, don't you worry, you're going to be just fine now."

I began to write again, although my arm was feeling heavy.

I HEARD HIS VOICE

"Well, it could have been Tristan," Clair said. "He's a paramedic who helped bring you in and he did stop by this morning to ask how you were. And, if you ask me," she said as she leaned a little closer, "he is a bit dreamy."

"Honey," Mom interrupted, "do you need anything for the pain?"

YES.

I had forgotten about the pain momentarily, intent on learning who this mystery man was. *Hmm…Tristan.*

Claire quickly set herself into motion. "That's what I'm here for." She smiled and quickly headed towards the door. "I'll be back in two shakes of a lamb's tail!"

I looked at Mom and began to write again.

WHAT HAPPENED?

"You don't remember, dear?" She and Dad both had a

concerned look on their face. "There was an accident."

WHERE AM I?

I knew I was in a hospital room, but this room looked different from the local hospital in our small hometown. There seemed to be much more commotion outside the door when it was opened… too much commotion.

"You're in a hospital. Do you remember your graduation gift—the trip to Paris?"

I fought through the fog that invaded my brain, trying desperately to remember anything since graduation.

At that moment, Claire came back through the door carrying a clear liquid bag and a syringe. After injecting the syringe into the IV in my arm, she removed the near empty bag from my I.V. pole and replaced it with the full one. Mom explained to Claire that I was having trouble remembering things.

"Oh," Claire smiled her dimpled smile at me. "It's probably a good thing you don't remember the accident. I am sure it was quite a traumatic event for you." She seemed to think that twelve weeks of lost time was no big deal.

My eyelids were getting heavy as Claire recorded readings from the machines beside my bed.

"She needs rest," I heard her whisper to my parents as they quietly made their way to the door, it softly closing behind them.

I scanned the room again before my eyelids failed and closed on their own. I lay still, listening to the sound of the machines. The pain began to subside as the medicine took over, leaving my body to relax into the mattress even though I felt weightless. I thought I could feel someone still in the room; but my head was too heavy to turn, and I couldn't seem to speak any words.

"Sleep, Courtney," was all I heard from the soft voice before I drifted again.

****

I dreamt of sitting next to a pond, the water still as glass except for an occasional ripple from a diving toad. He sat beside me on an outstretched blanket. I lay back, staring up at the blue sky, only an occasional cloud drifted by. He leaned over me, smiling. His face was beautiful, so perfect. For several minutes, he gazed down at me. He traced his finger around the curve of my face, lastly brushing it across the contour of my mouth. I waited for his kiss, longing to feel his lips against mine. My pulse intensified as he drew nearer. The feel of his warm lips and the weight of his body sent a sudden warmth that traveled throughout every cell. When he pulled away, a smile returned to his lips. I reached up to pull him close to me again. My lips parted to speak his name but nothing came. My eyes grew wide as his image disappeared and, once again, he was gone.

****

I awoke, slightly embarrassed by the fact that I had been dreaming, intimately, of a guy I didn't even know. He was so perfect though. I could still feel the tingling sensation throughout my body, left over from the dream. *God, there was something seriously wrong with me.*

My parents and Dr. Andrews were sitting in the room discussing my injuries. From the sound of their conversation, it appeared I was improving. From the intensity of the pain, I still felt like I was dying. The wounds to my head were not severe. The doctor's main concern was my right leg. There had been a great deal of blood loss but he was pleased with the improvement. I would be able to return home soon, maybe a week. It seemed that my heart rate was stable and my injuries could get more attention at home with physical therapy. It would take months to heal from the wounds but the prognosis was good. The doctor lowered his voice to a whisper that I could barely hear.

"With her memory loss she seems to be experiencing, it may be better if you avoid mentioning any details of the accident. Her body needs time to heal without reliving the trauma in her head."

"What if she asks?" Mom's voice was shaky.

"It's quite possible that she will remember over time but let it come to her. In the meantime, just ensure her she will be okay and the details are not that important. She needs to focus on her recovery."

I should feel happy about this conversation but the weight of my heart in my chest sank. I would never get the chance to talk with him. I need to know who he is, where he is from. I need more time. I worried, once I returned home, there would be no possibility of finding him again.

My parents came to the bedside, both smiling, obviously happy that I was awake and relieved at the doctor's words of reassurance before he left. I cleared my throat and Mom grabbed a cup of water that sat on the bed stand. I struggled to swallow even though the cool water felt good on the back of my raw throat.

"Honey," Mom began, "did you hear what the doctor said? You'll be able to return home soon."

I nodded, not quite certain that this was the news I really wanted just yet.

"Everything's going to be fine," she reassured me, obviously thinking I was more concerned about my injuries than finding out who he was. Her and Dad stood quietly beside the bed, either not knowing what to say or avoiding conversation for fear the accident details may slip out. "We're going to get a bite to eat while you rest some more," she said as she brushed a strand of hair from the side of my face. "We'll be back soon."

I smiled up at her and let out a weak "okay." It still hurt terribly to talk. I felt around on the covers and beside the bed for the small whiteboard Claire had left.

HOW BAD?

I searched their eyes, but Dad's head dropped to avoid my question. Mom smiled weakly before telling me that everything would be fine. I was left wondering how bad I looked.

I lay in silence as they exited through the door, listening to the sound of my own breathing. I hated hospitals. The odor was unique to every hospital I've ever been to. I had spent several days in one back home when I had a severe case of pneumonia. I had only been about seven years old but the memory has always remained quite clear. The boredom was the worst, followed by the sounds of the bedside machines, the nurses chatting out in the hallway, and the smell of disinfectant they used to sterilize the rooms. It was all quite vivid and no different in this hospital.

I closed my eyes, trying to imagine my bedroom. I could feel the warmth of my comforter, the softness of my mattress. I could imagine the numerous photos of my friends displayed on the vanity mirror. I envisioned the drawing that Jordan drew when we were in the third grade. It hung on the wall above my headboard. There were five of us in the drawing, all standing in a line, holding hands. We were inseparable friends, even back then.

I thought I could feel someone behind me, at the head of my bed. I listened carefully for any sound. Nothing. I opened my eyes and reached for the whiteboard.

ARE YOU HERE?

I wasn't sure if I'd get a response or if I had just imagined him there in the room with me. My heart sank as time seemed to pass by. I reached to wipe the words away with the palm of my hand when he whispered.

"Yes."

My heart began to race with excitement. I hadn't heard him

come in. I had been lost in thought. I wanted him here, close to me. I wanted to hear his soft voice, to see his beautiful blue eyes. I knew the heart monitor was giving my emotions away with the beeping noise picking up pace.

TRISTAN?

I wrote, obviously my hands were shaking after I looked at the penmanship. He moved to the chair next to the bed, sat down, and lowered his head. He remained quiet. I scribbled out another message.

STAY.

I couldn't believe I had written that, even though it was what I truly wanted to say. I didn't even know this guy, but I didn't want him to leave my side. He looked into my eyes after he read my message; a smile formed at the corner of his lips. He had one dimple that appeared in his right cheek when he smiled. *So beautiful.* His skin looked so soft; his eyes were so gloriously blue. As I remembered my dream, my heart raced again.

The machine that distributed the painkiller buzzed beside my bed as another dose drained into my veins. I wanted to stay awake. I needed to talk to him.

Just as my body began to feel heavy and I fought to keep my eyelids from falling, he replied, "I won't leave you."

****

I began to dream. This time I was dancing but not with my mother or father as I had done so many times as a child in our living room. I was dancing with him. He held me close in his arms. It felt as if time was standing still and the room was turning around us. His face brushed my hair. I could feel his breath on my neck. I was relieved that my first dance was with him. I had never experienced the awkward toe crushing dances that my friends loved to talk about, although I had wanted to. My parents disliked the closeness that young people displayed when they danced. They had always had plans in place whenever such an occasion came up. But, this dance with him was beautiful. There was no awkwardness at all. I could feel his heart beat against my chest. I felt so secure in his arms. This was the first time I had ever felt truly alive. He cupped the back of my neck with his hand and whispered.

"Courtney."

I looked up and gazed into his beautiful blue eyes, my lips parted to speak his name but nothing came out. In an instant he was gone and I was left standing all alone.

Brandy Walsh

Dreams are but mere fantasies, played out in the mind where we are the actors. If it is a good dream, we long to fall back asleep, to pick up where we left off, to see how the story unfolds. If it is a bad dream, we fight to stay awake; we lay in fear of what our minds will reveal to us. But that is all they are…just dreams.

Chapter 3

The Hospital

I continued to recover slowly. My throat was still hoarse and scratchy but the raw feeling had subsided. For the last several days, I had drifted in and out of consciousness, most likely due to the pain medication that flowed through my veins. I welcomed the buzzing sound the machine gave off each time a dose of morphine was distributed. The pain in my leg had a habit of waking me as the medication wore off. Several times I thought I sensed him beside my bed, although I did not hear him speak. Still, it was comforting to know he was there.

He never seemed to come to my room when my parents were around. In a way, I was relieved. I dreaded the confrontation this would cause. My parents spent many hours in my room each day, just sitting quietly. By 7:00 P.M. each night they would leave; I imagined to eat supper and return to their hotel room. I guess their 6:00 suppertime could be altered after all. It took a near death accident to do it, though. A nurse usually came in soon after with a pill to help me sleep; they said I was restless at night. I thought about him often and dreamt of him every time I closed my eyes.

Five days had passed since I first awoke in this room. The date on the nurse's board read August fourteenth. Mom and Dad had already left for the evening and Claire brought me the nightly sleeping pill. She filled the water jug beside the bed and talked for a few minutes before leaving to care for her other patients. I lay quietly, thinking about what the doctor had said. "It'll take months of recovery." Anger filled me. I had been looking forward to attending college, looking forward to the freedom. I wanted to meet new people, attend college parties, sporting events. Whatever had happened to me now stood in my way of freedom. I fought back tears behind my closed eyelids. The machine buzzed beside me and another dose of morphine would soon dry up the tears.

"Are you in pain?" he asked softly.

Again, I hadn't heard him come in. His beautiful voice sounded so caring and full of concern. I opened my eyes to see him standing next to the bed. A tear escaped as I tried to smile.

"No," I lied, but that wasn't why I was crying anyway.

"Will you tell me what's wrong?"

I wanted desperately to tell him what was bothering me. I wanted to tell him how confined I'd felt in my own home, never doing anything wrong, never getting into trouble, never being able to spread my wings. I wanted to tell him how angry I was, now that I wouldn't be able to go away to college. I wanted to tell him everything but... it all sounded so childish.

I studied his face, his eyes...so blue. My head began to feel heavy as the medicine worked its way through my body. I fought to stay awake, just to talk to him, just to hear his voice.

"I want to be free," I said softly as I drifted off to sleep.

Several times I awoke to see him standing next to me. I

suppressed the urge to reach out and touch his face. I didn't know anything about him. All I knew was that I wanted him to stay.

****

When morning arrived, my parents were already beside my bed. Dr. Andrews was also in the room checking over my chart. "Good Morning, Miss Courtney," Dr. Andrews said when he saw my eyes open.

"Morning," I replied weakly, my throat still hoarse.

"Everything looks good. There are no signs of infection," he continued as he read the notes in front of him.

He pulled up a chair beside the bed and leaned back, crossed his legs, and laid the clipboard on his lap. "How do you feel about going home?"

I contemplated this for a minute. What was there to go home to? I was positive I would be confined to my home with my broken leg. I desperately wanted to see my friends again, but I wasn't sure how soon, or how often, I would be able to see them. My parents had never allowed them to come over. Jess, Kari and Beth would probably be busy getting ready for college. Jordan had other obligations. He cared for his sister when he wasn't at work. At this point, there was nothing to go home to and every reason to stay here... close to Tristan. I looked at my parents; both wore smiles of excitement on their faces.

"Look," the doctor began as he leaned forward, "I know you're still experiencing a great deal of pain but you shouldn't worry about making the trip home. A nurse will accompany you on the flight."

I nodded and tried to smile. He looked over at my parents.

"Why don't we discuss the flight reservations and the accommodations we need to make for the trip? As soon as everything is in order, you can take her back home where she can get the physical therapy she needs." He looked back at me and smiled. "How's that sound? You should only need to remain with us for a couple days longer."

My heart sank. My thoughts went directly to Tristan, his blue eyes and soft voice. I would only have two more days to spend with him, two short days to tell him goodbye.

"We can discuss things further in my office," he said to my parents as he rose. "Courtney, you rest up. You'll be back in your own bed in no time."

Mom bent down and kissed my cheek and Dad patted my hand before they followed the doctor out.

I closed my eyes tightly, trying desperately to fight back the tears. The door opened quietly. I had hoped it was him coming back to see me, yet I didn't want him to see me crying. Claire walked in and my heart sank.

"Did I wake you?" she whispered. She was carrying a tray of food in her arms.

"No," I replied. I wasn't feeling hungry but she insisted I eat something to gain a little strength before the long flight. I had never had a liquid breakfast before. Chicken broth, applesauce, and jell-o accompanied with a glass of milk. She sat and talked while I ate. The food actually tasted good, probably because it had been months since any flavoring had touched my taste buds.

I wanted to talk to her about Tristan; I was anxious to tell someone. But, I wasn't sure if she would feel concerned and tell my parents. So, I remained quiet. She was so bubbly, talking about her life outside the hospital, where she lives, and her pet parrot. She talked about the good-looking male nurse that works the night shift. I listened to her describe him…tall with dark hair. He reminded me of my best friend Jordan. A sinking feeling settled in my stomach as I realized how much I really missed Jordan. I was sure, if Jordan knew I was lying here in the hospital, he would have swum across the ocean to be here.

"Something seems to be bothering you," she said, bringing me back to the present.

"It's nothing," I replied. "I'm just missing my friends, I guess."

"I'm sure you do," she said with sincerity. "You'll be home soon. Until you leave, I'll come in as much as I can. We'll have girl time and just chat. How does that sound?" she said with her unique bubbly personality.

"It sounds wonderful," I replied as she stood and gathered up the breakfast tray. I was beginning to feel tired again. There wasn't much to do in the hospital but sleep. I could watch the television, but that usually ended up being background noise anyway. It was hard to concentrate on anything with the medication running through my veins. I wasn't even that sociable with my parents while they were here. It was difficult to think of new things to talk about since most of our conversations back home had revolved around college and career. College and career were now put on hold, at least for the time being. Usually we sat in silence; mostly I slept.

When Claire left, I closed my eyes and relaxed. Thinking of Tristan was usually where my mind went while I was alone. I pictured his beautiful blue eyes in my mind. I imagined his soft voice talking to me. I had never felt this way about anyone before. I had never longed to see someone so much. If only he lived on the same continent as me. Once I returned home, it would be as if we were worlds apart.

The door opened quietly and I opened my eyelids just enough to see my mother peering through the door. I pretended to sleep so she would not feel obligated to come in and sit. This must be as boring for them as it was for me. At least they could go places and eat normal food. It was a minute or two before the door closed again. I could hear the hum of the machine that distributed my pain medication. My mind wandered back to him and his golden blonde hair that shined in the sunlight of my dreams. I was tired so dreaming of him would pass the time away, yet too many questions lingered in my mind. Who was he? Why did he come to see me? Does he feel the same way for me as I do for him? Am I falling in love with him? I had never been in love before but the feelings inside me were intense when he spoke, when he smiled. The butterfly sensation I'd heard so much about, the fluttering in the pit of one's stomach, was so very real.

"You're not sleeping," I heard him say with a slight humor to his voice.

I opened my eyes quickly to find him standing beside the bed. I smiled, slightly embarrassed.

"What are you thinking about?" he asked.

Because I was uncertain if he shared the same feelings for me that I had for him, I was reluctant to share my thoughts.

"I'll be going home soon," I said, sadness clearly dominating my voice.

"And you don't want to go home?"

I could feel the blood rush to my cheeks. I had led myself into the conversation after all. How would I explain the reasons for not wanting to go home? Why would anyone want to stay in some hospital room?

"I live in Kansas, in the U.S." I figured the best thing to do was use brief answers, see what his reply would be. Maybe he would confess to me his feelings, if there were any.

"And—" was all he replied.

Okay, the brief answers weren't working because his were briefer. I bit at my lip. I would just need to come out and say it.

"I want to see you again," I blurted out. "I live so far away though." Now I knew my face must have been blushing like a tomato. I looked towards the door, hoping my parents wouldn't walk in at any minute. His eyes turned towards the door as well.

"Your parents have left," he said before turning back to me. "They went to the cafeteria."

"How—?"

"I overheard them in the hallway," he replied before I could finish.

I felt relieved that they were nowhere around.

"Back to wanting to see me again," he said with a smile.

My stomach did flips. I didn't know if I could elaborate on the discussion any further. I couldn't believe I had been so forward. It seemed like an eternity had passed but I couldn't build up enough courage to tell him how much I liked him.

"Would you call me—if I leave you my number?" I figured this was a simple question.

He waited for a minute before responding. "Well, I happen to be taking a trip to the United States very soon. Wouldn't it be better if I came to see you—in Kansas?"

My eyes widened, my stomach did several flips. He obviously had the same feelings for me if he was willing to travel so far to see me again. Excitement grew inside me. Yet, it quickly diminished when I realized my parents would never allow a stranger to visit, especially a guy. Why did my parents have to be so controlling?

"I don't know," I said. "My parents are strict. They never allow anyone to come over, not even my friends." Surely he could hear the sadness in my voice.

"Hmmm—Well, I imagine I could stay out of sight. I have so far," he replied, grinning.

"I don't really know anything about you," I said.

"Do I scare you?"

"No," I said quickly. I had never felt anything but comfort when he was near.

"It's settled then." He smiled. "I'll come to see you—in Kansas."

I could feel the pain medicine working as my eyelids drooped.

"When?" I asked softly, fighting back sleep.

"Very soon," he whispered. "You should sleep now."

I looked into his beautiful blue eyes before sleep overcame me.

****

The same beautiful eyes gazed upon me as we danced in the moonlight. There were no sounds, no music. We didn't need music. Our bodies danced together in perfect rhythm. I lay my head against his chest, content with life, just happy to be with him. Voices cut through the night. Familiar voices that made my body stiffen. I pulled back to see where my parents voices were coming from as his image faded away. I frantically looked around but I was left standing all alone.

****

"Courtney," Mom said softly. "Honey, wake up."

She stood next to my bed. I scanned the room, but he had left.

"You slept through lunch. It's nearly supper time," she said. I tried to reposition myself in the bed. "Your nurse is going to bring you something to eat. They've upgraded you to a soft food diet," she said smiling, as if this was some kind of huge accomplishment on her part.

"Great," I replied, not real certain if a soft diet would be any better than a liquid diet. The door opened as Claire entered with another tray of food.

Mom rubbed my arm. "We're going to go back to the hotel for the night. All the arrangements have been made for us to return home. We'll leave the day after tomorrow, first thing in the morning."

I didn't feel as depressed as I had been when I first learned the news. He said he would come to Kansas. I prayed I hadn't dreamt our entire conversation.

"Okay," I said before she smiled at Claire and exited through the door.

The tray that Claire carried had two covered plates on it. She moved the bed table in front of me, laid one plate on top, and lifted the cover; revealing mashed potatoes and gravy, what appeared to be pureed beef and noodles, and chocolate pudding. She laughed as I turned my nose up. The chocolate pudding looked appetizing but the pureed beef and noodles resembled something a baby would barf up. I watched as she lifted the cover off her plate, expecting to see something quite a bit more appealing, maybe a steak or hamburger. Instead, her plate was filled with exactly the same things as mine. My mouth dropped and I looked at her in astonishment.

"Why are you eating that? Why not a hamburger or something good?" I asked.

"It would be rude to eat a hamburger while you had to suffer alone with this," she replied as she lifted a spoonful of glop and let it slide back off her spoon and onto her plate. She pulled out a salt and pepper shaker from her smock pocket and doused her food with both, offering me the shakers when she had finished. I gladly accepted. The food wasn't so bad once it had been doctored with seasonings; which I was sure she smuggled out of the cafeteria.

She had finished her shift and wanted to chat like she had mentioned earlier. Girl time lasted nearly an hour as I told her about my friends back home. I really did miss them. I was eager to tell them about Tristan. They had always tried to fix me up with various guys, none of which appealed to me. This one was special though. He was handsome, better than any male model on the cover of magazines. He seemed sensitive but very mysterious.

By the time Claire was ready to leave, I was exhausted. I took the sleeping pill she had brought to me but I knew I wouldn't need it. Eating supper and talking to Claire had been the longest I had stayed awake since the time I had first opened my eyes in the hospital. Sleep came as soon as the door closed behind her.

When morning arrived, I couldn't recall any of the dreams I had during the night. I hadn't woken once to see him next to me, and I realized I missed him.

My parents were already in the room. Throughout the day, there was a steady stream of nurses checking vitals and preparing for my departure. My hair had been freshly washed and braided. Claire had used her lunch break to apply a fresh coat of nail polish to my fingernails. The attention was flattering.

The doctor stopped in several times to discuss arrangements with my parents. I could tell how tense my dad felt whenever a minor detail was changed. I had assumed things would slow down as evening arrived, but I was wrong. Mom and Dad stayed longer than usual as the nurses disconnected machines. Claire spent supper with me again. I slept some throughout the day but always awoke to either my parents or nurses in my room. By nine o'clock that evening, the room was empty of all but me. There were no wires hooked up to me, no needles in my arms, the annoying heart monitor sat silent. For several minutes, I listened to the silence. I really missed him. I watched the door, hoping he would walk through at any minute. It was hard to stay awake. My leg throbbed with pain. The pain pills I was now taking weren't nearly as strong as the liquid morphine from the morphine drip.

The clock on the wall read nine-thirty. I closed my eyes. Why wouldn't he come to tell me good-bye? This could be the last chance I would see him before I flew home. I could feel the sleep pulling me down. "Good-bye," I whispered.

From a distance I could hear his beautiful voice. "Don't ever say good-bye," he said softly.

Life is funny sometimes. You can stare at the second hand of a clock and swear it moves slower with each click. At other times, you're positive it has sped up, flying out of control. Life, for the last eighteen years, has been the slow click of the second hand. For the last several days, the second hand has been an unstoppable force, gaining speed with its mission to return me to my home...to my prison.

Chapter 4

The Return Home

Morning arrived quickly. I had lost my opportunity to talk with him last night. Claire pushed a wheelchair through the doorway as the doctor followed close behind. Mom and Dad had been in the room before I had even opened my eyes. Everything was happening so fast.

Two attendants came in to lift me into the wheelchair. It was painful to move but not unbearable. As my broken leg rested against the leg rest, I could see the swollen purple toes that peeked out from my cast.

"I should have painted your toenails," Claire said as she noticed me staring at my foot.

"Yeah, you could have painted them purple. It would have matched with my toes," I said jokingly.

She wheeled me down to the hospital entrance. "Take care, Courtney," she said as she leaned down and gently hugged me, trying to avoid causing me any pain. "I hope you find your angel," she whispered in my ear. I looked up at her, a little confused. "You talk in your sleep," she said as she set the brakes on the wheelchair.

An airport shuttle van was waiting at the curb. The driver came around to help my father lift me up onto the middle bench seat of the van. I noticed bright new luggage bags in the back. I tried to make myself as comfortable as possible but the seat was not as soft as the hospital bed had been and sitting straight up was extremely uncomfortable. I wasn't sure how far the airport was but I had heard planes fly overhead occasionally so I knew the uncomfortable ride would not be that long.

Claire stood at the open door to the van. "Thanks, Claire," I said. "Maybe if I ever get out of this wheelchair, I'll come back to visit you."

"Oh, you'll get out of this wheelchair. Someday soon you'll be dancing again and it won't be in your dreams."

I flushed, realizing I must have talked quite a bit in my sleep. I waved goodbye as she stepped away from the curb and the driver slid the door closed.

I instinctively looked around the parking lot to see if I could see him standing anywhere, but he was nowhere in sight. My heart felt heavy as if I would never see him again. Mom and Dad discussed the delay on college and how they had already spoken with the dean. Is that all they ever think about…my future? Like always, they had everything taken care of, everything planned. My life would return to normal. Except now, they would have even more control over when I would see my friends. I was sure they would never let me see Tristan even if he did travel all the way to Kansas.

I looked up at the hospital as we began to drive away. I caught a glimpse of someone looking out of one of the windows. It could have been the room I was in; it may have been him standing there but I wasn't sure. He said he would come to Kansas but I had this horrible feeling I wouldn't see him again for quite a long time.

A tear rolled down my cheek. I remembered graduation day. I had not wanted to come to Paris, now I did not want to leave. The airport was only a short, twenty-minute drive. The driver exited from the van and removed the wheelchair from the back. He quickly slid the van door open and helped Dad situate me in the wheelchair. I was not looking forward to the long flight home. I had another reason, now, to dread the flight.

People stared at us as I was wheeled past the long lines of ticket holders. They were having their carry-on luggage scanned as we were escorted onto the plane ahead of everyone else. It felt awkward getting the first-in-line privilege. I gave many passengers an apologetic look as airport security guards asked them to step aside. Eventually I lowered my head as we moved forward. The flight attendant escorted us to a section of the plane designed for patients to sit comfortably. Quietly we waited as the rest of the passengers boarded the plane and the pilot announced over the speaker that we would be taking off soon. I felt like I was leaving my heart behind. There was nothing to return home to. I had never felt this way about anyone and now I was leaving him. My parents were obviously exhausted, and they dozed off about thirty minutes into the flight. A nurse sat across the aisle from me. She was, maybe, in her mid-thirties. She looked much like the flight attendants, the beautiful model type.

"Are you doing okay?" she whispered to me, leaning across the aisle.

"I could use a glass of water to take my pill." I had felt the pain medicine wearing off somewhat and I'd rather sleep through as much of the flight as I could. She stood and went for a glass of water from a cart in the rear of the plane. When she returned, I took the Vicodin and reclined my seat. I closed my eyes for a few minutes before I heard his voice.

"Are you in pain?" he asked with concern. My heart began to race with excitement. I looked over at my parents who were resting so quietly.

"Not really," I replied, barely above a whisper.

His voice came from somewhere behind me. He was close, maybe directly behind me. I couldn't turn around to see him and this was discouraging. I wanted to look into his eyes. I wanted to see his calming smile. How had I missed him board the plane? I was the first passenger on, yet somehow he had slipped past me and took a seat directly behind me.

"You're smiling," he whispered into my ear.

"Yes. I was afraid I was leaving you."

"You should stop being afraid."

"But why?" I needed to know what had caused him to stay by my side this entire time. Just then, the nurse looked in my direction. The creases that appeared across her forehead showed her confusion. She leaned across the aisle.

"Why what?" she asked.

"I'm sorry, I must be dozing off—talking to myself." I was surprised she had only heard my words and not his. I was talking just as softly as he was. I was glad she didn't notice him there. She would surely tell my parents I was having a conversation with the guy behind me. She smiled and told me to rest.

He whispered behind me again. "Yes, you need to rest."

The Vicodin was beginning to have an affect on me. I suddenly wished I had waited to take the pain meds. A panic began to wash over me. It seemed that every time I heard his voice, I was dozing off or on pain meds. I couldn't be imagining him! But, no one had noticed him. No one had ever seen him enter my hospital room. The nurse couldn't hear him talking to me on the plane. It's like he didn't exist but only in my dreams, only in my mind. I felt a sinking sensation in the pit of my stomach. I had one more question for him but I couldn't ask as long as the nurse was listening.

"Do you think I could get an extra pillow?" I hated to sound like a whiney, demanding person but I needed to get her away, just for a minute.

"Of course, dear," she replied, before retreating to the back of the plane again.

I leaned my head back once I knew she was far enough away.

"Are you real?" I whispered.

Time seemed to slow down. There was no answer from him. Maybe he was a figment of my imagination. This one question could have made his image disappear forever. Please answer. My heart began to beat faster. I wanted to say it louder, in case he hadn't heard me. I needed him to be real. I held my breath as I heard a noise behind me. Someone touched the back of my head and I stiffened as the touch startled me.

"Sorry, dear. I didn't mean to scare you. I thought I would slip the pillow behind your neck for you."

I looked up at the nurse and my heart began to sink. He had not answered.

"Thank you." I smiled at her as she sank back into her seat. It was quiet once again except for the loud beating of my heart against the wall of my chest. I could hear a child talking to his mother in another aisle. He wanted his sippy cup, and he seemed to get agitated with her response. I tuned the child and his mother out and tried desperately to quiet my heart.

"Yes."

I exhaled a deep breath at his reply. With that one answer, I closed my eyes and slept.

****

I awoke once during the flight to drink a cup of chicken broth the nurse had prepared. Even it was abstract of any flavor whatsoever. Salt was obviously not a condiment this nurse used often when preparing meals for her patients. I looked around on many occasions and observed several passengers peering in my direction. They showed a look of pain, more like sorrow, when my

60

eyes met theirs. I was suddenly sure I looked deformed. How ugly I must appear to all the passengers on board. My mind took me home to my friends and their gossip. Jess had a word for people whose beauty appeared well below average. Gargoyle. I looked like a gargoyle. I lowered my face and salty tears began to stream from my eyes. I had never thought of myself as beautiful, although my friends would point out which guys were interested in me. Kari wished her hair would fall like mine and she searched the stores to find a color to match it exactly. Beth had always been amazed at how little make-up I wore. Jess swore I must secretly work out to have the slender figure I carried. I wonder what my friends would say now. I must look hideous. I reached up to brush aside the loose strands of hair that had fallen from my braid.

"You are beautiful."

Could he possibly know what I was thinking? I looked over at my parents to make sure they had not heard him. Dad was reading a magazine and Mom was resting with her eyes closed. He thought I was beautiful, even when other's stared at me in disbelief. Even my parents couldn't hold their gaze on me for very long. I still had gauze taped to my head. I knew one eye was still swollen. It was sore to the touch, which told me it was surely bruised. My lip would burn when I drank the chicken broth. I couldn't possibly be beautiful, but he thought I was, and honestly, that's all that mattered to me right now.

The nurse removed the tray in front of me and handed me

another painkiller. I swallowed the pill. It was still difficult to get the pill to slide past my tonsils. I wondered when I would be able to eat normal food again. I struggled to swallow one pill; I couldn't even imagine biting into a taco. I missed eating tacos and my mouth watered at the thought.

I tried stretching, but a pain shot through my side that interrupted that much needed stretch. I sank back against the pillow and closed my eyes. Escaping to my dreams was all I wanted to do for the rest of the flight. I could dream about lying on the beach with him or dancing under the moonlight. Every time I closed my eyes, he was there. He was not hiding in my dreams. He always held me close, whispering my name. His body was tone, perfect. Every muscle defined. His fingertips outlined my lips.

The pilot's voice filled the air and invaded my dreams.

"Good evening, ladies and gentlemen. We are approaching the Kansas City Airport and will be beginning our descent shortly. Please fasten your seat belts. I hope your flight was enjoyable."

The seatbelt light came on and there was a rustling throughout the plane as the passengers all obeyed the pilot's request. The nurse came to check my seatbelt, which I had not unfastened through the entire flight. Why would I? It's not like I could go anywhere.

When the plane touched down on the runway, the jolt shot pain throughout my body once again. I winced a little and Mom reached over and took my hand.

"I'm okay, Mom." I smiled at her to reassure her that it wasn't that bad. We waited as the plane slowed and came to a stop at the departure gate. The seatbelt light disappeared and the nurse rose to fetch the wheelchair.

Once again, the passengers had to wait as I was wheeled off the plane. I hated the attention I was receiving, but I was probably more anxious to depart the plane than any of them. My body ached from being still throughout the entire flight.

There were people waiting to assist us when we exited. The nurse stayed with us until Dad fetched the car, and two more gentlemen retrieved our luggage. I didn't see Tristan after I left the plane. There was a lot of commotion around us as people hurried to their next flight or to the luggage belt. As we neared the outside doors, I frantically searched through the faces. How would he know where to find me? My heart began to race again. I couldn't lose him now, at the airport. Our home was several hours away.

Dad glided the car to a stop in front of the doors and they began loading the luggage in the trunk. I sat alone, trying to turn. My palms began to sweat and I frantically thought of ways to stall until I saw him, until I knew he was following me. The pain was intense as the blood rushed through my body. My adrenaline was racing and a panic began to wash over me.

"I will not leave you, Courtney."

Nobody was looking my direction as I let out a sigh of relief. He was there, behind me, although I couldn't turn to see his face.

"Do you know where I live?" I whispered.

"I will."

And then he was gone. I was lifted into the back seat and we began the long drive home. I had gone to Paris. I did not have the opportunity to see any of the sights. I did not visit the Eiffel tower. I did not tour any of the museums. I did not take a gondola ride down the river. I found the man of my dreams. I didn't really know who he was or anything about him. The trip was worth it, even the injuries were worth it, as long as I had a chance to get to know him.

Brandy Walsh

For the first time in life, I proceed into the unknown. Everything has always had a plan. A plan for what to wear, when to eat, what classes to take, and when I'll fall asleep. It's frightening and exciting at the same time to, for once, not have a plan.

Chapter 5

Back Home

The drive home would be an uncomfortable three hours. I couldn't lie down in the backseat because, no matter where I lay, something hurt. I couldn't sit up straight because there was no room for the bulky cast in front of me. Sitting at an angle, resting against a pillow stuffed behind my back, with one leg draped across the seat and the other resting on the opposite floor mat as me, was the only spot in the entire car where I could sit without wanting to down the entire bottle of pain killers. Yet, in this position, there was nothing to see. I was directly behind Mom so I couldn't see the road ahead of me. Everything that passed by the side window went by so quickly that it was just a blur. I wasn't sitting up straight enough to see out of the back window, to whatever I was leaving behind; the only thing for me to look at was either my mangled legs or the side of Dad's head. I closed my eyes so I wouldn't have to look at either.

I had asked Mom after we left the airport if she had my cell phone, recalling I had slipped my phone in my purse before graduation. I could remember graduation day but I still had no memory of what had happened once we arrived in Paris.

"We'll have to get you a new phone," Mom said without turning around. "Yours was damaged."

I sulked in the back seat, wishing I could call Jordan.

Dad pulled the car into our driveway, stopping just in front of the garage door. It was routine for him to pull the car completely inside and punch the door remote before ever getting out of the car but, once again, routines must change. It was quite obvious that it would be too difficult to maneuver the wheelchair in such a tight area.

I craned my neck around, hoping to see one of my friends sitting on the front steps or a familiar car parked along the curb. But there was no one waiting. I realized my friends were probably totally unaware of my condition. Mom and Dad wouldn't have gone out of their way to tell them anything about my tragedy. Jordan probably assumed that I would return with stacks of pictures and memorabilia, which I had none of. All of my friends were most likely envying my travels as they've always done. Wouldn't they be surprised to see the condition I am in now.

Although I was exhausted, I couldn't wait to tell my friends about Tristan. Jordan would be the first one I would call. I didn't want to lie in my room the rest of the evening, so I asked Mom to grab the cordless phone and help me out to the back yard. After waiting through the numerous messages on the answering machine, most of which were left by those annoying telemarketers, Mom placed the cordless phone on my lap and wheeled me towards the sliding glass door that opened up to the back deck. Outside we have a beautiful gazebo set within a patch of full-grown trees. I've spent numerous hours out there reading, sometimes late into the evening. I was astonished to see a wooden ramp covering the stairs from the back deck and the steps up to the gazebo. Dad came up behind us, a large smile across his face. He traded spots with Mom and wheeled me down the ramp from the deck, guiding the wheelchair down the sidewalk and up the second ramp of the gazebo.

"I know how much you love it out here, and I didn't want you to sneak out and try to drag yourself up those steps. I had Bob McCarthy and his boy come over and build these ramps before we returned home. They don't look too steep, do they?"

"No, Dad. Thanks. It's perfect."

So there were at least two people in town that knew I was in a wheelchair. I wonder how much information my dad had given them. Probably none. I sat through a few minutes of awkward silence as they both gazed down at me. I fidgeted with the number pad on the phone before they turned and retreated towards the house, waiting as they disappeared inside before I dialed Jordan's number.

"Hello?" I heard the sound of Jordan's deep voice ask on the second ring.

"Hey," I said.

"Courtney! You're back!"

He made it sound like I had been gone for years. This trip was, by far, the longest I had ever been on and I was just as excited to hear his voice.

"You have to tell me all about the architecture there! I bet it was awesome! Did you see the Eiffel Tower?"

Leave it to Jordan to ask about architecture.

"I didn't have a chance to see anything," I replied. "Something happened."

"Wow, Courtney, what's wrong with your voice? What happened?" His voice changed from excitement to worry. Obviously, the news had not traveled through our little small town.

"I was in some kind of accident. I don't really remember it so it's a little hard to explain."

"Oh! Jeez, Court! When can you get away so we can talk?"

Jordan knew my parents all too well. Allowing him to come here would be out of the question. I knew there would be no possible way for me to get away for a while, though.

"I can't really leave," I said. "I'm stuck in a wheelchair. I'll try to explain about the accident tomorrow, but I wanted to tell you that I met someone over there."

"You're in a wheelchair?!" he hesitated for a minute before continuing. "Wait—you met someone? Who?"

I thought he would be a little more shocked that I was in a wheelchair, but I was eager to tell my best friend about him. I wasn't sure what to tell, though. Tristan hardly spoke. I wasn't even sure if he was even from Paris; he spoke English with a slight accent that I couldn't quite place.

"Well, his name is Tristan. He's a paramedic that helped me

after my accident. I don't know much else. He's perfect, though. You should see his eyes. They're so amazingly blue and his voice makes me melt each time I hear it. He was even on the same flight home. You know, I've never felt this way before. I think I might be falling in love with him."

It went deathly quiet on the other end of the phone.

"Jordan? Hello?" I looked down at the phone to make sure I had not lost the connection. Jordan was probably the only person I would reveal that last part to, at least for a while. Jess, Kari, and Beth would surely want to meet him immediately and I'm positive they would find him as irresistible as I did.

"Yeah, Court, I'm here. Wow, in love, huh? With someone you just met? Do you even know much about him?"

It did sound a little weird now that he said it, but I didn't have to know everything about him to know how I felt when he was near. Fate worked in mysterious ways.

I could sense someone watching me and I looked towards the sliding glass door on the deck. I expected to see my parents, but no one stood behind the glass.

"Hey, Jordan. I need to go, but I'll call you again soon."

We said our goodbyes. I looked around and caught a movement by the trees. My heart began to pick up pace. He stepped out into the opening and walked to the gazebo with such grace. I couldn't take my eyes off him. I worried about what my parents would say when they saw him out here. I was waiting for them to make a scene. I was sure Dad would come out threatening to call the police and have him arrested for trespassing.

"How did you find me?" I asked, speaking barely above a whisper. "I mean, I didn't see you following us."

"You didn't want me to find you?" He said this with a joking tone to his voice.

Of course I wanted him to find me. It's all I could think about on the drive home. He came up into the gazebo and sat on the bench facing me. We sat there in silence for several minutes. He continued to smile at me, never once focusing on my bandages or bruises. I felt so relaxed and safe sitting here with him.

"You know," I began, "some people may consider this stalking," I said with a smile.

"What do you consider it?" he asked in the same joking tone.

I blushed. My emotions were clearly showing on my face. I wanted him here. I liked him…a lot.

"I can go away—if you want me to," he said. "I don't want to seem too persistent."

"No! I mean—I want you to stay. But—"

"But?" he asked.

"I don't know much about you. All I know is your name."

He looked down for a few minutes while I waited. "There's really not much to tell. I'd rather learn everything I can about you. What do you do, in your spare time, when you're not lying in hospital beds in other countries?"

I laughed. "I want to tell my friends about you but I don't know what to tell them."

"I like what you told Jordan." He smiled.

My face flushed and I'm sure the color turned a tomato red. I didn't realize he had heard my phone conversation.

I did nearly all of the talking for the next two hours. The moon rose directly overhead and the temperature had dropped ten degrees. I told Tristan of my life here in Kansas, my friends, my dreams of things I wanted to do and places I wanted to go. He listened so intensely to every word, every detail of my life. I had always visualized my life as boring. Yet, he seemed so interested. It was interesting with him in it. Suddenly I began to feel like anything was possible. I could find love, despite the walls my parents had built around my personal life. There he sat, in my back yard, talking with me as if I was the only person in existence on earth. The light from the deck could not cut through the darkness that engulfed the gazebo. I felt free, safe; I finally felt love for the first time.

Mom and Dad emerged on the deck below the light. My pulse began to race, as I was sure they would see him when they approached. I turned to look his way and he was gone, just like in my dreams. He slipped past the trees as quietly as he had arrived. They wheeled me to the house and helped me climb the stairs to my room. It was awkward and painful and I couldn't wait for the day when this bulky cast could be removed. As I painfully made my way past the dresser, I caught a glimpse of myself in the mirror. I stood, shocked, gazing at the swollen, bluish yellow blotches on my throat, my face, and the rest of the exposed skin of my battered body. I did not look as bad as I first imagined, though. They were wounds that would heal...someday. I was not a gargoyle. There would be scars, this I was sure of, but I was not disfigured. I sat on the edge of my bed and continued to stare into the mirror. If I stared long enough, maybe I could will the bruises and scars to vanish.

"Honey," Mom whispered, "you're still very beautiful and everything will heal."

I looked up at her. I had never really heard her tell me how beautiful I was. It just wasn't something said in our house. We talked about schoolwork, college, jobs, but never about me being pretty. Whenever school shopping came around, I'd find a top that would accent my figure a little or jeans that fit a little snugger; she'd always shake her head. She'd comment if I applied a little too much make-up, even though the other girls at school wore twice as much as I. They rarely turned on the television because the commercials were selling sex. Now she told me I was beautiful, when I was bruised and swollen. Did the accident soften her up a bit?

I looked back at the mirror. They closed the door behind them and I felt alone. Tristan had left. It was too late to call my friends. My parents seemed distant or afraid to really talk to me. I wished I knew the details of the accident, but after what the doctor had said to my parents, I knew they would never come out and tell me. They may fill in the blanks if I recalled most of it but it would be useless to try to drag the information from them. I tried to remember anything, even the slightest little detail, but nothing came to me.

It occurred to me that my parents weren't hurt. Not even a scratch. We had gone to Paris on a vacation together, but why would I be apart from them? This is something I would ask them first thing in the morning. Maybe their answer could spark some memory of the events. I wasn't sure I wanted to know everything, but maybe whatever I did learn could help me understand why Tristan was now in my life. I knew I was falling in love with him. I knew I couldn't live without him.

I grabbed the glass of water my parents had set beside my bed and swallowed a pain pill. I was wearing shorts and a t-shirt and I decided that was good enough to sleep in. I lay back on my pillow, closed my eyes, and searched for the first memories that were hidden somewhere in my mind. Graduation day.

It was sunny and warm. Our graduation ceremony was outside. I remembered the sun feeling warm against the red graduation gown. I began to remember the feeling of disappointment. I would miss the parties. I had looked forward to the graduation parties. I remember the plane ride. The blue ocean, how blue the ocean looked from this view, like Tristan's eyes. I searched and searched through my lost memories but the next memory I had was his eyes, his face, and his smile. I remembered there being pain, an excruciating pain; but his presence calmed me, calmed the pain. Why couldn't I remember anything else?

My head began to feel heavy and sleep would surely fall on me soon. His blue eyes lingered in my mind.

****

His face was so beautiful, and now, so familiar. He ran his fingers through my hair, tucking loose strands behind my ears. His palms rested on each side of my face as he drew me near. His lips were warm and soft against mine. My heart was beating faster and my cheeks flushed hot under his hands. My legs felt weak and he wrapped one arm around my lower back and pulled me closer. I could feel myself passionately running my hands through his hair. I was in love with him. I gazed into his eyes. I could feel his hold on me loosening before he disappeared.

****

The morning sun shone bright through the curtains and breakfast smells rose up from the kitchen. I lay there remembering the dream I had last night. I longed for him to be with me. I missed him terribly. I missed his voice. I sat up in bed and looked at myself in the mirror again. I looked better. A night of rest in my own bed had done a world of good. Most of the swelling had gone down and I looked refreshed. I lifted the gauze on my forehead to observe the wound underneath. It was ugly with black stitches that reminded me of Frankenstein. My bangs would cover whatever scar it left behind, though. I looked at the small supply of make-up I owned and contemplated covering up some of the bruising that remained. I dabbed at the foundation and looked back at the mirror. I was startled to see his reflection staring back at me. Instinctively I turned, but my room was as empty as it was when I first awoke. I turned back towards the mirror and saw only my face staring back at me. Had I imagined him there? I dreamt of him so much, it wouldn't surprise me if my sub-conscious saw him while I was awake as well. I covered what I could with my make-up and called for someone to come help me tackle the stairs. I knew the horrible wheelchair would be waiting at the bottom.

The day was planned out and I dreaded being away from him. I was to see the local doctor about my leg and the various other injuries I had. I knew I would need to tell my parents about him soon. We wouldn't be able to sneak around behind their backs forever. It would be weeks before this cast could be removed and I wanted to spend my days with him, even though I would most likely be confined to my home. They had dreams of me attending college and becoming someone important. I had dreams of being with him, forever. I couldn't imagine going off to college somewhere and never seeing him again. I'm sure he felt the same way. I could see it in his eyes. I would think of something, soon.

****

The doctor's visit took longer than I had expected. He had scheduled more x-rays and I had read nearly an entire magazine while sitting in the waiting room. With the technology these days, I was sure my initial x-rays in Paris had been sent over the internet. I was relieved when he came out and called us into a consultation room. I had never really liked this doctor. He never spoke to me, always to my parents. This time was no exception.

"Well, Mr. and Mrs. Nacoal, it looks like Courtney's breaks will heal nicely."

Breaks? I was not told there was more than one break in my leg. I guess that would explain why the cast went nearly to my hip.

"The damage was extensive," he continued, "but after comparing the x-rays, it looks like she may make a full recovery."

"How long?" I asked. It felt awkward speaking up since he had never addressed me personally, but I needed to know and I wasn't sure whether my parents would ask this extremely important question. "How long do I need to wear this thing?"

His eyes did not meet mine. "Two months, maybe longer."

There would be no possible way I could stay home for two months. I would go insane. I imagined a few more weeks but not two more months!

"Are you kidding me?!" I yelled. I looked over at my parents, their mouths dropped open at my sudden outburst, and I turned back to him. "I am not wearing this thing for two more months!" I know I sounded like a spoiled child, throwing a tantrum because I wasn't getting my way, but two months seemed like an eternity in this hot, itchy thing.

"Miss Courtney, your leg had been crushed and several bones had…"

"Uh hum." My dad cleared his throat politely but I could tell his intentions were to shut the doctor up before he revealed too much. The doctor straightened and smiled at me. "The good news is that you've already grown to your adult height; and apart from possible mild discomfort later, you should have full use of your leg."

I stared at him. There was a question of whether I would have full use of my leg? My head spun a bit as I imagined never being able to walk right. I heard them exchange a few more comments about medication and therapy, but my mind was not absorbing the conversation. I sat in my wheelchair quietly as they wheeled me back out to the car. We made several stops on the way home; to the pharmacy, then the grocery store, and finally the cellular shop. Each time I waited in the car with Dad while Mom ran inside to get the things she needed before we headed back home.

"Mom," I said as we entered the house, "why weren't you or Dad hurt in the accident?"

She paused briefly, and then began pushing me out to the back yard. "It's best not to talk about the accident right now. It will come to you someday, and we'll cross that bridge when it does."

That was all I would get and I realized, no matter what question I asked, they would never willingly offer any information.

Mom had laid the book I had been reading before graduation

down on the bench, and she rested the new cell phone on top of it. I watched her walk back into the house, and I sank lower into the wheelchair. My own personal prison. The only connection I had to the outside world was this small cell phone. My friends would be enjoying the summer before going off to college somewhere. Swimming at the nearby lake was a favorite summer pastime for everyone in our small town. The only time I had ever gone to the lake was with my parents and I had to bug them continuously until they caved. I had never gone with my friends, though, so my absence would not affect them.

I picked up the phone, thinking of whom I would call, but the only person I wanted to talk to was Tristan. The news at the doctor's office had depressed me and I was in no mood to talk to my friends. Tristan would make me smile. The sun broke through the trees and I felt the warmth against me face. A tear escaped my eye and glided down my cheek. I tasted the salt as it soaked into the corner of my mouth. My life was at a standstill. Two months in this cast and God only knows how long I'd have to go to physical therapy. I would not be going away to college like so many others in my graduating class. Maybe the following spring semester.

"We really should stop meeting like this," he whispered in my ear.

I turned to see Tristan smiling as he stood up. My sorrow drained away instantly. I wanted to throw my arms around him and tell him how happy I was that he was in my life. That would have probably made me look a little too desperate, though. He sat on the bench in front of me and asked me about my day. I told him everything the doctor had said. I had thought he would seem upset that I would be confined to this house for such an extended period of time.

"You need time to heal." His smile was genuine. If he was okay only seeing me at my home then I was okay with it too. I enjoyed sitting in the gazebo with him. I was thankful it wasn't winter.

"I guess you're right. I just wanted to be able to do things, go places."

"But you have your whole life ahead of you. Don't rush it. I'm not going anywhere."

Where are you staying?" I asked.

"I found a place, don't worry."

That was all I needed to hear. As long as he was here with me, I could make it through the months of confinement. He asked about the school I had gone to and about the colleges I had looked into. He wanted to know my favorite color, favorite food, favorite music. He was so interested in my life. When I thought he ran out of questions to ask, he always had another one right behind it. I felt like I was the center of his world. I knew he was the center of mine. But I knew nothing about him.

"Tell me something about you." I asked, eagerly.

He leaned forward and lowered his head. I wanted to reach

out and touch his hair but he raised his eyes to mine. The expression on his face had turned very serious, and I began to wonder if something was troubling him.

"I didn't have a life before you. My life began the minute I saw you," he said.

It was the sweetest thing I had ever heard, but when I stared deep into his eyes, I thought I saw a hint of pain.

"I am happy to be here with you now, Courtney. You are my life. If I lost you, I would have nothing."

He leaned forward. I closed my eyes, knowing I would feel his kiss against my lips. My body felt warm and the rhythm of my heartbeat increased. I remembered his kiss from my dream last night, and I longed for his kiss now.

"Hey Court!" Jess's voice rang out from the deck. I opened my eyes and he was gone. I turned to Jess who was running down the walk towards the gazebo. The silhouette of my mother stood in the doorway.

"Oh. My. Gosh. You really look like hell." Her hand flew up to her mouth and she whipped around to make sure my mother hadn't heard. "Jordan called today and said you were in an accident," she said as she slid onto the bench seat next to me. "You've got to tell me what happened. I asked your mom but she really didn't have much to say. It's weird, though, because she just opened the door and let me come in. Can you believe that?!"

Yeah…very weird…my parents never invited any one of my

friends to come in. Mom smiled and waved before she disappeared back into the house. I scanned the yard to see where Tristan had went, but he was nowhere around.

I sighed. "Hey, Jess," I said as I hugged her. "Sorry I didn't call. It's been kind of tough since I arrived home."

"It's okay. I tried calling you a couple of times, but your phone was off; so I thought I'd attempt getting past your parents. It was really quite easy though." She laughed. My friends always found it difficult to deal with Mom and Dad. In fact, most adults seemed uncomfortable around them as well.

"So tell me, what happened? Did the plane wreck?"

"No, I'm not really sure what happened, and it appears that no one has any intentions of telling me." I knew my friends would try to help me remember what happened, but they didn't have any information to go on either. It was up to my broken head to figure the entire mess out. Even though I was glad to see her, I didn't want Jess to stay long. Spending more time with Tristan was higher up on my priority list. And if my parents had allowed Jess to stop by, I had to convince them to allow Tristan over as well. I didn't want him to keep running off the way he did.

"I'm getting kind of tired. Can we get together another time? It'll be soon, I promise."

"Yeah, Court, that's okay. But you know Jordan seemed a little worried about you. He said something about you meeting someone who followed you home. Is there something you want to tell me?"

I fidgeted with the book that was still on my lap. I was eager to tell my friends all about him, but I guess I was feeling a little selfish. I wanted to spend every minute with him, alone. I didn't want to share him with anyone else, not yet at least. Her eyes were pleading with me to reveal just a little information about this mystery man, so I caved.

"Oh my gosh, Jess," I said as I leaned in and grabbed her arm. "He's really wonderful! He has blonde hair, and his eyes are prettier than the sky; he's so handsome. I absolutely melt each time he looks at me." I pretended to fan myself, just to add a little more clarity. "He's built, like he works out every day. God—and his voice—it's so soft." I did a quick scan of the tree line. "He was just here," I whispered.

"So where is he now?" she asked as she looked around the yard. "Can I meet this mystery man? I mean, it's the first time you've ever talked about anyone like this. He must be someone unbelievable."

"Oh, he is. I don't know where he went. I want to introduce him to my parents, but I'm a little nervous." I knew she understood.

"Yeah, I would be too, but they seem a little different now. Your mom actually smiled at me when she answered the door! Isn't that just some crazy shit?!" She laughed, but maybe she was right; maybe they were a little different now.

I told her what I knew about Tristan, which was very little. I promised her that she'd meet him soon. She helped me get back up to the house and we said our good-byes.

I went to the kitchen to help Mom with supper. I tried to summon up enough nerve to talk to her about Tristan. I knew my life would be easier…and the days would pass by much quicker…if they knew about him and allowed him to come over.

"Mom," I looked up at her while she browned the hamburger, "I really need to talk to you."

It's funny how one tragic event can change a person's perspective on things. Ideas, beliefs, things that were so important one day can be so trivial the next.

Chapter 6

My Imagination

"It was great seeing Jess today. Do you think, because I'm stuck in this wheelchair, that more people could stop over?" I didn't want to use the age card but I was prepared to if needed. I am eighteen, technically an adult.

She lifted her head and stared out the kitchen window.

"Mom?"

"Of course dear." She smiled down at me.

Wow, that was easy. I didn't want to push it but I had to know if she'd let a guy come over. I was prepared for a fight, but what came next shocked me.

"What if a guy wanted to stop by, Mom? Would that be okay if we sat in the gazebo?" She looked up at the wall, appearing to see through it, not at it, like she was remembering some lost memory.

"Are you referring to Jordan?" she asked.

"Well, yes, I would love it if Jordan could stop by. But, I was hoping that other people could stop over too. I'm not going to be able to see many people now that I'm in this wheelchair, and since I won't begin college this fall, I would like some contact with the outside world."

She was quiet for a minute while she contemplated what I had just said. "I don't see the harm in that. I don't want any boys in the house though, especially when we're at work."

I was excited…more than excited. This accident had really changed them. I was beginning to think my injuries were the best thing that had ever happened to me. I couldn't wait to talk to Tristan.

Supper seemed to drag by; I was too eager to slip back out to the gazebo and wait for him. When we were done eating, I gathered the plates from the table, put them on my lap, and wheeled them out to the kitchen. The sink was too high for me to do any of the rinsing, but I was able to load the dishes in the dishwasher after Mom rinsed them.

"I'm going out to the gazebo," I said, as I turned and headed for the sliding glass door. I was learning to maneuver in the chair pretty well. The ramps off the deck and the one that went up to the gazebo weren't too awful steep that I couldn't handle them on my own, but Dad caught up with me before I made it out the door.

"Hold on. I'd really like you to build that arm strength a little more before you work on the ramps alone. I don't want you rolling off the deck and down into the trees."

I could see Tristan standing by the tree, but Dad had obviously not noticed him. Once Dad disappeared back into the house, Tristan came up into the gazebo.

"I don't know how you manage to go undetected all of the time, but you won't have to hide anymore. I talked to Mom; she doesn't have a problem with company."

He was standing directly behind me when he leaned down and

whispered in my ear. "She may have a problem with me."

I turned in my chair and looked at him, shocked by what he had said. There shouldn't be any reason why they would have any more of a problem with him than anyone else who may stop by. Except...I would have a hard time not staring at him, controlling myself from kissing him, never wanting him to leave. I may accidentally give it away that I was madly in love with him, and that would probably cause them to think I'd choose him over college...which I would.

I could introduce him as a friend, at least until I could move around a little easier. They would grow to love him; I would make sure of this. Hopefully.

Mom appeared on the deck, and I looked at Tristan. "Don't go," I said to him, nearly pleading with him.

"Courtney? Are you on the phone or something?"

"No, Mom. Why?"

"Well, I heard you out here talking."

It wasn't quite dark yet, and she could surely see him standing right behind me. I turned to look at him again, just to make sure he hadn't slipped away. My heart was beating a little faster, but I was determined to introduce him to my family.

"No, Mom. I was just talking to Tristan."

She continued to stare at me like I had lost my mind. I turned and looked at him as he watched my mom's expression. He lowered his head and gave me an apologetic look. I didn't understand what was happening at the moment. I turned back to Mom.

"Courtney, this isn't funny."

"What?" I had no idea why she was staring at me this way.

"There's no one here," she said. I turned and faced him again.

"Yes he is, Mom. He's right here! Tristan, say something to her."

"She can't see me, Courtney," he said.

"What? What is that supposed to mean, she can't see you? That doesn't make sense!"

"This is ridiculous, Courtney!" Mom's voice rose. "It's time you go inside and lie down."

"Why can't you see him?" I yelled.

Dad came running out the back door. "What's going on?"

"Dad, tell me you can see him!"

"Who?"

Panic washed over me; nothing was making sense. Mom and Dad began talking; and I looked up at Tristan, pleading for answers. Dad started to turn the wheelchair towards the ramp. I reached for Tristan, but my hand passed through his arm. My hands began to shake; my whole body was shaking. Everything around me began to spin.

"Courtney, I love you. I'm not going anywhere."

His face, the sky, my parents, everything began to darken and disappear.

****

I awoke on the couch with a cool washcloth across my forehead. I could see Mom standing next to Dad while he talked on the phone.

"Yes, Doctor, she insists someone was with her in the yard. Uh huh." A long silence. "Could the head trauma be that severe?" He was listening intensely to what the doctor had to say. "We'll bring her in first thing in the morning." I heard the phone lay back on the receiver before Mom asked what the doctor thought.

"They want to do a CT scan. The injury to her head may be causing her to imagine things, hallucinations."

My stomach felt sick. I couldn't be imagining him. He's real! He has to be real!

"I'll go pick up the prescription at the drug store, and then we'll get her up to bed," Dad said as he grabbed his car keys and headed for the garage door. He was only gone twenty minutes.

When he returned, I took the small pill the doctor prescribed, and Dad carried me up the stairs to my room. I pretended to fall asleep so they would leave me in peace, alone with my imagination. There were too many things going through my mind. I lay in silence, staring towards the window. Mom and Dad's conversation had played over and over again in my mind. "...*causing her to imagine things...severe head trauma...hallucinations.*" He seemed so real. I'd carried on entire conversations with him. If he wasn't real, I'm truly crazy. That's what my parents were afraid of, that I'd gone crazy.

What if I have? Could I be happy being in love with someone I created from my own mind? Tears began to roll down my cheeks. I would never leave my room again. I couldn't face the world when I had all the drama I needed right inside my own head. My heart ached like I had just lost the most important person in my life…my only true love.

I buried my head in my pillow, and I for the pill to pull me into dreamland. Panic washed over me again because I knew I would surely dream of him. I couldn't handle much more of this. I wanted him to be real. Maybe I had wished for him so hard that my mind had begun to believe there was someone really there.

"Courtney."

I turned my head to the side to see him sitting in the chair. He was leaning forward with his face buried in his hands.

"If you're not real, then go away and stop tormenting me."

"Courtney, I don't mean to torment you. I am real."

"Nobody can see you, though!"

"You can."

"That doesn't mean you're not someone I'm imagining, according to the doctor."

"But you're not imagining me."

"How do you know that? How am *I* supposed to know that?" My voice was getting more frantic, but I kept it low so my parents would not return. My head began to ache, and I felt the gauze at the side of my temple.

"I don't know how to convince you, but I will."

"Is your name even Tristan? Did Claire see you at the hospital?" I began to feel sick because I knew what the answer was.

He lowered his head again. "No," he replied.

"So who are you?" I asked.

"I don't know," was all he said.

Maybe the doctor was right. I had imagined him.

I lay there for a long time, staring at him. I was lost, my memories were lost, and now my future with him was lost. Tears rolled down my cheeks.

"I'm sorry," he whispered. "I should have told you they wouldn't be able to see me. I didn't want to scare you, though."

I studied his face, the crease in his brow that told me how sincere he was, the sadness in his eyes that begged for forgiveness. If he wasn't real, I had one extremely vivid imagination. I didn't respond to his apology for keeping this a secret. In fact, I didn't say anything.

I closed my eyes and dreamt.

Brandy Walsh

The mind is a mysterious thing: how it works and thinks, plans, and calculates. But when something happens, some sort of trauma, the mind can be your worst enemy. It gives you false hope; it makes dreams seem real and turns every day into nightmares.

Chapter 7

Tiffany

The visit to the doctor only confirmed my fears even more. He spoke of head trauma and pressure against my skull. I told him my head did not hurt that often. It hurt when I touched it or throbbed when I was upset, but other than that, it felt fine. Yet, I did the CT scan the doctor had ordered. Although the doctor viewed the CT scan results, he wanted a radiologist to look them over, which would take another couple of days. I dreaded knowing the truth, hearing that my own brain was creating him in my mind. I didn't want him to go away…to disappear forever. But I didn't want to be crazy either.

The ride home was filled with silence. I wanted to lock myself away in my room; no visitors, no phone calls, just me with my crazy imagination. I lay in bed listening to the murmurs of my parents downstairs. I knew they were discussing what the doctor had said. It would be a couple of days. In just two short days, I would know I was crazy. But the doctor would fix it, and I would be okay. He would be gone. But I didn't want him to go. I didn't want to live life without him. My heart began to ache again. Why couldn't he be real?

I turned on my side and looked towards the chair. He sat quietly watching me.

"Talk to me, Tristan. The doctor says I'm imagining you.

Please talk to me. I don't want you to go away, and I'm scared that this will all end soon."

"I won't go away," he replied as he shook his head. "I won't leave you."

He rose from the chair and lay down on the bed facing me. We watched each other in silence. I wanted to reach out and touch him. I knew my hands would not touch his flesh. I knew my lips would not feel his. I remembered the dream I had of kissing him. It was so passionate. I just couldn't believe I had imagined it all this time.

I closed my eyes and fell asleep, hoping he would still be there when I woke. I dreamt of us dancing again. He whispered such wonderful things to me. He had always hoped he'd meet someone like me someday.

When I awoke, several hours later, he was still there. He reached out to touch my face. Although I couldn't feel his touch exactly, I felt the sensation of it on my skin; so soft, so gentle. I was confused, but I knew I needed him. I needed him in my life forever.

My parents brought up my lunch, and then, several hours later, my supper. I was lost in my own world, but I was happy here. I was with him. The following day passed much the same way, just lying in bed talking or staring at one another. He may be just a dream, but he was my dream. I would cherish every minute I had with him…until the doctor made him go away.

Jess and Beth stopped by later that evening. My mother had led them to my room, although she knew I didn't want any visitors. They both sat on the edge of my bed, quiet at first; probably searching for the right things to say, maybe wondering why I've stopped calling them.

Jess mentioned her visit to the college and how her mother broke down in tears because her little girl was growing up. Beth told me about the new guy who recently moved in three houses down from her. "He is what I would call some serious eye-candy," she said as she fanned herself. I smiled at her spontaneous hot flash, and the mood felt a little lighter in the room, that is, until Jess asked about Tristan.

I lied and told her he had to go away for a few days. She had obviously filled Beth in about the love of my life, and they both couldn't wait to meet him. I didn't have the heart to tell them I was actually crazy, that I had imagined him all this time. Someday they would know the truth. I would have to tell them eventually.

After they'd left, Mom and Dad came in to talk. They had received a phone call from the doctor. It appeared there was no pressure build up. The doctor had discussed another possibility about the visions, though. My body was under so much stress that my mind was playing tricks on me. He recommended another medication, this time an antidepressant. They talked about spending more time together because the doctor was worried that I spent too much time alone. I didn't know what they expected from me. There wasn't a lot that I could do in this wheelchair, but following the doctors orders, they had rented several movies. Mom had even bought a few puzzles for us to work on. They had it all planned out...so prepared all of the time. They would fill *my* free time, so I wouldn't have time to imagine *him*.

Their plans had backfired, though. Every movie we watched, he watched with us as well. He'd either sit beside me on the couch or in front of me on the floor. In the evening, he'd lie next to me in my bed, talking about the movie. We laughed about the comedies, talked about the stars of the movies, and discussed which previews we liked. We'd make a list of other movies we wanted to see. Mom would gladly go to the movie rental place and rent what was on the list, thinking all along they were my choices and I was letting go of my imaginary guy. Although Tristan and I did not talk to each other during the movies, we talked for hours at night. I had somehow convinced Mom to put a folding table in my room for one of the large puzzles she had bought. I told her that spending every waking hour with my parents couldn't be healthy for a teenager either, plus, working on a puzzle alone would occupy my mind. Late in the evening, Tristan and I would work on the puzzle together. He would point at a puzzle piece and point to where he thought it would fit and I would put it in its place.

We spent every minute together. His image did not fade or disappear. In fact, we grew even closer. My friends stopped by often, and he'd sit next to me in the gazebo while they talked about boys, shopping, and school. They had asked about him on several occasions, having no idea he was there; but they eventually stopped asking. I imagined they must have thought he was like other guys; guys who say they'll call and never do. But he wasn't like other guys, and they would never get the chance to know that.

He even accompanied me to my doctor's appointments. It was strange having him stand beside me when the doctor asked his questions.

"Have you been having anymore visions?" he'd ask.

"No," I'd reply, trying not to smile because I knew Tristan was smiling right beside me. When we'd arrive home, Tristan would tease me about what the doctor had said. Several weeks had passed, and the bruises had disappeared. My injuries had all but healed and scars began to replace them. I had always worried that I would awaken some morning and he would be gone as well.

One evening, after watching a movie, a love story about growing old, Tristan and I lay in bed, quietly. It seemed that neither of us wanted to bring up the topic but we both felt it lingering. I broke the silence that surrounded us.

"Tristan—I wonder—am I going to keep growing older while you stay the same?" I could tell he didn't know how to answer. "What I mean is—if you're just—someone I've imaged, do you think I will imagine you getting older?"

"But I'm NOT just someone you imagined. I am real," he replied.

"But I don't know that for sure. I'm beginning to think you won't just disappear, but I can't touch you. I can only see you...and hear you. If you are real, then who are you? Why can't anyone else see you?" We had avoided this very conversation for weeks.

In fact, he seemed more real every day to me. We had spent so much time together that we had memories of our own. When he reached over to touch my face, I would close my eyes and imagine his fingertips lightly touching my forehead, my cheeks, my chin, then brushing across my lips. I knew he wasn't really touching me.

"I will prove to you that I'm not just in your mind. I'll find a way. Just, believe in me for now. Trust me."

I wanted to, I really did.

When the morning came, the day began as usual. We lay next to each other, saying our good mornings. I would manage to get into the bathroom to get ready before Dad would come upstairs to help me down for breakfast. This morning seemed different when I sat at the breakfast table, though. The mood was a bit quieter, and my parents watched with a little more intensity. When I had finished, Mom began to tell me about another appointment I had today. I couldn't remember having a doctor's appointment scheduled, but there had been so many of them, I may have forgotten. Dad had taken the day off work to drive us to the city. I hadn't yet seen a doctor in the city, and that made me uncomfortable. I slid into the back seat next to Tristan. He leaned closer to me to talk, not that he needed to.

"I don't feel good about this appointment," he said.

I looked up at him. I didn't feel good about it either. I was worried that my parents had learned something more about my leg. Maybe it wasn't healing properly. Worse yet, maybe there was something that a specialist had seen with my head injury. My head had been feeling fine, though.

We pulled up in front of a mental health center. My heart began to race. An aide from the hospital met us at the car.

"Mom, what's going on?"

"We're worried about you, dear."

"Why?" I began to feel sick.

I was wheeled into a meeting room where a doctor stood waiting for my arrival. He spoke slowly and directly to me.

"Courtney, it appears that you may still be having your visions, and your parents are very concerned."

I looked over at them. How could they know I still saw him? I never spoke about him when they were around. I never looked his way when we watched movies. I had been very careful.

"Honey, we've heard you talking late at night like someone is in your room. We just want to get you the help that you need."

"No! What are you going to do? Leave me here? You can't leave me here! Mom! Dad! I don't want to be here!"

The doctor nodded towards my parents, and they both stood to say good-bye. The attendant waited at the doorway with my luggage. A lump began to form in my throat, and I wanted to scream, but no sound would escape. I turned and looked at Tristan who stood beside me. He was just as shocked as I. Tears well up in Mom's eyes as she leaned down to give me a hug and kiss on the cheek. This couldn't be happening to me.

After they left, the doctor proceeded to tell me about the tests he needed to perform, the sessions I would need to attend, and the medications I would be taking. Although he was sitting directly in front of me, he seemed to be talking to me from so far away. I began to feel abandoned. The only person who still stood by my side was Tristan. He had always kept his promise. He would never leave me. But he wasn't real, and the doctor was determined to make him disappear…forever. I didn't want him gone; I needed him in my life.

"Tristan," I said softly as they wheeled me down the empty hallway. The walls were white, yet it felt like a dreary and lonely place. I turned to look for him, hoping he had not left me as well.

"I'm here," he said softly. "It'll be okay."

I had my own room. There were no pictures on the white walls. There was no window to look out, only a bed, a dresser, a chair, and my belongings. I was given the medication that the doctor had ordered. This made me tired. I lay on the bed while Tristan sat at the foot of the bed. I listened to the sounds of footsteps echoing down the hallway. Occasionally, a patient would cry out from another room. I was afraid to talk, afraid to say anything to him. I knew he felt the same way. If I was caught talking to him, they would surely keep me in here longer. Maybe I did belong here, but I still didn't want him to go away.

I slept most of the day. When I had awoken, the doctor came in to talk to me about my visions. He asked many questions, but I refused to answer him. Maybe I was being childish, but I wasn't ready to admit to him that Tristan wasn't real, and I didn't want to hear him tell me any different. I was happy. So I let him talk...then leave.

A nurse brought in a tray of food. She introduced herself as Tiffany. If I needed anything, I could push a button at the head of my bed and she would arrive shortly. I didn't speak a word to her either. I just lay there, staring at nothing. At least that is what they thought. I had actually been watching Tristan the entire time. He still sat at the foot of the bed. What was he thinking about?

When the nurse had left, he turned to me.

"Don't say a word. We don't know who could be watching. We'll figure this out."

I didn't know if there was some way that the doctors or nurses were watching, but I did what he said.

"I'm going to have to first figure out a way to convince you that I'm not just a part of your imagination."

I didn't think that would help my situation because the doctors and my parents would always be convinced that's all he was, a figment of my imagination. But I listened to everything he said. I wasn't sure how he would do this, but he truly believed he did exist in some form or another. Or, I imagined that he thought he really did exist.

"You can't talk or nod when I say something. Let the doctor think the medication is working. Let him think that I am no longer here. I don't want them to keep trying different treatments on you. It's not fair, what they've done to you."

A tear rolled down my cheek. He truly did care about me. If I wasn't already insane, I would surely go insane in this place.

He came over and sat on the floor beside the little twin bed. We were both prisoners in this place, but at least we had each other. This would be a little more difficult, though. I could not do any of the talking, and he had no past that he could talk about. The days passed slowly. Occasionally, the nurse would wheel me out to a large room that had a television set mounted high on the wall. I missed the evenings watching movies with him. The doctor would come in and observe me, but I left no hints that Tristan was always sitting close by. I never looked Tristan's direction when others were around.

Tiffany would try to make small talk. On occasion, I would answer her. She asked me about my friends or about the music I liked. She seemed to be in her early twenties. I learned that she had only been working here six months. She had a very friendly personality, so it was hard not to like her. I wanted to be angry with her, because she was just another person that wanted me to be a prisoner here. But I did like her. She talked to me like I was a friend, not a patient. She would come into my room and talk about her life. She had a small Pomeranian dog that she called Tinker. She carried pictures of him and showed him off as if he was her child. She went to church every Sunday. Her and her boyfriend, Daniel, have been dating two years. Someday they planned to marry, but he was attending medical school far away, and life was too hectic. I began to enjoy her daily visits to my room and I opened up a little more each time. I never spoke of Tristan, though.

The other patients in the hospital seemed much different from me. Some would cry out for no apparent reason, which scared the crap out of me if I was nearby. I quickly learned who to avoid. There were some patients who would just sit and stare; their blank looks were very eerie. I often wondered what they were thinking, if they were thinking at all. I wondered if they were trapped inside their own head with no escape. I felt sorry for them, living such a solitary life, talking to no one. Was this how I would end up some day?

I sat by the window in the television room, or dayroom as the staff referred to it, watching the birds flutter from the trees only to return to their same perch a few minutes later. It was quiet in the dayroom today. Several other patients were here as well, although the wall seemed a bit more fascinating to them than the birds outside. Tiffany pulled a chair up beside me.

The hospital had a pet healing day when staff would bring in small animals, such as cats and dogs. They called it therapy. Tiffany was excited to bring her dog.

"Most Pomeranians are a little high strung, but not my Tinker. He'd rather curl up on your lap and sleep." She smiled.

I was anxious to meet Tinker. It would be nice to hold a dog on my lap. I had never owned a pet; my parents thought they were a hassle that infested your house with fleas and chewed up everything in sight. Everyone I knew had some kind of pet. Jordan had a dog, Kari and Jess both had cats, and Beth had an obnoxious ferret that stole her car keys every night. She was always late for school because of him. We gave her a key alarm finder last year for her birthday, one that would beep when you pushed the little remote. We thought it was the perfect present but she went and lost the remote for it or, maybe, the ferret stole that as well.

The next day was pet healing day, and Tiffany planned to bring Tinker to my room by 9:00 A.M.

Tristan and I lay next to each other in bed that night. He spoke and I listened. He seemed to like Tiffany also. "There's something about her. She seems like a very genuine, trusting person. Maybe she could help us."

I knew there was no way she could get me out of here; it wasn't a power she had. Only the doctor could release me and that was only when he was convinced I was better. I closed my eyes and waited for morning.

I woke early and began to read the book my parents had left me. Tristan sat at the foot of the bed. He wanted to hear my voice, so I read aloud. He listened and smiled at times. I could tell he enjoyed the book as much as I did. I laid the book down after a while and rubbed my eyes. He began reading where I had left off. My eyes widened. I had not read the book yet, and I didn't know what would happen next in the book. Tristan read to the end of the page and stopped. He looked up at me and smiled. I turned the page and left the book lay on the bed. He read the next page. My heart began to beat faster. I wanted to scream with excitement. I wanted to reach out and grab him. He had to be real! I couldn't be imagining what was in a book I had never read, which meant...I wasn't imagining him!

I could hear Tiffany in the hallway talking with another nurse. She had obviously brought Tinker with her. The other nurse was telling her how sweet her little dog was.

"Do you believe that I'm real now?" he said as he smiled. "I told you I'd find a way to convince you."

"Oh, Tristan! This means I'm not crazy! How do we convince the doctor?" I whispered with excitement.

"I don't know but, for now, you need to keep pretending you don't see me. Someone's coming."

I shifted my eyes away from him and towards the door just as Tiffany entered, carrying Tinker in her arms. Tinker was so small and adorable. His tail wagged when he saw me, but his eyes moved to the end of the bed where Tristan sat. He began barking with a high-pitched yapping sound. Tristan looked at me and stood; the dog watched and barked as Tristan walked to the other side of the room.

"What's the matter with you, Tinker?" she asked, trying to turn her small dog towards her face. But the dog was squirming so much in her arms. She walked to the bed and sat next to me, petting Tinker to calm him. She placed him on my lap, but Tinker was too interested in Tristan. He'd growl under his breath, then bark his shrill little bark again. Tiffany gazed in her dog's direction and quickly looked back at me. Realization began to set into her expression.

"Courtney," she whispered, "is he in here—in the room?"

I looked at Tristan. It felt right to tell her.

"Yes."

Friends are people you can trust with your deepest secrets. They'll laugh with you, cry with you; they'll even lie for you.

   "Oh, what a tangled web we weave…when first we practice to deceive." – *Walter Scott*

Chapter 8
Valerie

She continued to stare intensely in Tristan's direction as if she were trying to focus on something. Yet, I knew she wouldn't be able to see him. She turned back to me. "I have rounds to make, but I'll be back as soon as I can." She gathered the little dog up in her arms with excitement. "Courtney, I believe you. I promise I'll be back soon. We need to talk." She looked again in Tristan's direction and smiled before she exited through the door.

"Tristan. She knows you're really here," I whispered with excitement.

"Yes, I think she does."

"What now? Do I tell her everything about you?"

"I think so."

I was so happy that someone else at least *knew* he was here with me. And, I was relieved to know I wasn't crazy. Tristan lay next to me on the bed while we waited for Tiffany to return. We didn't talk for fear of the doctor or another staff member walking by the open doorway. Tiffany returned just before lunch carrying two trays.

"Okay, I went to the kitchen and grabbed a couple of hamburgers, fries, and some chocolate cake for us. How's that sound?" she smiled. "You know, meatloaf was on the menu today," she laughed as she said this.

"Thanks."

"I thought I'd spend my lunch hour in here with you and—"

"Tristan." It felt strange being able to say his name, out loud again, in front of someone. I lifted off the top of the hamburger bun. She had put ketchup, mustard, tomato, lettuce, and onion on it. I took a bite and was relieved to finally taste seasoning again. I dipped my fries in the pile of ketchup on the tray. The food tasted so good. I had hardly eaten anything the entire time I'd been here. We both ate quickly and still had fifty minutes left of her lunch hour to talk.

"Tell me about him—about Tristan."

"I don't know what to tell. He's the sweetest person I've ever met." I looked at Tristan who stood at the foot of the bed. I could tell he was enjoying this.

"What does he look like? Is he a spirit of some kind? Can you see through him?" She had so many questions.

"Um—no—I can't see through him. He looks normal, I mean, he's just like you and me, but he's— (I whispered when I said this) gorgeous." He let out a small chuckle and I rolled my eyes. "He has blonde wavy hair. His eyes are such a pretty blue, like the ocean. He has a dimple but only in one cheek. He's perfect."

Tristan cleared his throat and I turned to look at him. "I wouldn't go that far," he said.

"Why not?" I asked him with a little sarcasm to my tone.

"There's the little problem with not being able to touch me."

"Yes. That does kind of present a problem." We both laughed at this and Tiffany gazed at me, amazed.

"What did he say?" She was eager to know the entire conversation.

"Well, he says he can't be considered perfect because I can't touch him."

She looked towards the end of the bed. "When did you first start seeing him?"

"I'm not sure, maybe when I had my accident. He stayed in the hospital room with me."

"So what is he then? A ghost? Maybe he's your guardian angel."

I looked back at Tristan, and he had a look of confusion on his face.

"Well, Tristan can't remember anything before he met me. He doesn't remember his name. I just call him Tristan because I thought he was someone else at first. We love each other, though." I looked back at Tristan and he smiled at me. "What does a ghost look like? Have you ever seen one?" I asked her; curious because I didn't think Tristan looked like a ghost.

"I don't know. I've never seen one myself. I'd always imagined you could kind of see through them, though." She thought about this a minute, then asked me about my accident.

"I don't remember the accident, and the doctor in Paris convinced my parents to let the memories come back to me on their own. He said it was too traumatic to push them."

"Hmmm…" She thought in silence for another minute. "There's someone at my church that I can talk to. Maybe she has an idea." She looked at her watch and gathered up the trays. "I wouldn't say anything to the doctor about Tristan. He wouldn't believe it even if everyone else in here did. He'd just think we were all crazy. You know doctors, there's always a logical explanation for everything." She closed the door behind her when she left.

Tristan sat down again at the foot of the bed. I waited for him to say something, but he remained quiet, lost in thought.

"Tristan?"

He looked over at me with worry on his face. "Courtney, Tiffany seems to think that I am some kind of spirit or ghost or something. Is that what you think?"

I sat there contemplating what he was asking me. I had been so worried that he was just part of my imagination, and I was finally happy that someone believed me. What if he was a ghost, though? What would that mean for us? I couldn't be without him.

"I don't know." I finally answered. "Let's wait to hear what this person at her church thinks. You're real and that's all that matters to me right now."

"But, if I'm a ghost—or spirit—or angel, how can you be happy being with me the rest of your life?"

"It doesn't matter what you are; I will be happy with you either way." I smiled at him as he lay on the bed next to me.

We spent the rest of the day in silence. Tiffany checked in several times before her shift ended. At five o'clock, she came in and sat down in the chair next to the bed. She had shut the door behind her, so I knew she planned to tell me something important, something she didn't want the doctor to hear.

"Okay, you're going to have a visitor tomorrow. Her name is Valerie. You'll really like her. She's excited to meet you and Tristan. I arranged for you to visit with her outdoors, in the courtyard. You should have a little more privacy out there."

I was relieved that someone could possibly give us some answers. I wasn't sure how long I could go on pretending that he just didn't exist. Even if I couldn't talk to my parents or the doctors, or even my friends for that matter, at least I could talk to someone.

After Tiffany left, the evening seemed to drag on like tomorrow would never come. I ate supper in the T.V. room. I was tired of being in the wheelchair, although I was getting around pretty good in it. I started counting the weeks that had passed since the doctor first said I would be in the cast for two months. I figured it had been about five or six weeks, but I'd need to look at a calendar to be sure. My leg itched terribly. At seven o'clock, my parents stopped by. We sat in an awkward silence for nearly an hour. My friends had been calling the house and stopping by on a regular basis. Rehabilitation for my leg is what I've been doing this last week. Like always, my parents had it all planned out. They wouldn't want people to think they had a crazy daughter. They had left me a new book to read and promised to stop by again tomorrow evening. I returned to my room and read the book aloud for several hours. I knew I would have to reread it later sometime because the words I read were not sinking in. I could tell Tristan's thoughts were somewhere else as well. He seemed so distant today. I had figured he would be happy that he was able to convince me he was real, but something seemed to hang over him like a dark cloud.

****

I awoke from my dream to the smell of breakfast lingering in the hallway and seeping through the crack under my door. I closed my eyes, longing to step back into the dream again. Tristan and I were walking along a beach, while the moonlight danced across the water. He held my hand in his, our fingers intertwined around each others. Our pant legs were rolled up to mid calf as we carried our shoes in our free hand. I had never felt this happy before in my life. Right before I awoke, he had turned to face me as though he had something to say. I needed to know what he was going to tell me. My body longed for his tender kiss. But I couldn't will myself to sleep, no matter how hard I tried.

I opened my eyes and scanned the room. I quickly sat up in bed, my heart pounding harder. Tristan was gone. He had been so quiet the night before. Maybe he didn't love me as much as I knew I loved him. I never thought he would leave, though. I had gotten used to waking up beside him. I leaned over and pulled the wheelchair closer to the bed. Frantically, I climbed in the chair and wheeled myself out to the hallway. I could see people in the dayroom gathering at tables to eat breakfast. My blood was pumping through my veins with such fierceness. I moved the chair forward, as fast as I could. Please Tristan, be standing by the window looking out. We had enjoyed watching the birds flitter from one tree to another on many occasions. I turned the corner when I reached the dayroom, but Tristan was nowhere in sight.

"Miss Nacoal?" A male voice from behind startled me. "Are you looking for someone? You seem to be in such a hurry."

I turned to see one of the male attendants standing in a doorway. "Um, no. Well, yeah, I was wondering if Tiffany was here today." I knew I had to create some kind of lie. He would never believe I would come rolling down the hallway with such speed for no reason.

"Oh! She is, but she's speaking with the doctor right now. She said something about bringing your breakfast, though. Are you feeling any better this morning?" he asked in a genuine sort of way.

"Huh?" His question caught me off guard.

"I'd heard you were feeling a little under the weather. Tiffany was worried about you. She said she thought you may need some fresh air; spend the day outside instead of being cooped up in here." He looked towards another doorway where a steady rhythm of humming had emerged. "I can understand—believe me."

"Oh, yeah. I think that would help me a lot." I turned to the sound of a door opening followed by voices.

Tiffany and the doctor emerged from the doorway. "Yes, Doctor. I will be out there the entire time," I heard Tiffany say before she turned and began to walk towards me. Another figure emerged in the doorway, and my heart jumped when I realized it was Tristan. He had been eavesdropping on their entire conversation. I was so happy to see him that I couldn't control the smile that widened across my face.

"Courtney, wow, you look so happy to see me," she said with a laugh. "Are you hungry? I can bring you something from the kitchen."

"I'd like that," I replied.

She took off towards where the breakfast smells were coming from, and I wheeled myself back to my room as Tristan walked beside me. Before I entered the room, I looked back down the hallway to make sure no one was watching. I spotted the girl in the room next to mine peering out from around her door. She quickly hid out of view once our eyes met. I closed the door behind me and looked at him.

"You really scared me," I whispered.

"Sorry. You were sleeping so soundly, and it looked like you were really enjoying that dream you were having. I do hope it was about me," he said with a sly smile creeping up at the corners of his mouth.

I felt the heat move to my face. My dreams were always of him. I couldn't imagine dreaming of anyone else.

"Anyway," he continued as if the blushing in my cheeks was confirmation enough, "Tiffany poked her head in the doorway this morning when she got here. It's weird, you know, because I know she can't see me, but she talked to me like she knew I was right there."

"What did she say?"

"Well, she said, 'Tristan, follow me.' I didn't want to leave you in case you woke up, but I was really curious about what she wanted me for."

"Well?" I was now just as anxious, if not more so, to know what Tiffany was up to. I leaned in closer to him.

"She had me listen to her conversation with your doctor. It felt kind of wrong standing there, but I was glad I did. I think she has him about convinced that you don't see me anymore." He smiled as he said this.

Just then, the door opened, and Tiffany emerged with a tray filled with pancakes and maple syrup. My heart was beating rapidly from her sudden entrance.

"Did he fill you in on everything?" she whispered after she set the tray down on the stand.

"Does the doctor really believe I don't see him anymore?" I asked.

Her expression beamed with delight. "So he did follow me!"

she exclaimed. "I wanted him to hear what I told the doctor, just in case the doctor asked you questions. Tristan can fill you in on the details. I think you will get out of here much faster if I help to convince the doctor that you're not seeing things anymore."

I was relieved she was on my side. I knew it wouldn't be long before I could go home now. I enjoyed Tiffany's company, but I really wanted out of this place. I quickly ate breakfast and got ready for the day. My visitor would be here soon. Tiffany wheeled me outside into the warm sun and took a seat on a bench next to where she parked my wheelchair. We watched the squirrels dart to one tree after another. It was entertaining to see them play amongst themselves. Occasionally one would stand and look towards us but our presence did not alarm them in any way. They did seem to keep a close eye on Tristan, though. One of the bigger squirrels would start chattering at him if he moved, and Tiffany thought this was quite funny.

"Tristan," she'd say, "They're cussing you out." We laughed at this. It felt so good to finally be outside.

Valerie arrived around eleven o'clock. I had half expected a very prim and proper church-going girl, but her wild flower-girl attire took me by surprise. She wore her long, black hair flowing more than halfway down her back, and she had several tiny braids with ribbons intertwined in them. Her clothing was colorful; she must really stand out in church. But she was friendly and full of life. She brought books about spirits and life after death. Her bangle bracelets, she had at least ten of them on each arm, clattered when she handed me the books.

"Usually," she began, "there's a reason they are still here on Earth. Your Tristan has some kind of unresolved issue. Once he is at peace with this, he will move on to Heaven."

I looked at Tristan who had taken a seat on the ground next to the wheelchair. He folded his arms on his knees and lowered his head.

Valerie, of course, couldn't see that this information was bothering him.

"Has he mentioned anything that has been troubling him?"

"No," I replied. "He doesn't remember anything about his life." My heart began to feel heavy. I didn't want him to go anywhere...not even to Heaven...at least, not yet...not for a long time. My eyes began to well up with tears. I swallowed back the lump that formed in my throat. "Valerie," my voice cracked, "how do we find out what is causing him to remain here?"

"Well," she began but paused again briefly. "This seems like a really strange case. What I mean is, most of the time the spirit knows exactly what is holding them here and they try very hard to communicate with us. Usually they know who *they* are. Many times, they don't seem to know who *we* are. But your Tristan knows you, yet doesn't know himself; it's all very odd."

Tristan looked up shaking his head. "I don't feel like there's any unresolved issues keeping me here. I am here because I am in love with you, Courtney. Tell her this. Tell her that love is why I am here," he insisted.

"Couldn't he be here because he wants to be—because he loves me? Isn't that enough?" I asked. "Does there have to be unresolved issues?"

She looked at me with a great deal of curiosity. "Did you know him before your accident?"

"No," I replied. "I had just arrived in Paris when I had my accident."

"Well, it just doesn't make any sense. Spirits do not just fall in love with the living. I guess anything's possible, though. I'll have to research this a little more. Can I visit you again soon? I'd like to try to communicate with Tristan myself if it's possible."

Tristan laughed when she said this. "I don't know what she thinks I'm going to say to her that I wouldn't say through you." He sounded a bit agitated.

Tiffany and Valerie talked quietly between them about when we could all meet again. Tiffany was worried that the doctor would be concerned about a séance happening on hospital grounds. They agreed it would be best to wait until I was released from the hospital. I began to have doubts about all of it. I didn't want Tristan to resolve any issues and move on. Maybe I was being selfish. I was in love with him, though. I knew he loved me. I could live the rest of my life with him. Even though I would never have a wedding or get my first kiss, except in my dreams, I was okay with this. I didn't want anyone else.

"I'm not going anywhere—just tell her that—tell her I'm not going anywhere," he said with determination, as though she were the one making the final decision.

Valerie stood to leave.

"Tell her, Courtney. Tell her I'm not leaving you," Tristan said.

I grabbed Valerie's arm and she sat back down next to me. "He says he's not going anywhere," I told Valerie softly.

"I don't think he has much choice in this—that is, if he truly is a spirit of some sort. They're not meant to walk among us, not for very long anyway." We all sat in silence at these last words. "Look, I'll gather more information," she said. "Until then, see if he can remember anything from his past."

After Valerie left, the three of us remained outside for a while longer. Tiffany knew I was upset about the things Valerie said.

"You okay, Courtney?" she asked.

"I don't want him to go," I whispered back, trying not to cry.

Tristan spoke out of his silence. "I'm not going anywhere, Courtney. I'm staying right here with you, forever."

"But Tristan, if you're supposed to go to Heaven, shouldn't we find the reason why you're still here?"

"First people thought you were seeing things and they were wrong. How do you know for sure that I'm a spirit of some kind? What if they're wrong about this?"

"What else could there be? You were confident that you were

real but you're not confident about this. You know this is a possibility!"

I could tell he was getting agitated. Maybe he was scared. But, this made sense. No one else could see him. I knew he wasn't angry with me, but he seemed to close up within himself.

I turned to Tiffany and smiled weakly. "Maybe it's best if we only worry about getting me out of here for now."

"I agree," she said. "There's no reason why we have to rush to find the answers." She pushed my wheelchair back to my room while Tristan followed at a distance behind us.

The best thing for me to do was focus on getting out of this place. There was nothing at all wrong with me. The only thing abnormal about me was that I was in love with a ghost. Really, how bad was that? Most of the people in this place were practically catatonic. I wondered what they were like without being extremely medicated. I wondered how many of them were actually just like me. Maybe they had a ghost following them around. Several of them did talk to themselves. There's the girl whose room was next to mine. She would talk all night long. Maybe there was someone in her room after all.

I couldn't handle sitting in my room much longer. I wasn't sure what the doctor expected from me, but I doubt he approved of me spending all my time in my room. He couldn't possibly expect me to lighten up and become friends with everyone, when most of the people in here stare right through you. I should have opened up more with the doctor, though. I'd had a dreary personality, and I'm sure if that had changed, he'd think things were much better with me. In fact, I would change my mood with everyone.

****

My parents sat at one of the round tables in the T.V. room. There was no better time than the present to show everyone the new me.

"Mom, Dad! I'm so glad to see you! Tiffany took me outside today and it was just wonderful. You should have seen the squirrels playing! I can't wait to get out of here and start spending more days outdoors. And when this cast comes off, it's going to be even better. Has Jess, Beth, or Kari stopped by? I miss them so much!"

My parents stared at me in shock. Maybe I laid it on a little thick with a bit too much enthusiasm. I turned around and looked at Tiffany to save me.

"Hello, Mr. and Mrs. Nacoal, my name's Tiffany. Courtney's been talking my ear off. She's told me all about you and her friends. She even mentioned that she would be attending college in the spring."

"Well, Tiffany, it's very nice to meet you." They were both smiling, obviously relieved to know their daughter wasn't a nutcase after all. I bet they were just thrilled to know I had plans of still going off to school.

Their faces were full of hope and love as they turned back to face me. I hated deceiving them, but I just had to get out of this place. I could see Tristan out of the corner of my eye, but I didn't dare look at him. They would be watching my every move. I would, most likely, be walking on eggshells around everyone from now on.

"Oh, Courtney," Mom began. "You seem to be doing so well. You're friends have been calling continuously. That young man, Jordan, stopped by several times. He seems very concerned."

Tristan rolled his eyes, but I stayed focused on my parents, focused on my happy demeanor, and completely in tune with everything and everyone around me.

Mom and Dad stayed for supper. They told me about all of the local news happening in our small town. It wasn't gossip to them if there was even a hint of fact to it. The Bennington's that live down the street just had a baby boy; Chance Lyle weighed seven pounds, eleven ounces. Haylee Cantrel got accepted to Yale. Haylee was little Miss Perfect in school; the class president and queen of debate. She received straight A's, but, rumor has it, and there were plenty of rumors that circulated in homeroom on Monday mornings, she was quite the partier. One Saturday evening, when her parents were out of town, she threw a party and drank an entire bottle of Vodka to herself...so I heard. I also heard she had to have her stomach pumped, but rumors could really get out of control in our little school, so I wasn't sure if any of it was even true. I never did like Haylee, though. Shannon Booker was in a minor car accident with old man Fitzgerald. Mr. Fitzgerald should have had his driver's license revoked years ago, but he managed to keep it, even though he drives 15 mph in a 35 mph zone. Mom said the cops determined it was her fault because she rear ended him, but I wondered if she was just trying to give him a nudge to get him to drive a little faster. There were so many mornings I was nearly late for school because I was stuck behind him. I always figured he should have a slow moving vehicle sign on the trunk of that four-door clunker.

We had a very enjoyable visit; but it began to get late, and my parents still had the drive home to make. Before they left, they promised they would see me tomorrow.

I had just returned to my room when the doctor came in. As soon as I'd seen him enter, my palms began to sweat. I hadn't had a chance to get all of the details from Tristan about the meeting earlier between the doctor and Tiffany. I knew I was going to screw this up.

"Calm down." I heard Tristan whisper from somewhere behind me. Easy for him to say, it wasn't his sanity on the line here. And he knew everything that had been discussed; I didn't.

"Miss Nacoal!" the doctor began, "how are we feeling this evening?"

"Um—good."

The doctor gave me a quick nod. "Uh huh, just good?"

"Courtney," Tristan whispered, "tell him about your day, about sitting outside and seeing your parents."

"Well," I began, "Tiffany took me out to the courtyard today.

That felt really nice; I needed to get out in the sun a little. We watched the squirrels and talked for quite a while."

The doctor pulled the chair up and sat down, crossing his legs as though he planned to stay awhile. He looked down at his tablet and an awkward silence lingered in the room. "Uh huh. It says here you had a visitor while you were outside."

"Oh yeah, Valerie stopped by." I was unsure what to say about Valerie. I didn't know her, and I was sure he didn't want to know what we were really talking about.

"Is Valerie a friend of yours?" He asked.

"Yeah, I met her at church," I answered quickly.

He wrote a little in his tablet before he looked up. "What church do you attend?"

My head began to spin. Why had I said that? Surely he knew that my parents and I didn't go to church on Sundays. It's not that my parents didn't believe in God, it was just something they didn't speak about.

"Um, well, she's actually from Jess's church. Jess is a friend of mine. I had actually met Valerie when Jess and I were at the library one afternoon. She said she was coming to visit someone else when she saw Tiffany and me sitting outside."

"I see. Do you worry that she may say something back home? After all, I believe your parents have been telling your friends that you were going through rehabilitation for your leg."

"No, I asked her not to say anything. She won't. But someday I plan on telling my friends anyway. After all, I am better now. We'll all get a good laugh out of this in the future."

He smiled, obviously pleased with my response.

"How was the visit with your parents?" he continued.

"Oh, it was wonderful! They stayed for supper and filled me in on all of the news back home." I began to relax a little. He continued to write in his tablet. I dreaded being analyzed, my every word picked apart. Yet, I knew I had to put on a good show.

He laid his tablet on his lap and leaned forward. That's when he hit me with the big question.

"Courtney, when's the last time you envisioned—um—" he flipped though the pages and stopped, looking back up at me... "Tristan?"

My heart stopped. What was I supposed to say? Tristan! My head was screaming.

"You don't remember. Tell him it's been several days," Tristan said from somewhere behind me.

"Hmmm," I began like I had to think about it a bit. "Well,—I don't know for sure. It's been several days, but I can't be positive."

He watched me closely. What if he could tell when someone was lying? Of course he could tell, he's a psychiatrist! He would be able to analyze the behavior of someone lying. Isn't that what they're trained to do?

Tristan must have suspected this too. "Look him directly in the eye and smile. Don't look down."

Another awkward silence but the doctor smiled back at me and stood.

"Well, Courtney. It seems that things are improving a little. Would you agree?"

I nodded, keeping my eyes on his. With that, he exited. I let out a long sigh of relief. Tristan stepped around to the front of the wheelchair.

"I'll be right back. I want to see what he wrote in that little notepad of his."

"You're beginning to enjoy this snooping thing, aren't you?" I whispered.

He let out a small mischievous chuckle and disappeared through the doorway. It's too bad I hadn't known him in high school. Test days would have been a whole lot easier. I smiled at the thought of that. I still had college ahead of me, maybe. Yet, I knew I would never ask him to cheat for me. He could quite possibly end up being the best study companion, though. But I could hardly study with him if I had to share a dorm room with roommates. I decided, the only way I would attend college was if I had my own room. There would be no way I could pretend he wasn't there for that length of time.

We had talked about college on several occasions, back in the beginning, when he first came here. But that was before I'd found out he was a spirit. This definitely changed things. I would absolutely HAVE to attend college now. I would need some way to support myself my entire life. I didn't plan on working at the small town grocery store forever.

Tristan walked back through the open doorway with a grin stretched across his face that said, *I know something that you don't!*

"What?" I pleaded.

He looked back into the hall to make sure no one had heard me. I really needed to be more careful. We waited quietly for someone to emerge but no one did. I didn't want to ruin my chances of getting out of here. I thought about wheeling myself over and shutting the door but changed my mind, thinking it may look a little suspicious. The suspense was killing me, though. I used my puppy dog eyes on him and he rolled his.

"You are so pathetic," he said, jokingly.

I smiled at him and positioned my hands as if I were praying.

"Okay, okay, you win. He made a note to call your parents in the morning. Obviously, you have the ability to fool even the doc. You should become an actress." He laughed. "He doesn't think you are imagining me anymore, and all of this probably came on due to stress from your loss of memory, postponing college, and your lack of mobility. So, basically, what he's saying is—I am stress." He gave me a little wink.

"That is the last thing you could ever be," I said, smiling back at him. "And anyway, it doesn't matter what he puts down on paper, as long as I'm getting out of this place."

This was the best news I'd heard all day. I wanted to jump up and down and scream with delight but this stupid cast made that impossible. Plus, the nurses would come running. I would be going home soon! And it wouldn't be long before I could get this bulky cast off. Things were beginning to look good; life was beginning to get back to normal. I was in love with the most wonderful man, and it didn't matter to me that he was a spirit.

Half of the lights in the hallway turned off. This was usually the cue to everyone that it was time for bed. I looked at the clock. 10:00. I wheeled myself over to the door and quietly closed it. I spent very little time in the bathroom brushing my teeth and combing my hair. There was too much excitement in my head, and I couldn't wait for tomorrow to get here. I shut the light off, positioned myself next to the bed and slid in under the covers. Once I was comfortable, Tristan came over and lay beside me. Just enough light illuminated from the clock to allow me to see the troubled look on his face.

"I love you, Tristan."

"I love you," he whispered back, "with all my heart."

That was all I needed to hear before I drifted off to dream of him.

Some things are better left unsaid, unheard, and unseen.

Chapter 9

Going Home – Again

I could hear voices in the hallway when morning came. The smell of breakfast worked its way to my room, and my stomach made a hungry growl. I looked towards the chair where Tristan sat, staring at the palms of his hands. He had been pretty quiet after Valerie's visit yesterday. I watched him for a long time. His face looked so sad. She had upset him with her lost spirit idea and it was obvious that he was struggling with this. I loved him. It didn't matter. I would be with him forever, no matter what.

Unless he did figure out why he was still here. What would we do then? I wasn't sure I could live without him. I know he says he wants to stay with me, but what if there is no choice?

This horrible feeling washed over me. What if I had to go on without him? A tear formed in my eye just at the thought of this. My days would be lonely, and my nights would be unbearable. We'd spent every hour…every minute together. We danced in my dreams, every night. Last night's dream was so vivid, so fresh in my mind. I had felt him, his warmth, his breath against my neck. He would always be the only one I would love. My heart belonged to him. If he had to leave, my heart would surely whither and die.

The door opened to my hospital room and Tiffany flipped the light switch on. I wiped the tear from my eye and sat up as she approached. She was smiling but worry crossed her face when she reached the side of the bed.

"Are you okay, Courtney? What's wrong?"

"It's nothing, really." I looked over at Tristan who was now staring at me, concern on his face as well. "Really, I'm fine." This was directed at both of them, and I tried to smile. I was being such a baby about this, crying over something that hasn't even happened yet. Yet. That was the key word. In my heart, I knew it would happen. I ran my hands through my hair, trying to detangle the mop. I was certain I looked like Medusa.

Tristan approached the bed and knelt down beside me. "You're truly beautiful in the morning."

I rolled my eyes at him and let out a weak laugh.

"You're beautiful all the time."

"Beautiful, right. Look who's being the actor now. I should sleep with a hair brush beside the bed."

"Uh hum." Tiffany pretended to clear her throat. "I don't mean to interrupt this beautiful moment that you two *must* be having, but I have some news for you."

This got my full attention, and Tristan stood as I sat up further in bed.

"Tell me!" I was anxious to hear this news. It wasn't often that she came into my room without knocking.

She laughed. "You're parents are already here, talking with your doctor."

I had forgotten about what the doctor had written last night.

He must have called them later in the evening or very early this morning. I looked at the clock. 8:00 A.M.

"Oh my gosh! I've got to get cleaned up and pack my things!" I began to pull myself out of bed into my wheelchair.

"Slow down! You're not supposed to know what's going on yet. I saw them arrive just a few minutes ago," she said.

I finished getting into the wheelchair and wheeled myself to the bathroom. "I won't say anything. Apparently, acting should be my profession." I looked over at Tristan and stuck out my tongue. "I'll just get ready for breakfast and act surprised to see them."

"I'm so happy for you, Courtney. I just couldn't wait to tell you." She started for the door and turned back. "You want some eggs and bacon?"

"Yes, I'm starving! Um—Tiffany?"

"Yeah?"

"Has Stacy, the girl in the next room, went to breakfast yet?"

"No, I don't think so." I could see the curiosity on her face, but she smiled and walked out into the hallway, shutting the door behind her. I turned to face Tristan who now had a smile on his face. He was so beautiful. He never changed. His hair, his skin, his eyes. My heart beat faster every time I looked at him.

"I'm going to get ready. I can't wait to go home, but I want to talk to Stacy before I leave."

"She can't see me either."

I looked up at him. I heard my neighbor talk to herself so

many times. He must have known what I was thinking. I did want to know if she could see him. If she could really see other people, maybe they were spirits like Tristan.

"Are you sure? Did you try talking to her?"

"I could hear her talking last night. I entered her room. She just continued to talk. So, I walked in and stood in front of her. She didn't even look at me. I told her my name but she still didn't look at me. Courtney, she looked right through me like I wasn't even there."

"Who was she talking to?"

"There was no one else in the room, Courtney. It was just her."

I don't know why I needed her to see him. I guess I wanted her to confirm that he was one of them...that he was just like one of the spirits that spoke to her. But she didn't see him. Maybe she didn't see anyone.

I went to the bathroom and looked at myself in the mirror. I laughed and shook my head. My hair was so wild; it really did look like Medusa. I questioned what Tristan saw in me.

He was lying on the bed when I came back out, staring up at the ceiling.

"I'm going to miss this place, ya know." He turned to look at me and smiled.

"Well, you can stay," I told him, sarcastically. I wheeled myself to the door, keeping my eyes on him. He jumped off the bed and followed me out. There were several patients in the T.V. room eating breakfast. Tiffany sat at a table with another nurse and smiled when I entered. She got up and moved the chair that sat next to hers so I could pull up my wheelchair.

"I'll go get your breakfast. Make yourself comfortable."

When she got to the breakfast cart, my parents and the doctor entered the room. I made myself look surprised to see them.

"Mom! Dad! What are you doing here so early?"

They came over and sat across the table from me. The nurse that had been sitting with Tiffany rose and left so the doctor could take her seat. Tiffany arrived with my tray and set it in front of me.

"The doctor called us this morning. He thought it would be good for you to come home. We wanted to get here as soon as possible," Mom said.

"I'm going home today?"

"As soon as we get your things packed and sign some paperwork."

I looked over at the doctor. He continued to study my expressions. I hated being watched; it made me nervous, he made me nervous. I turned back to my parents, worried that he would read something in my eyes or my expression that would change his mind about my sanity. My parents stared at me, obviously waiting for some kind of confirmation to what they had just said.

"I can't wait to go home. I miss everyone so much. I want to sleep in my own bed again." I smiled my best smile. I really was excited, but I felt like one of those people who knew about the surprise party beforehand. It's very difficult to act surprised when you were expecting it.

I ate my breakfast quickly and Mom and I returned to my room to pack my things. Dad went to take care of the paperwork and bring the car up to the front. In the mean time, Tiffany came in and handed me a note. This was really happening. I was really going back home where I could watch whatever I wanted to on my own TV. I could call and text my friends whenever I wanted. I could finally sit outside in the gazebo. I knew it would be difficult for Tristan and me. My parents would watch every move I made, but it would be easier at home than it was here. My parents would go to work every weekday and we'd have the whole house to ourselves. I opened the note when Mom turned to put my clothes in my suitcase.

Call me as soon as you can.

555-1200

Tif

I folded the note and put it in the pocket of my shorts. I looked back at the room before I wheeled myself out into the hallway. I would make sure to never return. I would just have to be careful.

Stacy stood in the doorway of her room. I wish I knew if she really saw the people she talked to. If she did, I knew how she felt. People thought you were crazy. I hated that feeling. I felt so sorry for her. I was leaving because I was obviously better at acting than she was. She smiled at us when we passed. I thought I saw a movement in her room and my heart skipped a beat.

"Mom." I turned to her. "Do you think I could meet you out front? I'd like to say good-bye to Stacy."

"Sure, dear." I watched Mom walk down the hall and enter the elevator. I looked around; it was now only Tristan and me.

"What are you doing?" he asked.

"I thought I saw something in Stacy's room," I whispered back. "What if I can see the people she sees? Even if she can't see you?"

He looked back at Stacy. "I don't know, Courtney. Can't we just let it go and be happy? What if whatever she sees isn't such a good thing?"

"Well, no one can see *you* and you're a good thing." I turned my wheelchair around and proceeded to Stacy's room. She looked so fragile and scared; her eyes never quite met mine. I stopped in front of her.

"Stacy, my name is Courtney. I'm going home today, and I wanted to say good-bye before I left." She looked down the hall but never said a word. I leaned to my left a little so I could get a better view of her room.

She startled me when she spoke. "Can't you all just go away!? I want to be left alone! I'm tired of talking to you!" she hissed.

I backed my wheelchair up. I could see the rage in her eyes.

Tristan stepped in front of me as she started swinging wildly at the air.

"Go, Courtney!" Tristan shouted.

I started wheeling myself to the elevator and only looked back after I punched the down button. Stacy was coming down the hallway with several staff members catching up to her. The elevator was near the nurse's station and the nurse behind the counter had to release the elevator doors to open. My heart was fighting its way out of my chest. Tiffany came up as the other staff members restrained Stacy. She grabbed hold of the back of the wheelchair and pushed me into the elevator, quickly stabbing the ground floor button. When the doors finally shut, we both let out a sigh of relief.

As the elevator made its way down slowly and my heart returned to normal, Tiffany spoke quietly. "You don't belong in here but... Stacy does."

I looked up at her. "Why is she so different than me?"

"She's here, not only for her safety, but for everyone else's as well."

I couldn't quite understand what she meant.

She continued, "She sees something, whether it's in her own mind or not, but whatever she sees is not good."

I looked down and wished I had never approached her. It was my fault that she got angry.

"She doesn't know who's real and who's not," Tiffany said.

The doors opened on the ground floor, and I could see my

parents waiting outside next to the car. The warm air flowed through the doorway, and I felt a sudden overwhelming sense of relief.

Tiffany leaned down to whisper something in my ear. "You and Tristan take care and call me soon."

Tristan! Where was he? I looked around frantically, but he was not outside with the rest of us. My parents helped me into the backseat and folded the wheelchair up so it could be placed into the trunk. Tiffany stood at the open car door while my parents slid themselves in the front seat. "Bye, Tiff," I said as she backed away. Tristan stepped around her and slid into the backseat beside me.

"All is well?" Tiffany asked.

"Yeah, everything is perfect." Tristan appeared relieved that the ordeal was finally over. Tiffany closed the door, and my parents pulled the car away.

The ride home was quiet and peaceful. We pulled into the driveway, and Jordan stood from where he'd been sitting on the front steps. I was excited to see him. The last time was graduation. It felt like an eternity. I rolled the window down quickly and called to him. "Jordan!"

He ran to the back passenger door. He looked tired; dark circles outlined his eyes. His hair had grown quite long and he looked like he hadn't shaved in a week. This was definitely not the Jordan from high school. His hair was always a little longer than most guys' but he'd always been clean shaven. I remembered back when he first started growing hair on his face; it was probably freshman year. Just a few hairs and he began shaving. He was maybe only fourteen then, but no one has ever seen a hair on his face since.

"Court! Oh, my God! You're home, finally!" He flung the door open and scooped me out of the car. He swung me around, and my cast narrowly missed hitting my dad in the back. Laughing, I wrapped my arms around his neck while he carried me over to the trunk where Dad lifted the wheelchair out.

After placing me in my seat, he grabbed my bags from the trunk.

"Why don't you take Courtney out to the back, Jordan," Dad said. "We'll take her bags on up to her room."

I turned to look at Dad, shocked that he was being so accepting of Jordan.

"No problem, Mr. Nacoal," Jordan replied. He began wheeling me around the small walkway that would take us back to the gazebo.

"I'll bring you two some lemonade," Mom said as we wheeled past her.

"Thanks, Mrs. Nacoal. That sounds great!"

Things were beginning to feel a little strange. My parents were never so welcoming towards a guy. It felt good though, having Jordan here.

After we settled into the gazebo, Mom brought us lemonade

and sugar cookies and patted Jordan on the back before she turned and left. I looked around to see if Tristan had followed us out but we were alone.

"What was that about?" I looked at Jordan.

"What?"

"What do you mean 'what'? You know 'WHAT'! Mom patting you on the back and Dad—what the heck?! It's like I'm in the twilight zone!"

Jordan laughed. "I guess they're kind of used to me. I've been stopping by quite often. I've been really worried about you, Court. I didn't even know you were coming home today."

"Then what were you doing here?"

"Just waiting—for your parents to come home. I called this morning, like I do every morning, but they didn't answer. I got a little worried. I've been stopping by around six o'clock every night."

"So what have my parents been telling you?"

"They said the injuries to your head were a little more severe than originally thought. You were seeing a psychiatrist. Some kind of in-patient thing."

Wow, I was really surprised they had been so open with him. They were good about covering things up, making everything appear normal.

"Yeah, um, I'm better now. You look like crap, though. Did you decide that personal hygiene just wasn't your thing anymore, or

145

are you going for the rugged look now?" I smiled at him to ensure him that I was only joking.

"I've been a little preoccupied." He ran his hands through his hair. "Don't you worry, though; I'll be looking hot again tomorrow."

We both laughed. I had always felt comfortable around Jordan. If I could tell anyone anything, it would be him. He would never judge me or reveal any secrets. I wasn't quite ready to fill in the details, though. There was a lot left to figure out.

His phone rang, and from the sound of the conversation, it was his mom. She needed help moving a desk.

"Hey, Court," he said when he flipped his phone shut, "I'll be back tomorrow after you get your cast off."

"What?!" This took me by surprise. "Who said I'm getting my cast off tomorrow?"

"Your parents told me the other day. You have a morning appointment."

"They never told ME!" That was strange. Now I felt like they were telling the world everything and hiding it all from me. I was relieved to know I would soon be out of this wheelchair.

"What else have they told you?"

"Nothing really." He smiled and began to wheel me down the ramp and up to the deck.

Mom stepped outside. "Leaving so soon, Jordan?"

"Yes, Mrs. Nacoal. Mom needs my muscles." He smiled at her

and told Dad good-bye.

I looked over at Mom after Jordan closed the front door behind him. "So, what's this about a doctor's appointment tomorrow?" I asked.

"Oh! That's right! You may get your cast off tomorrow. We didn't mention it while you were away because we thought we might have to reschedule, but it looks like, now that you're home, plans can go ahead as scheduled."

"Finally!" I said. "This cast is really making my leg itch." It looked like I'd have to turn to Jordan for the important information. I wheeled myself into the living room, grabbed the remote and surfed through the channels. A psychic commercial caught my attention. I hesitated a bit on it, and moved on. I had never believed in psychics before, but I had never believed in ghosts either.

Mom and Dad left after mentioning something about getting groceries and a few movies. Tristan came over and sat on the couch.

"So, tell me about Jordan." He looked at me.

"Oh, he's like the best friend anyone could ever have. I'm just so surprised Mom and Dad are finally okay with him coming around. I've been friends with him since second grade. They've never trusted any guy, especially one that claims to be just a friend."

"And you trust him? To be just a friend, I mean."

"Tristan! Do I detect a hint of jealousy?" I laughed. "Of course he's just a friend. After all, I don't think he's really into girls."

"Ha, he's into you! Look at him! He hasn't slept in a week, ever since you went to the hospital. I think I have a little competition, that's all." He looked at the television like the conversation was over. I wasn't giving up so easily, though.

"There is NO competition. I love you. And Jordan is just a friend."

He looked at me and lowered his head. "You're right, there is no competition. I can't compete with him. He can open the doors for you, pick you up; he can touch you, Courtney. I can't do any of those things."

"I've decided what I want. I want you. Not Jordan, just you." I looked at the television this time, hoping to end whatever tension was going on between us.

The rest of the day was spent in silence. Mom, Dad, Tristan, and I watched two movies. On occasion, I would catch him staring at me. I knew I could never love someone as much as I loved him. Jordan was a friend, my best friend. I had never had feelings for Jordan any other way. Tristan was right, though. Jordan looked drained.

I was ready to sleep in my own bed. I laid my head back against the pillow and closed my eyes. Tristan had been sitting in the chair since I entered my room. I waited until I could hear my dad's snores from down the hall before I turned to him.

"Tristan, please don't ever leave me." I waited patiently for his reply.

"I won't."

I know he said the words, but there was something different about how he said them. It's like he said them, and then they just drifted away.

I shifted to my side to stare at his silhouette in the darkness. A warm sensation traveled through my body. *He was so beautiful. He was my angel, my very own personal angel.* He smiled and stood, walking across the floor so gracefully. He lay in the bed next to me, and I closed my eyes to dream of us dancing. I could feel him in my dreams. I could feel his hair, his skin, his warmth. I dreamt of his fingers touching my face. I opened my eyes. His fingers really were traveling across my face as they did in my dream, but I could not feel their touch. I closed my eyes again.

Brandy Walsh

Something bad always seems to accompany the good, like it's some balance to life, to existence. You can't have the good without the bad; or the bad without the good; or life without death; or friends without enemies.

Chapter 10

Unwanted Kisses

I waited in the doctor's office, anxiously anticipating the removal of the cast. Tristan stood by the far wall. I had asked my parents to remain in the waiting room, and they reluctantly agreed. I needed to see my leg before anyone else. I wasn't sure what to expect, but I didn't want to deal with their expressions and optimism.

The doctor strode in carrying his clipboard. "Looks like you'll be getting this thing off today," the doctor stated, still not looking me in the eye when he spoke.

I waited quietly as he used a small saw to cut away at the length of the cast. After he had made another cut down the other side, he began to lift the top off. I didn't look right away. I felt the cool air of the office hit my exposed skin. I looked at Tristan. He was watching me, not at what the doctor was doing. He smiled. I slowly looked down to see what looked like someone else's leg. It was raw, chapped, and badly scarred. My left leg was tan, even though I had not spent a great deal of time in the sun this summer. But, my right leg was deathly pale.

The doctor's voice startled me from my gaze.

"It looks good, considering the amount of damage that had been done. The doctor in London did a wonderful job." He looked up at me and smiled. Eye contact for the first time.

"Paris," I corrected him.

151

"Oh, yes. Paris. Well, they did a superb job. I just need to grab some crutches and I'll be right back." He turned and left, the door softly closed behind him.

Tristan moved to my side and knelt down beside my newly exposed leg, his hand outlined the scars that intertwined with one another. He lowered his head and sunk further to the floor.

"Tristan?"

"I'm so sorry, Courtney."

"Oh no, you are not going to start feeling sorry for me."

He let out a deep sigh.

"It doesn't look that bad, does it?"

He looked up at me. "You are beautiful; every part of you is beautiful. No scar would ever make me think any differently."

The door opened and the doctor entered, carrying two crutches. I leaned myself into the crutches and put a little weight on my right leg. A sharp pain traveled up causing a wave of dizziness in my head.

"Your leg hasn't been used in quite some time. You'll have to take it easy; you'll need to strengthen those muscles with therapy."

He held the door open as I awkwardly hobbled past. I placed nearly all of my weight on my left leg as I went the length of the hallway with the doctor close behind. My parents stood as I entered the waiting room, and their eyes drifted to my scarred up leg. The color in my mom's face drained as she sank back down into the chair. Dad hadn't moved, hadn't breathed.

"Jeez! It's really not that bad!" It was my turn to be optimistic, I guess. I was just so relieved to have the itchy cast removed. I was finally mobile again, without wheels.

"She will need some therapy to strengthen her muscles," the doctor stared, "and the scars will fade over time. Her leg looks much better than I had anticipated, Mr. and Mrs. Nacoal."

They shook the doctor's hand and I hobbled my way to the door. I really hated hospitals...and doctors. I just wanted out of here. It wasn't over yet, though. There would still be several weeks of physical therapy.

I climbed in the backseat of the car and laid the crutches on the floorboard. I looked over at Tristan, who looked sad and withdrawn. Mom and Dad drove to the pharmacy to pick up an ointment that the doctor prescribed for the scars.

I had forgotten that Jordan said he would stop by today after my appointment. He was sitting on the front step, clean shaven with a new haircut.

"Look who's here," Tristan said with a trace of irritation in his voice.

I bit my lip and, without turning my head, looked at him out of the corner of my eye.

"What?" he said, shrugging his shoulders.

I rolled my eyes and reached for the door handle.

Jordan approached the car. "Court! Did you get it off?"

I opened the door the rest of the way and let my leg rest

outside the car door.

Jordan looked down and smiled. "It looks good!"

Leave it to Jordan to say something looks good when it really looks horrible.

"You do too," I said.

He smiled again and stepped back so I could position myself on my crutches. He looked like he had finally slept.

We went out back again, and this time Tristan followed close behind.

"So, I was wondering if you and I could go to dinner. I already asked your parents. They seemed okay with it, that is, if you are."

I looked back at the house and saw Mom and Dad standing in the doorway. This was definitely not like them. They never liked Jordan; they never liked the idea of me dating. And this was definitely not like Jordan. He had never asked me out on a date before. He'd never hinted that he even liked me.

"Jordan, I can't. I mean—"

"Why not? It doesn't have to be a date, just two friends hanging out."

"I don't know, Jordan."

"Is this about that guy you met in Paris?"

I looked up at him. I couldn't lie to him. He has always been my best friend. I guess I didn't know him as well as I thought. Tristan was right; he did have a thing for me. I wondered how long he's had these feelings. How could he have kept them hidden like that? How could he just go on pretending to be a friend?

"Yes." I looked back at the house to see if my parents were still standing at the door. They had left and I felt it was safe to fill Jordan in on my secret. He would need to know, and I trusted him not to tell anyone.

"Jordan—" I began. "Tristan is here. No one else can see him but he's with me—all the time." I watched his expression turn from jealousy to bewilderment.

"That doesn't make sense, Courtney. How can he be here, but no one can see him?"

"We think he's a—spirit—maybe."

"We?"

"Well, the nurse at the hospital realized that he wasn't part of my imagination. He's really here."

Jordan sat in silence, his elbows resting on his knees while he twisted his hands as if he was trying to flatten wet clay. I turned to look for Tristan and found him standing several feet away, near the large weeping willow tree. I knew there was nothing he could do to help me convince Jordan he existed. Jordan was my friend; I should know what to say to him. At least, I thought I would know what to say. Right now, though, I was at a loss for words. How could I convince my best friend that not only do ghosts exist, but that I was in love with one?

"You do believe me, don't you?" I asked.

He shook his head without looking at me.

"Jordan, I'm not making this up. I'm not imagining him." I was pleading with him now. "You have to believe me; just try to understand."

When he raised his head, I tried to decipher the emotions that read on his face...in his eyes. Anger? Hurt? Disbelief? Maybe a combination of all three.

"Help me to understand, Courtney. Help me to understand what in the world is going on with you—going on in your head. You expect me to believe that a ghost is following you around? You expect me to believe that you're in love with someone that only you can see? You don't have to make this shit up just so you don't have to go out with me. Just say you don't like me in that way."

"That's what you think?!" I yelled at him. "You think I'm making things up so I don't have to go out with you? Grow up, Jordan! Of all people, I figured you would be the one with the open mind. You would be the one person who would believe me." I turned my body so I wouldn't be facing him when the tear fought to escape my eye.

"You're serious," he said with a hint of compassion in his voice. "You really believe there is someone, or something, that is hanging around that nobody else can see. That's why you went to the psychiatrist. That's why they sent you away, isn't it!"

Anger was building up inside me again. "I don't just BELIEVE, I KNOW!" I spat at him. "I see him, I hear him, I dream about him. I want him here, and he wants to be here. Is it that hard to believe? Tiffany believes me and so does Valerie, and they don't even know me as well as you. I'm not making this up, and I'm not crazy!"

"Who in the hell are Tiffany and Valerie?" he asked, confusion clearly showing in his expression. He probably thought I was making these people up as well.

"Tiffany's the nurse at the hospital. Valerie is a friend of hers that knows a great deal about spirits."

"Jeez. And you think you're in love with him? You think you're in love with a spirit?"

I nodded. We sat in silence. He shook his head and stood up to leave.

"Jordan, please. I'm sorry."

"It's just not natural, Courtney. It's not right!" And he walked away. I heard his car start up in the front before he sped off.

Tristan walked up to the gazebo and sat down on the bench beside me. We sat in silence for several minutes before he spoke.

"Do you think he'll say anything?"

I shook my head, slightly, in case my parents were watching. I'm sure they wondered why Jordan had left so suddenly. I didn't know how to fix this. Jordan caught me by surprise. Surely he would come around. He has always been there for me.

I grabbed my crutches and managed to make my way to the house, up the stairs, and to my room. I didn't look at my parents when I passed them, and they didn't ask any questions. I wasn't sure how I would explain it anyway. Tristan and I worked on an unfinished puzzle of Cherubs. How ironic. Neither of us spoke.

After supper, I told my parents I wanted to spend the evening in my room, probably go to bed early. I was really tired and thinking about Jordan being upset was depressing me. I wanted to be happy. Tristan was with me, my cast was off, but my best friend walked out on me. I lay in bed with my television on; background noise was all it was. Tristan sat in the chair with his eyes closed. My pain was having such an effect on him, and I felt a heavy sadness weighing on me. Here I had run Jordan off, now my depression was bringing down the one person I truly loved.

I heard my parents go up to bed. I shut the television off so I could hear when Dad began snoring. Tristan still sat in the chair, his head lowered.

"I love you," I whispered to him. He looked up and shook his head. "Tristan."

"I love you too, Courtney. But Jordan's right, it's not natural."

"Do you think I care? I don't want to be without you. I would live alone in the wilderness with you if I had to."

"I don't ever want to be without you either, but this is going to be difficult, for you and me both."

"It'll get easier; I know it will—eventually."

He came over and lay next to me. Tomorrow my parents would leave for work. We could talk tomorrow, get past what was

causing both of us pain. Jordan would come around. And if he
didn't, it would be something I would have to live with.

I closed my eyes and found myself walking along the shoreline
with Tristan. Our fingers intertwined. We laughed and held each
other until I woke to the morning light making its way through my
bedroom curtains. I looked at Tristan, still lying next to me. I had
always fallen asleep with him staring into my eyes. I had never seen
him sleep; yet, he appeared to be sleeping soundly. I turned to look
at my clock on the nightstand. 6:00 A.M. I listened as my parents
scurried around downstairs, getting ready for work. Mom climbed
the stairs and opened my door quietly. I pretended to be asleep, the
door shut again, and I heard her descend the stairs and close the
garage door behind her as she left for work.

I turned back to Tristan, his eyes open now.

"I didn't know spirits could sleep."

"I guess they do when they're tired." He smiled when he said
this.

"Do you dream too?"

"Yeah, I guess I do."

"What do you dream about?"

"Hmmm—well, last nights dream was about us. You came
walking down these winding stairs of a very large house. You
stopped in a foyer with a beautiful crystal chandelier that hung
from the ceiling. I scooped you up into my arms and carried you
through the house, grabbing a picnic basket on the way out. I

carried you and the basket to a blanket that lay out beside a pond."

"And—"

"I woke up. I heard the door. Was that your mom?"

"Yeah. They're both gone now, though. We have the whole house to ourselves."

"I guess if I was alive, that could be really fun." He smiled.

"You know, that doesn't matter to me. I'm just happy you're here with me."

"I am too. I just feel like you're missing out on so much."

"I'm not."

We stayed in bed until nearly 9:00. I told him about my dreams and how I could feel him when I was asleep. He had similar dreams. I heard the doorbell ring, and I slid myself out of bed. It rang several more times before I made my way down the stairs, maneuvering the crutches carefully. When I opened the door, Jordan pushed his way past and barged into the living room. "Hello to you too," I said as I closed the door and followed him.

"None of this makes sense, Courtney!" He was clearly agitated while he paced back and forth. I stood in the middle of the room with a crutch under each arm.

"What can he ever do for you? He can't provide for you!"

"I can provide for myself!"

"What about kids? Can he ever give you kids?!"

"No—but I never said I wanted kids."

"Do you think you can go through your whole life like this?

Pretending?"

"Jordan! Why can't you understand and just be happy for me?"

"Understand? Understand what? That you got a thing for some ghost?"

I stood there shocked. I turned away from him, realizing that he may never understand. I felt him step closer, his hand reached around to the side of my face, turning me back around to face him. I expected him to say he was sorry, that he was just having a difficult time grasping it all, I expected him to be my best friend… but he suddenly leaned down and kissed my lips, a hard, forceful kiss that took me off guard.

"Can your ghost do that?!" he yelled.

I reached out and slapped him across the face, losing my balance on my crutches. I began to fall backwards and Jordan grabbed my arms to catch me before I hit the floor. I pushed him away and sat on the floor. Tristan knelt beside me, anger filling his face.

"Where was your ghost then? How's he going to help you when you fall?"

"If you hadn't kissed me, I wouldn't have slapped you. Therefore, I wouldn't have fallen!"

"What is with you lately?!" he yelled.

"Me?! What in the hell is with you?! You were supposed to be my friend!"

He sat back on the couch and lowered his head into his hands.

We sat there in silence for a few minutes until he spoke again.

"I don't know how to deal with this, Courtney. I've liked you since the second grade. I never knew how to tell you. Then you went away on vacation and I had three months to miss you, really miss you. I came up with a million ways to tell you how much I liked you while you were away. But, then you come home to tell me that you're in love. Ya know, I think I could have dealt with that… eventually. I just can't deal with this. How in the hell did you fall in love with a ghost anyway?"

I looked over at Tristan who was now sitting on the floor next to me. His face was filled with sadness again. I didn't know how I fell in love with him; I just knew I was. The sound of his voice, his smile, the way my heart beat faster when we were together. How could I explain that to Jordan?

"He's here, isn't he?"

"Yes," I said as I tried to read the expression on Tristan's face.

"How am I supposed to compete with that? He can be around you every minute of the day without anyone ever knowing," Jordan said.

"This is not some kind of competition! I wish you would both stop being so jealous of the other!" I yelled.

"What? Your ghost is jealous?" He laughed aloud.

I could tell Tristan was getting angry. "Why don't you leave, Jordan? Come back when you can talk civil."

"Oh, I'll come back, everyday, until he—until *it* leaves." He stood and went towards the front door. "You sure you don't want to give me a kiss good-bye?"

I threw one of my crutches in his direction, and he laughed before he shut the door behind him. Tears began to well up in my eyes. Why did he have to act this way? He's never been like this. I wanted to hate him, wanting him never to return. He was just supposed to be a friend. My parents and Tristan were right. Why couldn't I see it?

"He's right," I heard Tristan say. "We can't keep going on like this, Courtney."

I turned to Tristan. "Tristan, I'm sorry. It's not supposed to be this way."

"How's it supposed to be? Do you think anyone will ever understand this?"

"I don't care if anyone understands! It's my life!"

"That's just it, it *is* your *life*. You're alive and I'm not! I can't be with you the way Jordan can."

"But I don't want to be with him. Please, Tristan!"

He spoke softly, full of pain. "I can't stop anyone from kissing you. I can't protect you. I can't even hold you to comfort you right now. I'm so sorry, Courtney. I want you to have a normal life, to have a family." He stood to leave.

"Please don't go. I need you," I said in between my sobs.

"You need someone who can give you so much more than I can offer. You need someone who can buy you roses and bring you breakfast in bed, someone who can actually hold you close. I can't do any of those things, and you deserve them. You deserve someone who will be with you, physically with you, through everything. I want to be that person, but you and I both know I can never be. I will always love you, Courtney."

He left me sitting there on the floor. Hours passed and my life was empty.

Void. Emptiness. Pain. How can a heart ache when it feels like it's been ripped from your chest?

Chapter 11

Acceptance

Each day that passed seemed like an eternity. My heart ached deep inside my chest as if all that remained was an empty void. I couldn't bear to go outside; to hear the birds singing and people going about their busy lives. I left the house with my parents only to go to physical therapy. Every day, I heard Jordan's car pull up and the doorbell ring. I held the pillow over my head to drown out the ringing of the chimes. I knew he would eventually leave… and he did. Throughout the week, I could hide in my room; hide from the world. Saturday was unbearable. I would drag myself out of bed to watch movies with Mom and Dad. Although they were there, I felt so alone. Many times, Mom would feel my forehead to check for a fever. For nearly a week, I told her I was just feeling a little under the weather.

Sunday morning I awoke to my parents standing at my bedroom doorway. They were holding gifts; my birthday gifts. I had forgotten about my own birthday. I was now nineteen… nineteen and alone. I pulled the covers up over my head; it was a childish gesture that I hoped would make them leave me alone.

"Would you like to invite your friends over later for cake and ice-cream?" Mom asked in her sweetest tone. NOW she wanted to throw birthday parties for me? NOW she wanted to have my friends come over to hang out? Just when I wished I was dead?

"No," I replied. "I just want to be left alone."

They closed the door quietly. My cell phone rang continuously throughout the day. I pushed 'ignore' as each one of my friends' numbers appeared. Eventually I turned my phone off and threw it on the floor where it skidded to a stop under my dresser. When I did finally make my way downstairs, I left the presents sitting on the hall table...unopened.

By Monday, Mom had decided it was time to see a doctor. She called into work to let them know she would be in later. I begged her to let me stay home, telling her that it would pass. She assumed it was just my hatred towards hospitals, though. After realizing I could not win this argument, I reluctantly went along. I climbed out of the passenger seat, balancing myself with one crutch. I had left the other one at home. I could get around better with just one now. Something caught my eye beside the brick entrance. I turned to see what it was, but nothing was there.

The doctor went through his normal routine; checking my temperature, ears, nose and throat. He listened to my heart. I wondered if he could tell it was broken. I imagined him telling Mom that I was suffering from a broken heart. "*It's not fixable,*" he would say. "*There's nothing we can do for her.*" There wasn't anything that anyone could do for me... nothing at all. What was the point in living if the one person I loved couldn't be here with me? Or in my case, the one spirit I loved didn't want to be with me anymore.

I could hear the doctor talking with Mom, "a touch of a

cold…maybe a stomach virus…plenty of rest." I wished I could go to sleep, never to wake again; like Sleeping Beauty, only to wake when she felt her true love's kiss. But I would never feel his kiss. I couldn't feel his touch. And now that he was gone, pain and emptiness was all I felt.

Before I climbed back into Mom's car, the sound of Jordan's car started up in the parking lot, just a few spaces down from ours. I looked in his direction. He was watching me. I turned away, angry, and climbed in quickly. Mom drove me home after a brief stop at the pharmacy for a new bottle of Motrin. She needed to get to work. She had missed a great deal of work these last several months, all because of me.

As we pulled into the driveway, I spotted Jordan's car parked a couple houses down from ours. I didn't want to deal with him right now. I didn't want to deal with anyone, especially *his* criticism. *He* was the reason Tristan left and I hated him for that. I calculated the distance from the car to the house and how much time it would take for me to get there before he reached me. I could see him sitting in the driver's seat and, after telling Mom goodbye, I made my move. Mom backed away, honked, and began slowly driving down the street. I didn't look his way, but I heard his car door slam and knew it would only be a matter of seconds. I could hear his footsteps approaching, and I picked up my pace. My leg ached with the amount of weight I was putting on it. I balanced myself on my crutch and reached for the front door just as his hand reached around me and held the door closed.

I turned with all the rage building up in me and screamed, "Go away, Jordan!"

"Are you sick? Why were you at the hospital?"

"It's none of your business—just leave!" I wanted to go up to my bed and hide from the world.

"What's going on, Court?"

A lump formed in my throat and my body began to shake. I knew I was losing it. The tears started flowing like a rapid moving stream. My chest ached and my body began to fall. I couldn't handle it anymore; I couldn't handle the pain of losing Tristan.

Jordan wrapped his arms around me and helped me sit on the step. He held me tight while I sobbed uncontrollably.

After several minutes, I began forming words. "He's gone, Jordan," I sobbed. "He left and I'm lost."

Jordan straightened up and pulled back, his hands still on my shoulders. "He's gone?"

I broke down again at the sound of him saying the words.

"Why? Why did he leave?"

"He left because no one would ever accept us. He couldn't give me what he thought I needed. But I needed him; that was all—just him."

Jordan pulled me close to him again, holding me tight to control my shaking.

"I'm sorry, Court. I'm so sorry. This is entirely my fault. I can't bear to see you like this."

He helped me to my feet and into the house. I lay on the couch while he grabbed an afghan and pillow from the nearby chair. He sat on the floor with his back resting against the couch. For a while, neither of us spoke a word. My shaking finally died away. I felt drained.

"We have to find him," he broke the silence without facing me.

I wasn't sure how he planned on doing that. Tristan wasn't someone you could call information and get a number for. Not to mention the fact that I was the only person who could see him. Going to extremes with a search party would be pointless. He left me here...alone. He didn't want me to find him. Jordan's suggestion seemed impossible. Yet, curiosity struck me. Why would Jordan want to find him anyway? Wasn't he happy that Tristan was gone? I sat up on the couch and Jordan turned to face me. Tear stains streaked his face.

"I thought this was what you wanted; I thought you couldn't wait for Tristan to be out of the picture," I said.

"I thought that too, but your pain is tearing me up inside." He looked sincere and he lowered his head. "I know I can't be with you, Courtney. I see now how much you love him, and it's killing me to let you go." He looked back up at me. "I've loved you for so long, but I would never forgive myself if I was the one that caused you this much pain."

I slid to the floor and wrapped my arms around him. I wished he could have come to see my love for Tristan before it had come to this. But Jordan was my friend; my best friend. I couldn't possibly hold this against him.

"So, what do we do now?" I asked. If Jordan had some kind of plan to his brilliant idea, I was all ears.

"What's the best way to find a ghost?" he said with his quirky smile.

"I don't know! He found me—I think."

"Jeez, girl. You've got to open yourself up to greater possibilities. You really are sheltered. I'm surprised you even accepted the idea he was real. Who are the only people you've heard of that can speak with the dead—besides you, that is?"

I thought about this for a few minutes. "I don't know—a medium maybe?"

His smile widened. "Know where we can find a good medium when we need one?"

I shook my head. Then I remembered Tiffany's friend, Valerie. She had never said she was a psychic, but she knew an awful lot about spirits. She sure fit the part. I remembered Tiffany's note. I had hidden it inside my jewelry box, under the bottom drawer.

Jordan and I climbed the stairs to my room, and I quickly pulled out the jewelry box drawer, spilling its contents on top of the dresser. He stood in the doorway, looking around at the pink canopy and furry pillows that lay across my bed. Stuffed animals sat in the windowsill.

"What?" I asked as he scanned my room.

"You're such a girl," he laughed.

I grabbed a stuffed dog and threw it at his head. He ducked as it sailed past him and landed in the hallway. I was glad to have my friend back. Now, if I could only get the love of my life to come back.

After Jordan fished my phone out from underneath the dresser, we sat down on the bed and dialed Tiffany's number. My hands were shaking as I punched the numbers of my cell phone. I looked at the clock, knowing she would be at work at this time. It was eleven-thirty. If this was her cell number, I may catch her at lunch.

"Hello?" she answered.

"Tiffany!"

"Courtney? Oh my gosh! How are you? How's Tristan?"

"That's why I'm calling. Tristan's gone."

"What do you mean, gone? Did he find out what was troubling him?"

"Not exactly, but something is troubling him. Can we meet with you and Valerie?"

"I don't get off until seven-thirty tonight. Do you want us to come over?"

"No—not here. I'd have to meet you somewhere."

I looked at Jordan and he nodded. "They can meet us at my house," he said, without hesitation.

We agreed on eight-thirty. "Tiffany," I said before hanging up, "I need Valerie to try to contact Tristan tonight. Can she do that?" I asked.

"If anyone can contact him, it would be her."

I gave her the address and closed my phone. I sighed and looked back at Jordan.

"We'll find him, don't worry." He smiled. "Guess I'll be telling your parents I'm taking you on that date after all."

"This is not a date!"

"I know that, but what are you going to say to them? That you are out looking for your ghost?"

He was right. A date would be the only logical explanation that I could give them.

"When we do find him, I don't have to like him—right?" he asked.

"*If* we find him! And I don't expect you to like him—just accept him."

"Yeah, okay. Whatever makes you happy."

"And no more kisses!"

"Ah, come on! You're asking quite a bit from me, ya know."

For once in this past week, things seemed a bit brighter. I was tired of feeling empty. At least, now, I had something to look forward to. And, to top things off, my best friend was back.

There were things Jordan had to take care of at home. He had promised to get the yard work done and work on his mom's car before she left for work. His mom worked nights, and he planned to drop his sister off at the neighbors. I went around the house after Jordan left, straightening up and putting a load of laundry in the wash. It was impossible to clean using my crutch, and I found the more I walked on my bad leg, the easier it became. I had to make Mom believe I was feeling much better. She'd never let me go anywhere if I was still under the weather. I wasn't sure what to expect tonight, but I was extremely hopeful. This was the only thing I knew of to do. I needed Tristan back in my life. I needed him to know that Jordan came to accept our relationship.

I watched the clock. Time seemed to stand still. I went to the hall table and began opening the presents I had left there: a laptop, a new purse, several new novels, and a present from Jordan. I opened the flat, rectangular present. A painted portrait of myself stared up at me inside a beautiful, cherry wood frame. Once again, I was amazed at how talented Jordan really was. He must have dropped it off yesterday while I was sulking in bed.

After grabbing a hammer and nail from the garage and having to make two trips up and down the stairs, I managed to get my gifts to my room. I set the laptop on my desk along with the purse and books. Above Jordan's sketch from third grade, I hung the newly painted portrait of me. Afterwards, I occupied myself with folding laundry and washing dishes; anything that did not require a lot of walking. Vacuuming would be a little too much at this point.

I decided to cook spaghetti for my parents. They could eat and relax while I dressed for my date. The aroma from the garlic bread and spaghetti sauce filled the house. My stomach growled so I sampled a little, making sure I washed my plate afterwards. I would need to give them the impression I was eating out. The house looked immaculate by the time my parents arrived home. I heard the garage door open, and I finished setting the table. They always arrived home at the same time. I think Dad waits in the parking lot where Mom works until she gets in her car, and then she follows him home. Most of the time, Mom would ride with him. He would just drop her off on the way. Today was an exception since she insisted on dragging me to the doctor.

They were both surprised, as I knew they would be. I usually helped around the house but, most of the time, it wasn't a voluntary ordeal. It was approaching six o'clock and they seemed eager to sit down to eat.

"You appear to be feeling better," Mom stated. "The house looks wonderful and supper smells great. What's the occasion?"

"Nothing really, I just had a little energy today after I took a nap. I wanted to help out and give you both time to relax."

"Thank you," they both said in unison as they exchanged looks of confusion.

"Oh, and thanks for the gifts," I said with a smile.

"Well, we figured the laptop would come in useful at college this spring," Dad said as he unfolded the napkin beside his plate.

They began eating as I went to the fridge and grabbed the milk.

I wasn't sure how to tell them I would be leaving with Jordan this evening. Do I come out and just say it? or do I ask for their permission? I had never asked to go on a date before.

"Aren't you forgetting something?" Dad asked.

I turned around, my mind scanned through things I might have forgotten. "Um—" I couldn't think of anything. I looked at him with confusion.

"A plate? Aren't you eating?" he asked.

I needed to mention it now. "Um—no. Jordan—well—he stopped by today and asked me out to dinner."

They both stopped chewing. Mom glanced at Dad before she laid her fork on her plate and wiped her hands on her napkin.

"That's wonderful!" she chimed. "Right, honey?" She nudged Dad who nodded in agreement before he continued to chewing. He was really a man of very few words. "Are you going dressed in shorts and a t-shirt or do you plan on changing before he arrives?" she asked.

I looked down at my clothes. If they knew I was going to summon up a spirit, they wouldn't have asked that question; but they thought it was a date, so date clothes was what I needed to find. I laughed a little and excused myself from the room.

What in the world would I wear on a date? If I knew Jordan, and I felt I knew him pretty well, then he would claim to be taking me to some fancy restaurant. Fast food would not pass as a date. I flipped through the clothes hanging in my closet. What would I wear to a séance? I grinned to myself. It sounded so mysterious and comical at the same time. I was anxious to see Tristan again, to have him back in my life.

My hand stopped at a white, sleeveless dress. I had always liked this dress but I hardly ever wore it. It wouldn't be something that someone would wear to a séance, I was certain of that. I pulled it out of the closet and held it up in front of me as I examined it in the mirror. It would definitely be something to wear to, hopefully, catch the eye of the man you love. It was perfect.

I slipped into the dress and examined myself in the mirror again. Many of the scars on my leg were hidden under the hem of the dress. One long scar stretched down the inside of my calf but, really, was not that noticeable. This dress was a good choice. I hoped Tristan would agree. I looked back at the mirror; my eyes gazed upon the tired, dull reflection that looked back at me. Dark, puffy circles rested underneath my eyes. There surely wasn't enough makeup concealer in the world to cover these circles. I slid onto the vanity bench, praying I could do wonders with the makeup I had.

The doorbell rang and I looked over at the clock. 7:30. Jordan arrived earlier than I had expected. I ran a brush through my hair and decided it was best to pull it up. This is the closest I've ever came to a date. I went back to the closet to search for a pair of shoes that I wouldn't fall and break my other leg in. I settled on a pair of white flats and made my way down the stairs. Mom, Dad, and Jordan stood waiting in the foyer. Jordan had a dumbfounded expression, almost as if he had never seen a member of the opposite sex.

"What?!" I snapped at him.

He grinned, "Sorry, you look really hot." He looked over at my parents quickly and back at me. "I mean, you look very beautiful." He stood there, obviously nervous, and amazingly handsome. He wore a pair of tan khaki's and a light green button down shirt.

I grabbed his arm and headed for the door. "Bye Mom, bye Dad." I wanted to get out of there before they had a chance to ask questions that I didn't have answers to; like what restaurant we were eating at.

"Midnight, no later," Dad said in a stern voice, obviously directed at Jordan.

"Yes, Mr. Nacoal," Jordan responded as he helped me out of the front door. I looked back to see Mom and Dad both standing in the doorway, apparently watching their only child grow up, and most likely not liking one bit of it.

I waited until we were seated in the car before I spoke. "Midnight?"

Jordan grinned, obviously pleased with himself. "I didn't know how long it would take. I told your parents we were going to the city to eat, then to a movie afterwards."

"What am I supposed to say when they ask about the movie?!"

"I've thought of everything. Don't panic. We're going to look up the reviews online before I take you back home."

He started the car and pulled away. I sank back in the seat and stared out of the passenger window. I thought I caught a glimpse of someone standing behind a tree. I sat up, straining my eyes to see who it was. My mind must be playing tricks on me. As we passed, there was obviously no one there. My heart fell. I was looking for him everywhere.

"Are you sure you don't want to make this a half date/half ghost hunting expedition?" Jordan asked with his eyes fixed on the road ahead. "I could take you to TGIF's. We have time."

I glared at him. "That's why you showed up so early!" I spat. "No, I'm not really that hungry anyway and remember—THIS IS NOT A DATE!"

"At least let's go to Subway then. I'm starving," He looked over at me. "I could resort to begging if you wished."

I rolled my eyes and caved. I could use a sandwich too. I wasn't sure how long this evening would take, and I didn't want to find out whether or not Jordan was a good cook. "Subway's fine, but let's get it to go."

We grabbed a couple of sandwiches and headed over to Jordan's house. His mom had already left for work, and she wasn't due back home until quarter after midnight. I could see his sister and the neighbor girl swinging on the neighbor's swing set outside.

His room was in the basement, looking more like a dungeon than anything. A perfect place for a séance, I thought. The walls were old brick and mortar with his paintings covering nearly half of them. The other half was lined with shelves that held hundreds of books from every genre imaginable; fiction, art, poetry, even children's books filled the shelves and were stacked in the corners.

A single light bulb hung from the ceiling. His room took up the entire basement. There was a full sized metal frame bed off in the corner with a night stand supporting a smaller lamp next to it. In the middle of the room sat a card table with four folding chairs.

He walked over to the card table, slid a chair out, and waited for me to sit down. He positioned himself in the chair across from me and lit a large white candle, setting it on a saucer in the middle of the table.

"What are you doing?" I asked.

He smiled and leaned back in his chair. "It's for the séance," he said as he took a bite of his sandwich.

"Looks more like a candle lit dinner." I glared at him from across the table. "How do you know if we need a candle for this thing anyway?"

"I don't," he replied, "Just in case."

My phone rang inside my purse. Tiffany had already clocked out and was heading over to pick up Valerie. I explained to her what had happened and why Tristan had left, that way Valerie would come prepared for whatever needed to be done. I closed my phone and my heart began to beat rapidly. I was anxious for them to arrive, but I was more excited to see Tristan again.

"So what does he look like anyway, your ghost?" Jordan asked.

I began describing him; his eyes, his skin, and the gentle way he spoke.

"Yeah, yeah. That's not what I mean. Can you see through him? Is he like—all fuzzy looking? What exactly does a ghost look like?"

"Tristan looks normal. I can't see through him. He looks just like you and me," I explained.

He sat there, quietly, digesting the information. "How do you think he died?"

"I don't know. He doesn't remember anything about his life at all." I went into detail about my stay in the hospital in Paris, how Tristan came to visit me, how he's been with me ever since. A feeling of sadness washed over me. I had missed him terribly this last week.

"But you can't feel him touch you," he said, looking directly in my eyes.

"I can feel his touch, just not in the way you're saying."

His forehead creased a bit.

"It's not the actual touch, the nerves in my skin or anything like that. It's the sensation under my skin, in my stomach, my heart, everywhere."

"I guess—I—I understand," he said as he looked away.

I could sense his pain, his jealousy, but I didn't know how to ease it. Jordan was my friend, my best friend, but that's all he was and I wished it was enough for him. I loved Tristan, and Jordan knew that. All that was left to say was answered by the silence that filled the room.

We heard a faint knock at the front door and we both made our way upstairs, Jordan a great distance ahead of me while I used my hands and my one good leg to climb the wooden steps. I imagined I looked like quite a sight in my white dress, crawling up the steps. Tiffany and Valerie stood on the front steps holding candles.

"I told you we needed candles!" Jordan exclaimed, obviously pleased with himself. I glared at him and he chuckled.

Tiffany still wore her nurse's uniform while Valerie was dressed in a flowing white skirt and a lacy white blouse with sleeves that opened wider around her wrists. She no longer wore the bangle bracelets. In fact, the only jewelry was a cross hanging around her neck. I introduced them both to Jordan.

We all followed Jordan back downstairs. After we were seated at the card table, Valerie began explaining the process.

"We all must be strong believers. There can't be any doubt that lingers in the room, for this could give off negative energy."

This would not be difficult for me; I was in love with a spirit. A year ago I would have probably given off negative energy, but not today. I was sure Tiffany did not harbor any doubt either. She was the one who introduced me to Valerie. The only person in question would be Jordan. I looked in his direction. He was listening intently to what Valerie was saying. Yet, he was the one who suggested we find Tristan. I felt confident that we all believed what we were about to do would work.

"Next, we need to charge the candles with our energy." Valerie passed each candle around and we silently held it before passing it on to the next person. When it arrived back to Valerie, she lit each one and placed them throughout the room. We did the same with the candles she placed in the center of the table. She explained how she would say a short prayer, both at the beginning of the process and at the end. She asked us to all hold hands and focus on relaxing. She stood and pulled the string that hung from the ceiling light. Now the only light that illuminated the room came from the positively charged candles that flickered on the walls. I could hear my heart beat louder, anticipating Tristan's arrival.

Brandy Walsh

"If you love someone, set them free. If they come back, they're yours; if they don't, they never were. — Richard Bach"

Chapter 12

The Séance

Valerie's voice was soft as she spoke.

"We have gathered here at this location this evening to open up communication with one particular spirit. He answers to the name Tristan. We only wish to speak with Tristan at this time." Valerie looked at each of us and asked us all to repeat after her. "Tristan, please join us."

In unison, the four of us softly chanted the phrase three times.

"Tristan, please join us."

"Tristan, please join us."

"Tristan, please join us."

Valerie lowered her head and we did the same. "We will ask questions that require a yes or no answer. If the answer is yes, we ask you to knock once. If the answer is no, we ask you to knock twice. Tristan—are you with us now?"

Silence.

"Tristan," she began again, "if you are with us, please knock once."

We sat extremely still, no one dared move. The stillness of the dark filled the basement, but there was no knock that would break the silence. We could faintly hear Jordan's dog, Bo, barking in the backyard.

"Everyone here, sitting at the table, please breathe in through your nose and out through your mouth. With each breath, will your body to relax and let the positive energy flow through you."

The sound of our breathing was the only sound we could hear.

"Tristan." Valerie paused briefly. "We invite you into our circle to speak with us. If you are with us, please knock once."

The room was deathly silent again.

"Can you give us another sign that you are present in this room?"

We lifted our heads, each one of us hoping to see some kind of sign. Nothing. The candles stayed lit, the flicker of the flame unchanged. The air around us remained calm. There was no unexpected draft or change in temperature.

"I'm sorry, Courtney. We need to close the circle now. If we leave it open, uninvited guests may try to come through."

My heart began to sink. This was my last hope. "Please, Valerie," I whispered. "Just one more try."

She smiled back at me, straightened up and closed her eyes. "Tristan, Courtney is here and desperately wishes to speak with you. Can you give us some kind of sign that you have joined us?"

Once again, there was silence and the sound of my heartbeat increasing, but nothing else. I began to worry that Valerie would close the circle. "Tristan," I began. "Please talk to me. I need you to come back. I need you in my life." A tear made its way down my cheek. We sat in silence for several more minutes. He didn't respond. My heart ached as I was losing all hope of ever seeing him again. I lowered my head in defeat, biting my lip to hold in my sobs.

"Before we close our circle, we want to thank all spirits who respected our wishes and allowed us to try to communicate with Tristan. We ask, if anyone else is here, that you go in peace." She raised her head and blew out the candles that still flickered in the middle of the table. Darkness engulfed us, until Valerie pulled the light string that chased it away. "You can let go of each others hands; this will break the circle and close the veil between the two worlds."

Jordan and Tiffany let go of my hands as I stared at the unlit candles on the table. All hope was lost. I had no way to reach him. Despair washed over me. The only way I would ever see him again was if I was like him.

"I'm sorry, Courtney," Valerie said with sincerity. "I don't know what else to do."

"I do," I said as Jordan turned to look at me.

"What?" Jordan asked.

"I have to go to him. I have to be like him," I replied. I lowered my head because I knew all eyes were on me.

"You have to WHAT?!" Jordan yelled.

"Jordan, it's the only way I'll see him again," I pleaded, hoping he would understand.

"Over my dead body! Are you crazy?!" Jordan shot out of his chair and began pacing the floor.

"I can't go on like this," I said softly.

Valerie leaned across the table and took my hands in hers. "Courtney. Suicide is not an option. There would be no guarantee where your soul would go. You have to start thinking rationally."

"I can't even think right now! Trying to reach him through a séance was my only hope!" The tears fell more quickly. "Maybe I don't have to die; maybe I have to be close to dying. That's how he came to me the first time, when I had my accident." I looked up at each of them. They weren't seeing things the way I did. I turned to Jordan who began pacing the floor again. "Jordan," I said softly.

"No way!" he replied. "No way are you even going to be close to dying. You're starting to make me think you have truly lost your mind."

Tiffany had been sitting in silence through the entire conversation but turned to ask Valerie a question. "What would be the reasons why he didn't join us?" she asked.

"There could be several reasons," Valerie replied. She turned back to me. "Courtney, was Tristan angry when he left?"

I thought about this for a minute. He seemed angry at first, but more at the fact that he couldn't do anything for me. "He wasn't angry at me; he seemed hurt. He may have been a little angry about feeling helpless."

"He might have been here, with us, but too angry to communicate," Valerie suggested.

I shook my head. "He would have said something if he knew I

went to these extremes to contact him."

"Is there someone in the room, then, that Tristan does not approve of?" We all turned to look at Jordan.

"Ah, come on! Don't tell me the spook is going to refuse to talk to Courtney because he holds a grudge against me!"

"It's a possibility. We should not open our circle again tonight, but we could try again soon, without Jordan, that is."

Jordan sat back down in the chair, obviously sulking at the thought of being excluded.

"There is another reason why he may not have communicated," Valerie said as she thought about this. "He may still be trapped in this world and not passed to the other side. We opened a veil between the two worlds, the one of the living and the one of the dead. He's been in our world; it's possible he still is."

This made sense to me. When he left, he still didn't remember anything about his past life. There was a possibility that he was still a lost spirit. But where was he? Was he searching for answers so he could cross over?"

It gave me new hope. I looked at Valerie. "How can I find him, if he's still here?"

"I don't know for sure. He may go back to where he first met you. He'll travel to his first memory, if he has finally decided to find the answers."

I would need to take a trip to Paris. How would I get away from my parents? This was something I needed to do and quickly.

"If you're thinking about going to Paris, I'm going with you this time," Jordan said. "I don't need you picking up any other ghosts along the way."

I glared at him as he sat smugly back in his chair, his arms folded across his chest. I didn't want to go alone, but I had doubts about bringing Jordan along. "What if he won't talk to me because you're there?"

"Well, if he's that petty of a ghost, you shouldn't be with him anyway," he said as he smirked at me.

Valerie stood and began gathering the candles up. "I really must be going. There's nothing else we can do tonight. If you two are going to Paris, I wouldn't mind tagging along."

"Me either," Tiffany said. "I have two weeks of vacation time I can use."

I felt a little better about the evening. There was still a chance that I could find Tristan, and it felt good knowing that friends would accompany me on such a journey.

We climbed the stairs and stood in the hallway to say our good-byes. Bo continued to bark outside, and Jordan went to the back to let him in.

"Bo, get in here! What is the matter with you?" Jordan shouted from the door. "Come on, boy!"

I walked to the back door to see if I could help. Most of the neighbors were probably getting ready for bed, and they would surely call the cops about a noise disturbance. Bo always came running when he saw me. Tiffany and Valerie followed close behind. I moved in front of Jordan who still stood in the doorway.

"Bo!" I hollered. Just then, Tristan stepped out of the shadow next to Jordan's car. "Tristan!" The blood rushed through my body, sending a warm sensation to my face. I ran out the back door and down the steps, stabbing pains shooting through my leg. "You did come!" I stopped right in front of him, knowing that I could not wrap my arms around him or I would surely fall on my face. His face was full of sorrow.

"Come to what?—your little date with Jordan?"

"Date?! This is not a date!"

"Then what would you call it? You got all dressed up, stopped to get sandwiches, and you've been at his house ever since. It's none of my business anyway; I'm the one who left." He turned to leave, again.

"Wait just a minute! How did you know we stopped to get sandwiches? Have you been following me?" I began laughing, hysterically.

"What?!" Tristan said. "What's so funny?"

"You've been here all along, haven't you? You've been at my house; you were even at the doctor's office. It was *you* behind the tree earlier tonight when we left!"

"I just didn't want to leave you, Courtney," he said softly. "I don't know how to explain it but I—couldn't leave. I know whatever this is isn't natural, but I do love you."

"Tristan, I got dressed up to see you," I said.

Jordan, Tiffany, and Valerie walked up beside me.

Tristan looked at Jordan and the others. "I think you should probably fill me in on what's going on," he said.

Tiffany and Valerie stood beside me smiling.

"I guess the spook's back," Jordan said.

I slapped him on the shoulder and turned back to Tiffany and Valerie. Tiffany turned in the direction that she assumed Tristan stood. "Well, Tristan," Tiffany began. "Courtney and Jordan called, hoping to find a way to contact you. I called Valerie and we agreed to meet here."

Valerie stepped forward, looking in the same direction. "We met here to perform a séance to open the communication back up between you and Courtney."

"A séance?" He looked at me. "You weren't going out with Jordan?"

"No, Jordan wants you here—with me. Don't you, Jordan?" I looked back at Jordan so he could reassure Tristan that I was speaking truthfully.

"If the little ghost makes you happy, that's what I want," he said, directed solely at me.

"Jordan! Can't you just be nice for once!" I exclaimed.

"Sorry." Jordan turned in Tristan's direction. "I think you should stay, for Courtney's sake. Obviously you're the one she wants, and she'll never be happy without you." He turned back to face me. "Better? You know, it feels really weird talking to thin air like this."

"Tristan, I would do anything for you to come back. My life has been so empty this last week. Please tell me you're going to stay."

"Yeah," Jordan spoke. "If you only knew what she was contemplating down there after this séance thing didn't work."

"What's he talking about?" Tristan asked.

"Nothing, really." I tried to think of something to change the subject, but Jordan wouldn't let it go.

"If she won't tell you, I will. She wanted to commit suicide so she could find you," he said, smugly.

"Is he telling the truth? Courtney, you can't ever think like that!" He stepped closer to me, laying his hands on the outside of my face. Although I couldn't feel his touch, I felt safe and secure with the tenderness I imagined. "I won't leave you again," he said softly. "I'll never go unless you tell me to."

"Um," Valerie interrupted. "You didn't hear us calling to you during our séance?"

Tristan shook his head no. I looked at Valerie and shook my head, repeating his response.

"He must still be trapped in our world," she said with a look of concern on her face.

"This is so exciting!" Tiffany chimed, "much better than knocking once or twice!"

"Yeah," Jordan began, "a real hoot. We need to move into the house. My neighbors are going to wonder why we're all out here talking to my car."

We scanned the nearby houses to see if there was movement behind the few windows that remained lit. Tristan and I followed the other three back inside. I was so happy to have him beside me. Tiffany and Valerie sat in the recliners in the living room, while Jordan, Tristan, and I sat on the couch, me in between the two.

Valerie still looked concerned. "I'm not so sure this is a good idea, having Tristan remain in this world." We all looked in her direction. "It's really not safe for him to stay very long."

"What do you mean, not safe?" I asked. "Not safe for whom?"

"It may not be safe for him. The longer he stays here, the harder it will be for him to cross over. Spirits are not meant to live among us."

Here she goes again with the "not living among us" speech.

"I don't want him to go anywhere," I said.

"Maybe we should speak with the pastor at my church. He could help us with this. I just think you should know a little more about what you're getting yourself into. And—Tristan should know what could possibly lay ahead if he remains here with you."

I didn't want any harm to come to Tristan. I didn't want to be the reason why something bad happened to his soul. I looked at him. He sat there, shaking his head.

"We'll go," I said. "We'll speak with your pastor."

"No, we won't," Tristan said.

"What could it hurt?" I asked.

"So you're suddenly okay with me having to leave here, never to return again?"

"No, I'm not okay with that. But—I think we should find out how long you do have, before it becomes dangerous for you."

"Maybe I've been here too long already," he said. "Maybe there is no *crossing over* for me."

That thought had never entered my mind. I wasn't sure what to do next. I sat back against the couch. Suddenly I felt confused. I didn't want to lose him. I didn't want to live without him.

"Valerie. Could you speak with your pastor? Could you find out if there is any way that Tristan could stay here, you know, in this world?"

"It's not like asking someone for a slumber party. You can't get permission to stay." She could read my sadness, though. "I'll talk to him."

"This doesn't have to happen right now," Tiffany said. "You should both be happy you're with one another. Enjoy each other. I'm so happy he didn't go away, even though I was looking forward to going to Paris with all of you."

"Paris?" Tristan asked. "You were planning on going back to Paris?"

"Only to find you," I replied.

Valerie and Tiffany stood to say good-bye. I walked them both to the front door and gave each a warm hug. "Thank you, both of you."

"You can call me anytime," Tiffany said softly. I watched as they both climbed into Tiffany's car and drove away. I could hear voices coming from the living room and I silently approached the doorway to listen.

"You know," Jordan began, "she said I don't have to like you; I only have to put up with you."

I knew Jordan couldn't hear Tristan's response, which I was very glad of at this moment. "I don't know what she sees in you, even as a friend," Tristan said. "You're just an obnoxious jerk."

I walked around the corner, smiling at each of them. Yeah, the two of them were a little bullheaded, but I was happy to have them both, the love of my life and my best friend, sitting in the same room, even if they weren't the most civil pair in the world.

Brandy Walsh

To the living, a lost soul is someone who has no clear path or direction in life. They seem to wander aimlessly, not towards anything in particular. A lost soul is someone who cannot find their way. What if the lost soul doesn't *want* to find their way? Are they still lost?

Chapter 13

Unanswered Questions

Once Jordan had dropped Tristan and me off at my house, I had assumed I would be able to sneak upstairs unheard. I was wrong. Dad sat in the living room, pretending to watch television. It had suddenly occurred to me that we had not looked up the reviews on any of the movies playing in the theaters. *Please don't ask about the movie,* I quietly thought to myself.

"How was your evening?" Dad asked.

"Oh—Dad, it was great but I'm exhausted. Can I tell you about it tomorrow? I'd like to go to bed."

"Well at least tell me what movie you went to see."

My palms got sweaty. I had no idea what was playing. I wasn't very good at lying either. "I'm trying to remember the title but—"

Tristan's voice whispered in my ear. "The Lake House."

Dad looked at me. I was sure he could read the panic on my face. "Oh, I remember—*The Lake House,*" I said.

"Oh! I've heard that was a good movie. What was it about again?"

"Tell him it's about two people who fall in love; they learn they live two years apart." Tristan whispered again.

"Um, well—" I began, "there are these two people who fall in love, but they find out they live two years apart."

"Yeah, I remember now. The previews for that one looked

really good. I'm glad you had a good evening."

"Thanks, Dad. Night!" I hollered as I made my way upstairs. I closed the door once I was inside my room. Tristan stood at the end of my bed, staring at the painted portrait that hung above my headboard.

"The painting really captures your beauty," he said, never taking his eyes off of it.

I could feel my face begin to flush. He was the only guy who had really called me beautiful. My friends told me how pretty I was, even mentioning that guys at school thought I was "hot." I sat on the edge of the bed and looked at myself in the mirror. I didn't see it. I always thought I was plain. Tristan sat next to me, gazing at my reflection in the mirror as well.

"Jordan painted it for me—for my birthday," I said as I turned to look at him.

"It's a wonderful gift. I missed your birthday," he said as he lowered his head. "I'm sorry, Courtney."

"You gave me the best birthday gift ever." I turned to him. "You came back; that's all I wanted."

"I won't miss another birthday as long as I can help it. I promise."

I could hear my father's footsteps on the stairs. I lay down in bed and Tristan lay next to me. My door slowly opened a crack, and then closed again. Within fifteen minutes, I could hear Dad's snores making their way through the thick walls.

"How did you know about the movie *The Lake House?*" I asked Tristan.

He continued to smile at me. "This last week has been torture on me too. I didn't have anyone to talk to." He laughed a little and continued. "Well, I guess I've talked to people but they were always one sided conversations. I told your friend Jordan off every time he stood on your front steps. By the way, did you know the little twerp talks to himself?"

I shook my head.

"At first, I thought he had answered me. I had just finished yelling at him to go away when he mumbled something. It caught me off guard a bit, I have to admit. I imagined for a second that he heard me."

"What did he say?"

"He asked why you wouldn't answer him. Then he sat down on the steps and started comparing himself to me. He's been in love with you for a long time. I don't blame him."

A sudden feeling of guilt washed over me. I felt bad for Jordan, hiding a secret affection for me that I had never known about. Then I come home from Paris to tell him I was in love.

"Anyway," he continued, "time is different for me. It doesn't pass by in minutes or hours, days or nights. I guess it just exists. But this time I existed in a state of nothingness, wandering around—empty. One minute I'd be watching you sleep, while another I would find myself in the movie theatre. I have even seen some movies three or four times."

I had felt the black hole of loneliness as well. Even though I had my parents to talk to, I avoided them as much as possible. "Well, in a way, I'm thankful. I had no idea what was even playing."

I knew I would sleep much better tonight, now that Tristan was here. I looked forward to dreaming about him, feeling his touch.

"Tell me what you and Jordan talked about. I mean, what made him finally come around?" He had obviously not been within hearing distance when I had my little breakdown on the front steps earlier today.

"I avoided him the entire time, up until today, that is. Then Mom took me to the doctor. Like the doctor would be able to diagnose a broken heart." I laughed a little. "But when I got out of Mom's car, Jordan was waiting down the street."

"Yeah, I saw him. I stayed back. Secretly, I was hoping you would slug him, but then he started hugging you and you weren't pulling away."

I imagined what it might have looked like to Tristan. "You were gone, Tristan. I just lost it. Jordan began to feel sorry for me."

"I wish I could hold you now. I want to be the one who comforts you. I guess Jordan was right; maybe I am a little jealous. I was so angry all day today, then seeing you leave with him tonight—I wanted to die." He laughed aloud at what he'd said.

"Just being here next to me is comfort enough. I *do* feel you holding me when I dream every night, at least when you're here."

He outlined my face with his fingers and softly whispered, "Dream, my love." And I did.

****

At first, the dream began as before. Tristan and I were walking, holding hands. We would stop, hold each other and gaze into each other's eyes. Our kisses were passionate, a fire growing between us, an uncontrollable blaze full of emotion. But the dream took an unpredictable turn. Tristan began releasing his hold on me. Our lips parted. I clung to him but something was pulling him away, something much stronger than me. "Tristan!" I could hear the sound of my own voice frantically screaming. "Don't go! Don't leave me here alone!"

****

I sat up, sweat beading on my forehead. Tristan stood next to the bed, worry washing over his face. My body filled with relief to see him beside me. Uncontrollable sobs escaped my throat.

"What is it? Courtney, what happened?" he asked as he knelt beside the bed.

I shook my head. "Nothing—yet." I looked into his worried eyes. "Oh, Tristan! I dreamt you were leaving. Something was pulling you away from me." I began sobbing again, quietly.

"I won't go," he said softly, his blue eyes full of pain. He tilted his head towards the ceiling. "I won't go!" he said again, filled with anger this time, not directed at me.

My heart ached for him. What could we do to stop it? My dream had been so vivid. There had been no way to hold on to him. A force, stronger than me, stronger than our love, would be what tore us apart. I could feel it and there would be nothing I could do.

"It was just a dream, just something you're worrying about," he said as he sat next to me on the bed.

"It scares you too, doesn't it?" I whispered back to him. I could see the worry crease across his brow. When he lowered his head, I knew. I knew he had dreamt the same thing. I knew Valerie's words lingered in the back of his mind. *"Spirits are not meant to live among us."*

"Tristan, what do you think could happen—if you stayed here too long?"

He shook his head.

I had to know. I had to know how bad it could be for him. Would he be a lost spirit forever? Would he change in some way? Would the gates of Heaven close on him forever? I had to know what would happen to his soul, his beautiful soul.

"Let's not discuss it; please Courtney. Let's just be together."

I could sense that the conversation was over. We could sit here and imagine what the future could hold, but we would never know for sure...not until the future became the present. That's when something *would* rip him from my arms. That's when my heart

would feel like it's been ripped from my chest…again. I sensed it. I could feel it. It was just a matter of time. But when? I tried to smile, to push the memory of the dream to the back of my mind. It wouldn't go. It danced in the open, taunting me every time I looked into his eyes. We lay awake for hours, neither of us wanting to say it aloud, neither of us wanting to talk about the end.

When morning finally arrived, the sunlight filled the room. Tristan smiled as I turned to face him. Something was different about his eyes. They were still a beautiful blue, but just a slight hint lighter than before. I imagined it was the lighting.

Over the next several days, Tristan and I spent most of our time reading, working on puzzles, and watching sappy love movies. We spent much of our time in my room. He had grown quite comfortable there, lounging on the floor or sprawled across the bed. I imagined if life had been normal for us, if Tristan and I could have ever married, this would be our life. We would have spent our time just being together, no one else. We were happy this way.

When my phone rang, and I knew that either Beth or Jess or Kari was on the other end, I pushed ignore more often than I answered it. The things they discussed were so trivial. They had no idea what real problems were. Kari complained about her new boyfriend wanting to spend time with his friends. Jess liked to discuss who was dating who. Beth complained about her clothes and how she needed another shopping trip so she could restock her closet. I didn't care about those things. Maybe, at one time, I would have sat for hours discussing their problems; But now, things were different. I didn't know how much time I had with Tristan, and I wanted to spend every minute with him.

Jordan didn't stop by for several days. I began to worry. I prayed that I didn't offend him or hurt his feelings in any way. He was the only friend that I could talk to right now. He was the only person, besides Tiffany and Valerie, who knew about Tristan.

There were several times over the last few days that I would catch Tristan staring at me, a torn, sad look on his face. We both sensed the other's worries. I was happy he was with me again, the loneliness nearly gone. Nearly. It was never completely gone. It was as if we both expected the loneliness to come back, and the next time it would be forever.

It was two o'clock in the afternoon when we decided to take a walk to the park. Therapy was going quite well and I could walk without the crutch. I still had a limp and my leg ached afterwards but I could tell it was getting stronger. The day was cool with a slight breeze. Children played on the park equipment while their parents stood close by, watching. We found a park bench near a patch of trees, out of the way. Normally, we would have just sat and enjoyed the day. We would have enjoyed the laughter around us. But something was bothering me. There were so many questions. The unknown had been eating at me. I needed answers. I knew he didn't have the answers, but I knew we needed a way to find them. I felt that my life was at a standstill, waiting for the unknown…waiting for him to be gone…to disappear.

"Tristan." I turned to look at him. He didn't respond. His gaze was set on the children. One small boy, about three years old, was being twirled around by his father. The little boy's laughter carried throughout the park. I smiled as I watched the father and son companionship. I turned back to Tristan to find his gaze set on me this time.

"We're going to miss out on so much," he said with a heavy sadness.

"I know." I lowered my head. This was the life I chose, though, and I wanted nothing more than him.

"You don't have to give up your life for me."

"I'm not giving up my life. You are the only life I want." I knew there would be a day when he would be gone. The only memories I would be left with were the memories we made together. I knew him only by a name that wasn't really his. "Can't you remember anything before you met me?"

He remained quiet, staring off in the distance as if he were searching for even a small remnant of who he once was. He turned back to me, shaking his head. "No," he said.

"How did you know you needed to be with me?"

"Can I ask you the same question?" he replied.

I thought back to the hospital room, feeling his presence there and knowing he could be someone I could love. His voice was so soft and calm. His eyes, his beautiful ocean blue eyes, were full of love, yet, full of sadness at times, too. I didn't want him to leave me. I just knew...I needed him. The dreams I had of him...of us... "I felt a love for you, Tristan, which I've never felt before. I felt safe with you."

"I felt the same thing, Courtney. But there was something else."

"What?" I asked eager to know what drew this beautiful spirit to my side.

"Something pulled me to you. I couldn't let you go. From the second you were in pain, I couldn't leave your side."

I looked into his eyes. The accident. I hadn't thought much about it but, now, memories of sirens and screaming came rushing back to me; memories of seeing him, memories of him telling me to wake up. He was there, comforting me when I was hurt.

"Do you remember anything about the accident—about when you first saw me?" I asked.

He shook his head. When he looked at me again, I could see the pain and torment in his eyes. "My very first memories are of you, lying there. There was blood everywhere. I didn't see anyone else. I didn't hear anyone else. I was terrified that you would never open your eyes. I don't know what happened. I have tried every day to remember something, anything that would explain the pain you had experienced. But I can't, Courtney, I'm sorry."

"I think we should talk to someone. Maybe I should be

hypnotized. If I could just remember, maybe it could answer a lot of the questions."

"What questions do you want answered? Are you searching for the answers of why I'm still here? Maybe I'm just here because I want to be with you. You know, answers are probably what I want to avoid."

"But why, Tristan?"

"Didn't you hear Valerie? I'm a lost soul. When I find out what's troubling me, I won't be lost anymore. I'll just be gone."

We sat in silence for another hour, watching the children laugh and play.

Some questions are best left unanswered; while some answers only create more questions.

Chapter 14

The Festival

The days were growing increasingly colder. Soon we would be confined to the comfort of the warm house. The winter months would be approaching soon, and winter had always been terrible here. Before winter arrived each year, our small town had its annual celebration. Most places would call it a county fair, but we called it the Wheat Festival. The women of our town would bake delicious pies, cakes, and breads. The town brought in a carnival equipped with rides and numerous attractions. There was always live entertainment and, on occasion, we would get some big name country singers to play. It was something everyone in town looked forward to throughout the entire year.

The festival was this weekend, and my friends were coming home from college to enjoy everything the town had to offer. It had been a ritual for all of us to go, ever since we were young children. My friends had been able to go without adults since they were twelve or thirteen. My parents, however, were never far away.

This year would be no different, especially since the accident and my little stay at the psychiatric hospital. But I knew they would want to sample the home-baked goods and watch the rodeo. I had made arrangements to meet everyone at the entrance to the fairgrounds this Saturday at noon. Jordan agreed to pick us up.

Mom and Dad were growing to like Jordan and didn't object to him taking me to the Wheat Festival.

I was looking forward to getting out of the house for an entire day. The tricky part would be not talking to Tristan. My friends were still unaware that I was in love with a spirit. Jordan had grown comfortable with me talking to the air, although he made his usual wise cracks about it.

I had been feeling shut away from the world for the last several months. Jess, Beth, and Kari were meeting new people, attending frat parties, and enjoying their freedom. Jordan had made the decision to postpone art school for a year or two, so he could take care of his mom and little sister. He still had a great deal more freedom than I did, however. He had a car, a job, and two good legs. I had none of these things. I was still unsure which road I wanted my future to take. I didn't even know if I wanted to attend college anymore. Mom and Dad wanted me to transfer my records to the local community college and stay close to home. I needed my own place, free to talk to Tristan as much as possible. Tristan and I spoke about this many times. He only wanted what I wanted; therefore, he wasn't any help in this decision. If I moved away to college I would be required to stay in the dormitory my first year. This would mean roommates and no privacy. If I chose to attend the community college, Mom and Dad insisted I stay home. This would mean parents and no privacy. I thought about getting a job and getting an apartment, but saving up for the deposit would take a good deal of time. My life was confusing. My friends were moving on and I was stuck at a standstill. Maybe the festival would be a welcome release for me.

Tristan seemed anxious as well, even though he had grown accustomed to spending so much time in my room. Our walks were mostly in silence, unless we stopped at the park bench nestled away in the trees. We had seen every movie and read numerous books. There were very few pastimes that two people could do in silence. I had been writing a lot in my journal, which I kept hidden in my closet in an empty shoebox. I'd written about my injuries and the slow recovery, about my struggles with my future, and my thoughts about college. Mostly, though, the pages were filled of Tristan and the love I felt for him. If Mom or Dad had ever come across my journal, I would surely be spending more time in the psychiatric hospital once again.

Saturday had finally arrived, and by the numerous phone calls, my friends were anxious to come home. They had so much to tell me about their college experiences. Jess had a new boyfriend. She wanted him to come home with her for the day, but he played ball for the college they both attended. "He's dreamy!" she exclaimed over the phone one night. "He plays football, quarterback. He wants to play pro after college." I had never heard her talk about football before. Now, she seemed to know everything about the game.

Jordan picked us up in front of my house at 11:30. It was only

62 degrees outside, but the sun was shining bright above. The warmth of the sun on my face made it feel warmer than it really was. I had brought a light jacket along; I knew as the day wore on and the sun began to set, there was sure to be a chill in the air. I told my parents it would be 11:00 P.M. before I would arrive back home. We planned to stay for the entertainment after the rodeo.

Jess, Beth, and Kari were all waiting by the entrance when we pulled into the dirt packed parking lot. I hardly recognized Kari with her new hairstyle. She had cut it short; it had longer strands that outlined her face and was fuller at the back. It was also colored a deep auburn. Bethany wore her same hairstyle but had lightened it so much that it was nearly blonde now. Her clothes also appeared to be a couple sizes too small. Her waist showed above her extremely tight jeans and her tight fitting low-cut shirt failed to cover the top of her lace bra. She was so excited to show me the new tattoo she recently acquired. It was a sun, stamped on the small of her back. It looked bright and painful and obviously only a few days old. Jordan seemed rather impressed by the tattoo, though, asking to get a closer look. Beth slapped him playfully and gave him a huge hug. Jess looked the same; her hair was pulled up in a ponytail, and she wore a bright sweatshirt that advertised the college she attended.

We gave each other hugs, all of us talking at once. They wanted to know how my leg was; I wanted to know how they were enjoying school, enjoying freedom.

"So," Jess leaned over to me, talking quietly so Jordan couldn't hear, "what's up with you and Jordan?"

I looked over at Jordan who seemed mesmerized by Beth's cleavage, and I rolled my eyes. "Nothing. We're friends," I told her. "He's the only one who hasn't gone away to school." I looked around to see where Tristan was. He stood back a few feet from the rest of us. When he caught my eye, he smiled; I quickly smiled back.

Kari grabbed my arm, as we all began to walk down the dirt path that took us into the fairgrounds. Every year we would make a quick walk through of the grounds to see what rides were there and which food stands we would be stopping at throughout the day. The rodeo wouldn't start until seven that evening; live music and dancing began at nine. Most of the rides were targeted at the younger children; merry-go-rounds and bumper cars, teacup rides and bounce houses. There were stands where you could throw darts or balls to win prizes and numerous food stands selling corndogs and funnel cakes. Everyone from town seemed to be out enjoying the festival. The children wore wristbands that their parents had purchased, which allowed them to ride as many rides as they wanted. It was a beautiful day and it felt good to be out in the sun, surrounded by friends.

At the far end of the fairgrounds, there was a funhouse full of mirrors. Next to it sat a small, brightly colored tent with a sign that read FORTUNE TELLING $5. I stopped in front of the tent and looked around at Tristan, who had been walking a short distance behind. He stood, shaking his head. This was the first time I had seen a fortuneteller at the festival before. The tent might have been here every year and I'd never noticed it. My mind began to race. Maybe this person held the answers to my questions of college and what lay ahead. I took a step forward as an old woman in bright clothing appeared in the tent's entryway.

"Would you like me to read your future, young lady?" she asked.

"Um—" I looked over at the others who wore confused expressions on their faces.

Jess spoke up. "No, we're just walking through." She grabbed my arm and steered me away.

"I'd like to know what my future holds," Jordan said as he stood there staring at the woman. She opened the tent for him to enter but Beth grabbed his arm and pulled him away as well. "What?!" he exclaimed.

Once we were all outside of hearing distance, Jess argued that it was a waste of money and we shouldn't believe in people like that. "They'll tell you things you want to hear," she said.

"So? What's the big deal?" Jordan asked. "It's better than someone telling me what I don't want to hear." Jess shoved him out of her way, jokingly.

We continued to walk through the grounds, stopping occasionally to throw darts at balloons or shoot a cork gun at targets. To me, this was a waste of money. Everyone knows that these games are fixed. If you do happen to hit several balloons, they give you the smallest toy. After winning again, you could upgrade to a bigger toy. By the time you had earned enough to trade in for the big teddy bear that hung from the tent, you had already spent nearly fifty dollars, much more than what you would have spent if you would have purchased the same bear at Wal-Mart.

Jordan managed to win a medium sized teddy bear that held a stuffed sugar bag in its paws, and he had only spent thirty-five dollars in the process. I rolled my eyes.

"Did you win that for Courtney?" Jess asked after he had picked out which bear he wanted.

My heart began to beat faster. I did not want him to agitate Tristan here in public. I turned to look at Tristan who was now glaring at Jordan, most likely wondering the same thing.

"No," Jordan said after a long hesitation. "I won this for my sister. She likes bears."

I let out a sigh of relief. We stopped to buy funnel cakes and sat at one of the many picnic tables far away from the noisy rides. I enjoyed hearing the laughter of the small kids, but Jess wanted to talk about Dustin, her quarterback boyfriend. She laid out pictures of him in his football gear, her and him at parties, and some that were taken in a picture booth you normally find in malls. It was obvious that Jess was in love. They had met the first day of college.

He was a sophomore, but they shared an economics class together. They started dating immediately, risking several times of being caught in each other's dorm room. I was both happy for her and envious of her at the same time. She was able to show everyone the man of her dreams. She could touch him, talk about him, and someday she may even plan a wedding with him. I could do none of these things. Very few people knew about Tristan. I could touch him and kiss him in my dreams, but that was it. We would never marry, never walk down the aisle and vow our love before God. Yet, Tristan was whom I wanted in my life. I turned to him and smiled.

After we finished eating our funnel cakes and caught up on everything that happened over the last several months, we started making our way around the rides and games again. We, once again, reached the funhouse with the small fortuneteller's tent beside it. The others planned on going in the funhouse; but I continued past and stopped in front of the old woman, who was now seated in her wooden rocker. She didn't say anything to me this time; she just simply smiled and waited.

Tristan's voice startled me when he spoke. "Courtney, don't go in there."

I turned to look at him; concern showed in his eyes and creased his brow. I looked around to make sure that the others had disappeared into the funhouse. Jordan stood on the steps to the funhouse looking down at me. Feeling confident that nobody but

Jordan and the fortuneteller could see me talking to myself, I whispered, "Why?"

"I just don't trust people like this. I don't trust anyone who claims they can see into the future."

"But Tristan," I began, "I just want to ask her about college— you know—what I should do. Where's the harm in that?"

Jordan approached beside us. "Yeah, Tristan, where's the harm in that?" Jordan said as he looked at me.

I glanced at Jordan and back at Tristan again. He had lowered his eyes and shook his head. The old woman stood and entered the tent. I followed Jordan inside and turned to make sure Tristan was still with me. He had followed us; however, he stopped and stood just inside the entrance to the tent.

"Sit, please," the fortuneteller began, in a very old and frail voice. "Your leg must be getting strained from the walking today. A terrible thing—that accident." She could have guessed my leg was strained; I still had a slight limp when I walked. I sat down in the wooden chair across the small table from her. Before I could ask her a question, she began speaking again.

"You are a very lovely lady, one who has found true love."

I turned quickly to look at Tristan who straightened a bit, but raised an eyebrow in question. I turned back to her and nodded.

"May I see the palms of your hands, my dear?"

I held out my hands for her to read. She held them in hers, gazing at them quietly for a minute. Her hands were cold but extremely soft. She closed her eyes. I looked at Jordan as the minutes seemed to pass. He shrugged.

"You have a long journey ahead of you. You and your friends seek answers; and answers will come." This was not making much sense; maybe she was referring to college.

Before I could ask, she continued. "You will live a long life, one with a beautiful home and the sounds of young voices at play."

I turned around to look at Tristan again, shock on his face this time. I pulled my hands away from the old woman. I knew I would never have children. I had chosen to be with Tristan.

"Trust in the things that cannot be seen, my dear," she continued, leaning towards me as she spoke. "I see a man in your future, a man with the initials—J.S."

I looked at Jordan, whose mouth had dropped open, and then I turned and ran towards Tristan, who was now making his way out through the opening in the tent.

"Tristan! Wait!" I yelled as he continued to walk. "Tristan! You said yourself that you didn't trust people like that. I don't believe anything she said!"

He stopped and turned. I could see the pain in his eyes. We were standing outside in the sunlight again; people began looking in our direction. It suddenly dawned on me; these people could only see me. Jess, Kari, and Beth came running up, and I heard Jordan approach from behind.

"Look, Courtney," Jordan whispered. "I know this is, you

know, important and can't wait and everything, but people are beginning to wonder what's up. We'd better get out of here before word gets to your parents."

"What in the hell are you two talking about?" Jess asked.

Jordan turned to face her. "Can't you see that Courtney is having an argument with her boyfriend?" he said.

Jessica looked at him in shock, and then to me with confusion. "I thought you said you two weren't dating?"

"We're not!" Jordan and I both yelled in unison. Then Jordan followed up with, "She's dating a ghost!"

The shock on all of their faces was almost comical.

I turned back to Tristan. "Can we just go somewhere and talk?"

He nodded and we both began walking to a place more secluded. There was a wooded area on the edge of the fair grounds, far enough out of the way that our voices wouldn't carry. I could hear Jordan and the others following behind us. He was filling them in on my secrets. There would be no use hiding it from them now anyway, they had already witnessed me talking to no one in particular. I wasn't sure how they would handle the information, but I was less worried about them and more worried about Tristan. What the fortuneteller said made absolutely no sense. I had to convince Tristan that she was making assumptions, probably because Jordan had been standing there.

We reached the edge of the woods where there was a log to sit on about fifteen feet in. I made my way through the dried leaves to the log, sat down, and waited for Tristan to sit beside me. We watched the others as they approached.

"I guess you have a lot of explaining to do," he said as Jordan and my three other friends approached, all looking quite skeptical.

I wasn't sure where to begin. I had wanted to tell them but I was afraid they wouldn't believe me. I looked up at Jordan. "What all did you say?" I asked.

"The truth."

I looked back at the others then back to Jordan again. "Did you tell them you believe it? Did you tell them you believe Tristan is here?"

"I told them you weren't crazy."

Jess stepped forward, looking around as if something or someone was going to jump out from behind a tree. "I don't understand," she said. "You're dating a—um—ghost?"

Tristan lowered his head to his hands. I didn't know how to comfort him with everyone standing here staring at me.

"This is really weird, Courtney," Beth said, in just a little more than a whisper.

My emotions were going haywire. I wanted to scream, cry, and run all at the same time. I was worried that none of them would believe me, scared they may tell someone and I would be sent back to the hospital, but most of all, terrified that Tristan would leave. My life had become more confusing than it was before walking into that tent. In a way, I was relieved my friends finally knew. I was just uncertain, at this point, what would happen after their shock wore off, if it ever did wear off. Several minutes passed by, engulfed in silence. The sound of Jordan's cell phone ringing startled us all. He walked several feet away to answer.

"Look, guys," I began, "I wanted to tell you, but I didn't really know how." My three friends stood, still stone faced, in front of me. "I really love him."

Kari shook her head. She had remained quiet since the ordeal in front of the tent. I began thinking, if things were reversed, if I had been the one to hear this kind of news about one of them, what would be going through my mind right now?

"They don't believe us," Tristan said beside me. "I can't even defend you from their skeptical stares."

Jordan walked up, flipped his phone shut, and slid it into his back pocket. "Let's go," he said to all of us. "I just have to drop off this bear with my sister. She and Mom are by the merry-go-round."

Jordan seemed confident and ready to take control of the situation. I turned back to Tristan, who still looked defeated and hurt. We both stood and followed Jordan and the others out of the trees and towards the rides. I could see my friends giving each other glances, and I wondered how I would ever convince them that I wasn't truly insane. It was hard enough for Jordan to accept it.

Jordan's little sister spotted us as we approached. She ran up to him and threw her arms around his neck so he could give her a big hug and twirl her around as she squealed with delight. He still held the bear in his hand. When he planted her feet back onto the ground, he handed her the stuffed bear. "For my sugar-bear," he said before he kissed her on the cheek. She squealed again and ran back to their mom, waving the bear in her arms. Jordan's mom waved at us and Jordan began walking back towards the parking lot. Jess, Kari, and Beth kept their distance before Jordan turned around.

"Are you all coming or what?" he hollered.

Tristan and I began walking after him. I looked at my friends as I passed by, the dumb-founded look still on their faces. They eventually started to follow, and I could hear their footsteps and whispers several feet back.

"Where are we going?" Jess asked as we reached the cars.

Jordan turned, smiled at me then turned back to Jess and the others. "I have something to show you—at my house."

I didn't know what could possibly be at his house that could help our situation. I looked at Tristan, who shrugged. Jess, Kari, and Beth all climbed into Jess's car while Tristan and I climbed in with Jordan.

We were nearly to Jordan's home before he spoke. "He's still here, isn't he?" he asked.

"Yes," I answered.

"Good," he said and smiled.

Jess's car pulled up behind Jordan's in the driveway and they all climbed out. I could tell, by the looks on their faces, they had been talking about this weird course of events. Maybe they had even been discussing my sanity. We quietly followed Jordan inside, but he didn't turn to the basement that would take us down to his room. He continued out the back door. His dog, Bo, began barking at the sight of Jordan. He ran the length of his chain, which tightened and knocked him back on his rear. This did not stop him from jumping up and down with excitement, though. Once we were all outside, Jordan gestured for us to follow him to the side of the yard. "Except Tristan," he said. The look of confirmation set on Tristan's face and he smiled at me.

"What are we doing?" Jess asked, shaking her head and following Jordan.

"Just watch the dog," he replied. The other three turned and watched Bo, who now continued to bark at, what they would think was, nothing at all.

"Tristan," Jordan said from across the yard now, "go to the opposite side of the yard."

I watched Tristan walk to the other side, next to the privacy fence that separated Jordan's yard from the neighbor's. Bo did not take his eyes off of him and continued to bark in his direction. I looked at my friends faces, their jaws dropped in astonishment.

"Now see if you can pet him," Jordan hollered. As Tristan walked towards Bo, the dog began to back away, yet continued to bark frantically.

Kari threw her hands up to her mouth and slowly turned to face me. I could only imagine what was going through her mind.

Beth whispered, "It's like Bo is barking at someone."

"He IS barking at someone," Jordan replied, a look of satisfaction on his face.

Beth smiled. "Weird," she said, "but if the dog can see him and Courtney can see him, why can't we see him? Does Courtney have some kind of—I don't know—canine sense?"

"Don't be a ditz, Beth," Jordan said in a playful tone. "If Courtney was part dog, she'd be barking at him too, not falling in love with him."

I looked over at all my friends. Beth still smiled, Kari still seemed a little in shock, and Jess stood shaking her head.

"This could be some kind of a joke, some trick you taught your dog," Jess said as she continued to stare in Bo's direction. "You expect us to believe there is a ghost here? Ghosts aren't real. The Boogyman isn't real. I stopped believing in this crap when I was like—I don't know—six years old. I'm not falling for it." Jess began to walk towards the house.

"Wait!" Jordan called after her. She stopped without turning back around. I could only imagine her rolling her eyes. "Okay," Jordan said. "If you think Bo is smart enough to learn a trick, as you call it, like that, then I'll just have to prove it another way."

She turned to face him again as she placed one hand on her

hip. "Waiting!" she sang back to him in a sarcastic tone.

"Just let me think!" Jordan replied to her.

I glanced over at Beth and Kari. We were all such good friends; but I knew, if we couldn't convince Jess that Tristan was real, they would side with her. I didn't want them to have to choose sides. This wasn't supposed to ruin our friendships.

"I've got it!" Jordan's voice broke through the silence making us all jump. "Your bag, you know that thing you carry on your shoulder that you stuff full of everything but your kitchen sink; the forbidden bag that no guy would ever want to venture to look in."

"Yeah, what about it?" she asked.

"Tristan can tell us what's in it," he replied.

"No, I won't!" Tristan called from across the yard before he began making his way towards me. Bo began barking frantically again. "Those things are off limits," he said as he stopped in front of me. "Has he seriously lost his mind?"

"I think it's a great idea," I said to him. "It's not like we're asking you to buy tampons or something. You're just going to tell us what's in her purse. Where's the harm in that?" Tristan looked at me like I was asking him to reveal KFC's secret recipe.

Jess walked over to the picnic table and laid her purse down. "Fine," she said. "If you all can tell me what's in my purse, I'll believe you." Her mouth set into a smirk as she backed a few feet away from the table.

"You have to open it," I said to her from across the yard. "He can't open your purse."

"This is ridiculous," she mumbled as she walked back to her purse and unzipped it.

I looked back up at Tristan who let out a defeated sigh before he turned and walked to the picnic table. I watched him as he leaned over slowly and peered inside Jess's purse.

"Where is he? Is he going to do it?" Beth whispered.

"Yeah, he's over there now," I replied. "He's not real happy about it, though," I said, trying not to laugh. We stood in silence for several minutes, everyone watching me, anticipating what Tristan would reveal.

"What do you see?" I asked him from across the yard.

"Um—makeup, hairbrush, a green billfold."

I repeated the list to the others.

"Every girl has those things in her purse, nice try," Jess said to me.

Jordan replied, "Well, he said your billfold was green."

"Any one of you could have noticed that when I took my money out today," she shot back at him.

"There are some other things," Tristan reluctantly said as he continued to peer inside her purse.

"What are they? What else do you see?" I asked excitedly.

"Um—" there was a long hesitation before he answered. "Those tampons you said you wouldn't ask me to buy. And, something else, but—I'd rather not say."

"What is it? What else besides tampons?" I asked again. Kari moved closer to me so she wouldn't miss what I repeated. Jordan started smiling; obviously hoping it was something really interesting.

"Well," Tristan said slowly, "I just don't think she would want me to say, at least not with Jordan around." He looked back at me. "Can't we find some other way of convincing her?"

"What could possibly be that embarrassing that she wouldn't want you to say? She said she would believe us if you could tell what was in there."

"Oh man, this is good," Jordan said beside me. "He has to tell us."

I looked over at Jess who was now biting nervously at her lower lip. I wasn't sure what Tristan saw, but I could tell she was uncomfortable. Jess's phone began ringing inside her purse and Tristan turned back to look at it.

"Someone named Pooky is calling her right now," he said as he shrugged his shoulders.

"Pooky's calling," I said to her before she turned and grabbed her purse, yanking her phone out.

"Dustin, I'm going to have to call you back," she said immediately into the phone. "There's something really weird going on. I'll call you later tonight when I get home." She blew kisses into the phone before she hung up. "Okay," she said as she faced us. "I believe you." She threw her cell phone back inside her purse and zipped it closed.

"Pooky?" Jordan asked, fighting back a smile.

"Shut up, Jordan!" she spat back at him. "Do NOT go there!"

"The only way I'm going to NOT go there is if you tell me what's inside that purse of yours. Obviously, Tristan's too respectable or whatever, but not me."

"Well, I guess he's a better man than you are!" Jess said.

We all laughed and Tristan and I made our way towards each other. Bo barked frantically again once Tristan began moving. "They believe us," I said once I reached him. He cupped his hands around my face and I closed my eyes, imagining his touch as I had felt so many times in my dreams.

Brandy Walsh

Life isn't always what we expect; it reveals secrets that stop us in our tracks, that makes us question all that we believe, that builds walls or tears them down.

Chapter 15

Revealing Secrets

We all followed Jordan back into the house. This time we turned and retreated downstairs to his dimly lit room. Beth asked me a million questions on the way down, never waiting until I fully answered the previous question. When we reached the bottom of the stairs, I gave Jordan a hug.

"What's that for?" he asked.

"For being so smart. For finding a way to convince them," I said.

"Hey, you'd do the same for me, if I was in love with a ghost," he replied, and then laughed. "Mom told me on the phone that she had accidentally left Bo tied up outside. She didn't want him barking all day long at every squirrel that taunted him from the tree. That's when I remembered how Bo reacted to Tristan. I figured if they couldn't see him, then Bo would convince them that he was here. I guess Jess is a little tougher sell, though."

Tristan stood behind Jordan shaking his head. "I don't understand it," he said as he looked at me. "He knows he's going to end up with you, but he still convinced your friends that I was here."

What the old woman said came rushing back to me. It had obviously never left Tristan's mind, though. "Jeez, Tristan! He's

235

not going to end up with me!"

"I'm obviously not a threat to him anymore," Tristan said. "I mean—if he knows you'll be with him in the end. You'll live in a nice home with children. Everything I can't give you."

"Just stop! I don't care about having children! Maybe we *will* have a nice house! Us—you and me! That old woman was a nut!" I screamed.

Jess looked at me in confusion. "What old woman? Who's talking about children?"

I could tell this one-sided conversation had been confusing them almost as much as the conversation was frustrating me.

Jordan walked over to the overstuffed loveseat against the wall and pulled it out to the center of the room. He then went around gathering up folding chairs and opened them up to face the loveseat. I continued to stare at Tristan as the others stared at me in confusion. I had to fix this, but I didn't know how. I had hoped the old woman would just tell me whether I went away to college or if I would even go.

"Uh hum." Jordan pretended to clear his throat as he stood behind the loveseat.

I walked over, sat down, and waited for Tristan to sit down beside me. I watched Tristan; everyone else stared in the same direction as me. Eventually, obviously feeling defeated, he came to sit beside me. Jordan held out a chair for the others to each sit in. He turned the one remaining chair around backwards, sat down, folded his arms across the back of the chair, and rested his chin on them. No one said a word at first. I was very near tears before Jordan spoke.

"First of all, do we all agree that Tristan, the ghost, is real?" he asked, looking around at Jess, Kari, and Beth. They all three nodded in agreement. "Okay," he continued, "I just want to say up front, I don't know how much faith I put in fortunetellers, but some of what the old woman said actually made sense."

"Yeah? Which part?" Tristan said, anger rising in his words. "The part where she has a nice home and children or the part where she ends up with YOU?!"

I turned quickly towards Tristan, ready to argue again, against what the old woman had said. Obviously, Jordan could sense the tension that was taking place on the love seat.

"Look, Tristan," he began again, probably hoping to cut Tristan off with whatever Jordan had assumed he was angry about, "Courtney is in love with you. The old woman said she had found true love. That much of what she said is true. She also said she would have a nice home and children laughing, or something like that." Before Tristan or I could say anything, Jordan quickly stated, "That doesn't mean they're her own children. Maybe they're neighbor children, or she adopted one or two."

I looked back at Tristan who now had a crease across his brow in thought. The others looked confused but were obviously listening intently. They hadn't heard what the fortuneteller said.

"I'm not good at reading between the lines on this next part, but didn't she say something about needing to find some answers?" He was looking at me this time instead of at, what he could see, an empty seat beside me.

"I don't know, yeah—something like that," I said. "She said I had a long journey, whatever that means. And that we would seek answers."

"Okay, so maybe the answers are what we're figuring out now. Unless we're supposed to help Tristan find the answers about why he's a lost soul."

"A lost what?" Jess said, in total confusion.

Jordan turned to Jess and said, "We'll explain later." He looked back at me. "Okay, so the journey and the answers are a little confusing. She told you to trust in the things that can't be seen. What if she's talking about Tristan? I know you can see him, but none of us can. Let's assume this crazy old woman isn't a nut. I mean, they never actually come out and say exactly what they mean."

"Yeah, I guess that makes sense—a little," I said.

"And about the last part, before you ran out of the tent, when she said she saw a man in your future with my initials; she did say that after the part where you have a nice home and children. So, that man doesn't even have to be someone you're with, she just saw him."

I was totally confused now.

"Why would she say she saw him if he wasn't some important part of her future?" Kari asked.

Tristan leaned forward; he obviously wanted to hear what Jordan had to say about this statement. I preferred to forget about the last part. I preferred to make the assumption that the old woman was a fraud.

Jordan straightened up in his chair with a look of concentration on his face. "Maybe," he began again, "I do play an important role, but not the role you all are thinking." He looked towards Tristan. Because he couldn't see him, it looked as though he was looking through Tristan and focusing on the wall behind him. "I will admit, I loved Courtney for a long time."

Kari and Beth had a look of astonishment on their faces at this news. Jess, however, smirked as if she had known this all along.

"It's obvious who Courtney is in love with. Yeah—a little strange, but who am I to judge? At first, the news was a little too much for me. I was losing out to someone who wasn't even alive. But, I've gotten past that. Plus, I wouldn't want you haunting me the rest of my life." He laughed at this before he said, "Just joking, no offense."

"What other important role does he think he'll play in your life?" Tristan said after he listened to what Jordan had to say.

"A best friend," I replied.

"Exactly!" Jordan exclaimed. "When I tried paying the woman, after you stormed out of the tent, she refused to take my money.

She said… 'Go, go! Your friend needs you.' Don't you all see? She referred to me as Courtney's friend! If she saw me as something more than that, she wouldn't have called me her friend."

"How do we know if anything this woman says is even true?" Kari asked. "Everything she said sounds a little vague, don't you think? She could have said any one of those things to any one of us."

"The accident," Tristan said, "she knew about the accident."

"She could have guessed that. I still have a limp," I replied.

"People can have a limp for many different reasons, Courtney. She specifically referred to the accident as a terrible thing," he said.

"Aren't most accidents terrible?" I answered back.

"Um—hello?" Beth said.

I realized that my friends were only hearing part of the conversation. I looked at Jordan. "Do you remember when we first walked in and she said my leg must be tired? She referred to the accident."

Jordan thought for a minute and then his face lit up. "I do remember that! What if this woman doesn't only see the future but can also see into the past?"

"You're both getting carried away now," I said. I looked from Tristan to Jordan. "This woman doesn't know anything! She's just guessing!"

"Jeez, Courtney." Jordan stood up and began to pace the floor. "You're the one who wanted to go in there, to find out about your future. Now *you're* the one being skeptical? Think about it for a minute. If she's the real deal, maybe she can give you answers about what happened to you. Maybe she can even help Tristan."

I stood up, anger boiling inside me now. "This is all crazy! You're talking like this old woman holds the answers to everything!"

"Maybe she does!" Jordan shot back. Tristan stood up, stepping in between Jordan and me.

"Maybe I don't want answers anymore!" I screamed. I didn't know why Jordan was getting to me. Everything he was saying about this old woman was driving me crazy. My head began to spin and my body began to shake with rage.

"Why don't we all calm down," Jess said with total control. "I see what's happening here." We all turned towards Jess. "We can't be for certain that what this woman said is true. And, even if she isn't a fraud, what she said can be read a million different ways. That's not even the issue right now, though."

I sat down to listen to what she had to say.

She turned to me and leaned closer. "Answer me this," she began, "why don't you want to know the answers now?"

I leaned forward and put my head in my hands. I was holding back the tears. There was a large lump forming in my throat, and I knew I would cry any minute. I couldn't say it. I couldn't tell them that answers may set him free. What if we were to find out what happened to me? What if we knew everything? Would Tristan still be a lost soul? Obviously, he came to me at a time when I needed him most; but why? Now I didn't want to lose him. I was being selfish. The tears begin to stream down my face. Tristan knelt in front of me.

"We don't need to know the answers," he said quietly.

I lifted my head and looked into his beautiful blue eyes. "I just don't want to lose you," I whispered back to him, wiping the tears from my face.

"You won't. I'm not going anywhere."

"You're okay with everything that old woman said?" I was a little shocked. He was the one who didn't trust her in the beginning.

"I don't know," he said, shaking his head. He brought his finger up to my face and traced a tear that had escaped my eye. "Jordan made some of what she said make sense."

I looked up at my friends who sat in silence. Several tears streaked Kari's face. Beth's eyes were watery. Jordan had sat back down on his chair. All were waiting quietly. I felt bad. I needed to apologize for the scene I made. I needed to apologize to Jordan for lashing out at him. This was all too much.

"I'm sorry, everyone. Jordan, I'm really sorry. I didn't mean to yell at you." I looked at each one of them, and I could see understanding in their eyes.

Jess was the first one to speak. "We can't even imagine what you're going through right now, what you've been going through since your trip to Paris. We believe you, though. Whatever you want to do, we're behind you. If you want answers, we'll help you find them. If you don't want answers, that's okay too."

I bit my lower lip. I did want to know what had happened to me. I did want to know who Tristan really was. I looked at Tristan who was still kneeling in front of me. "Maybe we could find out what your real name is," I said to him.

"Oh, well, I don't know about that," he said. I looked at him in confusion. He smiled and then said, "I really like my new name."

"No matter what we find out, you won't leave? You won't cross over? Or find your way? Or whatever it is you're supposed to do?"

"Not until you grow old and tell me it's time to go," he said. I looked around at all the waiting faces. They were all on board. Every one of them waited to know what the next move would be. As long as I knew I wouldn't lose Tristan, what would be the harm in searching for the answers?

"Okay. Let's do this. Let's find out all we can," I said, smiling at them.

"First things first," Jess began. "What is a lost soul?"

Jordan explained to the others everything that had taken place during and after the séance. He filled them in on Valerie's definition of a lost soul. Tristan still didn't agree with everything Valerie had said. He had told me many times since the séance that he didn't feel like he was supposed to cross over. Yet, he waited quietly while Jordan spoke. My friends learned about my unfortunate stay at the psychiatric hospital and how important it was that Tristan be kept a secret. When Jordan had finished, they all looked to me to fill in the gaps. I proceeded to tell them about first seeing Tristan. Over the next couple of hours, Jordan and I relayed to them my life over the past few months.

"This is so cool!" Beth said after we all grew silent again. "What does he look like? I bet he's gorgeous!"

Tristan laughed beside me.

"I know what he looks like," Jess said. The others turned to her in shock. "I can't see him," she continued "but Courtney told me about him when she came home in August."

I remembered back to the conversation I had with Jess in the gazebo, before I knew just what Tristan was.

"Blonde, ocean blue eyes, and muscular. Right, Court?"

I nodded, looked at Tristan and said, "But better."

"Well," Jordan said in a matter-of-fact voice, "he must be pretty good looking if she chose him over my sizzling hot body."

"Seriously?" Kari said. "Really? You did *not* just say sizzling hot body."

We laughed at Kari's comment, everyone but Jordan.

"Smokin' hot body," Jordan replied with a smirk as he flexed his tan muscles.

"I want one," Beth said as she sat back against her chair, crossing her arms like a child.

"What? My body or a ghost of your own? No way, one ghost is enough," Jordan said laughing. "And he's not something you can go to the store and buy."

"I still think it's romantic," she added. "You know, to have a spirit be in love with you. I mean, it's obviously love. Unless—"

"Unless what?" I asked.

"Unless there is a physical thing," she said.

"No, I can't touch him," I replied.

"Then it's true love—it's not about sex. That's all guys our age think about."

"Hey!" Jordan interrupted. "That is not true!"

"Whatever, Jordan. You're different. You've been in love with the same person for eleven years. Hello—we thought you were gay!" Beth said in her matter-of-fact tone. "Now that we know you're not, and Courtney is spoken for, I guess you're fair game," she finished with a wink before blowing him a kiss.

We all laughed. I could tell that Tristan had felt a little uncomfortable about the others talking about his looks in front of him, but even he relaxed and laughed at this bizarre conversation. He was getting used to Jordan. I didn't think he was growing to like him, but he was, at the very least, tolerating him; and that was good enough for me. It felt great to talk so freely with my friends again. I had kept so much of my recent life bottled up inside of me. Jordan had been the only other person I could confide in, besides Tristan. Now we all sat together again like old times.

We heard the front door close upstairs and the voices of Jordan's mom and sister carried down to us. Bo came bounding down the stairs at full speed, anxious to see if we were all still here. Before he reached our circle, he began barking again. Jordan grabbed him by the collar and hauled him back upstairs.

Tristan leaned over to me and whispered, "Promise me you'll never bring home a dog."

I laughed.

I realized it must be late. Everyone usually stayed to watch the rodeo, but it was difficult to tell what time it was in Jordan's dungeon basement room. Even in the afternoon, one would wonder whether it was daytime or evening. I looked around to locate a clock. A digital alarm clock sat beside his bed, illuminating the time. 10:30. I could hear Jordan's mom talking to him upstairs. "Why on earth would you have four girls down in your room?" she had asked. He laughed and replied, "Just catching up, Mom."

I stood as I heard his footsteps come down the stairs. "I need to start heading home. I told Mom and Dad I'd be there around eleven," I said.

Everyone else stood up as well. "I guess it's a little too late to go back to the fortuneteller tonight," Kari said. "Maybe we should meet again tomorrow and see what else she can tell us."

They all agreed. I felt a sinking feeling in the pit of my stomach. I wasn't quite sure I wanted to know what else the old woman had to say. I wanted answers, I just wasn't sure if I was ready for them yet. *Suck it up*, I told myself after we said our good-byes to Jess, Kari, and Beth. What could the old woman possibly tell us that would be worse than saying another man was in my future?

Brandy Walsh

Two paths. The first path, go to school, find a job, fall in love, and live happily ever after. Path two, cut down the underbrush and make your own path.

Chapter 16

Searching for Answers

Once Tristan and I returned home and retreated to the comfort of my bedroom, we went over the events of the day. He seemed a little more eager to start searching for answers than me. I still had an uneasy feeling about it, though. All these months I wanted to know what happened to me. Now Valerie's statement rang in my ears. *"Once he finds what he's looking for, he can finally let this world go."* I didn't want him to let go, not of this world *or* of me. He was confident, though, no matter what we learned, he'd be with me forever. I wasn't so confident. When I finally drifted off to sleep, the dream that proceeded only deepened my fears.

****

We were walking along a narrow dirt path that wound its way through the trees. It was just wide enough for the two of us. We had to watch our footing on this trail because, occasionally, a tree root jutted up through the dirt, threatening to trip us. Twice he grabbed me before I completely lost my footing. I had to mentally remind myself to watch where I walked, but it was difficult not to look at him while we continued on to our destination. So beautiful. His eyes were so blue, so hypnotizing. The sunlight peeked through openings in the timber. Birds sang from their nests high above. In the distance, the sound of a woodpecker hammered away at a hollow tree. We continued on this narrow path, deep into the woods. I didn't feel tired; there was no pain in my leg, no limp to my walk. He seemed eager to get to our destination.

"Where are we going?" I asked.

"It's a surprise," he said.

We had walked quite a distance, but the time seemed to pass by quickly. I could hear a faint roaring sound up ahead. It was not a sound made by a machine or that of an animal. It was a constant hum, a sound I had never heard before. He smiled at me and quickened his pace. As we grew closer, the sound grew louder. I could see an opening in the trees ahead. We made our way through to the clearing where I stopped and stared in awe at the glorious view in front of me. We stood atop a cliff; rapids were forcing their way below. The sound that had caught my attention earlier came from the waterfall, a *magnificent* waterfall that had a drop that must have been hundreds of feet down. A white cloud of water foamed at the bottom, yet I could feel its mist reach up to the perch we stood upon. The view took my breath away.

"It's beautiful," was all I could say as I stared on, transfixed on the cloud of water that rose at the bottom. I had never, in my life, seen anything quite like it. I turned to see if he was as captivated as I. His gaze was on me, though. A smile twisted on his mouth and shined brightly in his eyes.

"It's all yours," he said. He cupped his hands around my face and leaned down to kiss my lips. I reached up to comb my fingers though his hair and return his kiss. The kiss never came. He was being pulled away from me. I reached for him, to hang on to him as tightly as I could. My mouth opened to call his name but no sound escaped my lips. And, then…he was gone.

****

I sat up quickly in bed, my heart still racing with the fear of losing him. Tristan sat up beside me, concern on his face. Once I realized he was there, the rhythm of my heart began to return to normal but my body still shook uncontrollably. Tears began to escape down my face as I fought the lump that had formed in my throat. My chest ached. It took several minutes before I could begin to explain my dream, what had eventually become a nightmare.

"It's just a fear you have," he said, trying to comfort me. "I'm not going anywhere; nothing's going to pull me away from you."

I couldn't help but think there was a reason for these dreams. Every time I went to say his name, only to find I had no name to call him, he disappeared. Maybe if I knew his real name, if I could call out to him, I wouldn't lose him in my dreams. Obviously, in my dreams, I was aware that the name Tristan was not his. As I lay there, waiting for morning to arrive, I had made a decision. Although the fear of finding answers terrified me before I had fallen asleep, the fear of even losing him in my dreams, losing his touch, terrified me even more. My dreams were all that I had of his touch, the warmth of his hands, and the softness of his lips.

It was still dark at six o'clock. My parents remained fast asleep down the hall. I turned the laptop on in my room, not really knowing where to begin looking. I searched for online newspapers in Paris, France. Accidents. Obituaries. Unsolved murders. I began looking through the numerous deaths from August, the month I had awoken in the hospital. Nobody fit his description. I searched July's obituaries. Many deaths, but nothing that would make me think any of them were Tristan. I began searching May and June's. A few could be possibilities. A teenager, 17, drowned in a boating accident. Two boys, both nineteen, killed in a car accident. I couldn't be sure any of them were him, though. There were no pictures; no description of what they looked like. Just the things in life they enjoyed, their age, and surviving relatives. I had hoped I would find something solid to go on, some information that would lead me in the right direction. I was getting nowhere. I became so engrossed in my mission of giving Tristan a name; I hadn't realized he was standing behind me.

"Did you decide it was okay to start looking now?" he asked.

I smiled weakly. "Do any of these names ring a bell?"

He looked over my shoulder at the names that appeared on the screen. After several minutes, he shook his head. I could hear my parents moving about the house. How long had I been searching? I turned to look at the clock, the small hand on the eight, the large hand on the six. I had been searching for two and a half hours and felt as if I had gotten nowhere. Defeated, I turned the computer off. I needed to call my friends. After all, we were in this together now. Our mission…finding answers.

I dialed Jess's number and she answered on the first ring.

"I've been waiting for you to call!"

She really had no patience at all. From the sounds of our conversation, she hardly slept a wink last night. She made a list of places to start searching. The online websites were endless. Public death records, lost loved ones, online newspapers. Our first stop, however, would be the old woman at the festival. We were going back to the fortuneteller. Jess had already called the others. This time we would be meeting at the entrance at ten o'clock. Jordan had already agreed to pick me up. In a way, I was glad someone else was taking control. I had been content to leave things the way they were, and that was getting me nowhere. Now I was just along on this journey, hoping it would be a smooth ride and take me where I wanted to go, without losing any passengers along the way…especially Tristan.

Jordan arrived early, as usual. My parents were overly understanding about my spending all weekend with my friends. All but Jordan would need to leave this evening to head back to their schools. This time we were early, waiting on the others to arrive. When we finally saw Jess's bright red car pull into the parking lot, my stomach did a small flip. Soon we would be listening (and then deciphering) what the old woman would say.

Jess was now wearing a football jersey, obviously her boyfriend's sweatpants, and not a dab of make-up. It looked as if she had not slept at all; and her hair, once again, was pulled back in a ponytail.

"Jeez, Jess. Didn't you remember to sleep last night?" I asked. She gave a small laugh, mentioning that her mind was too preoccupied to sleep. Kari, on the other hand, looked very refreshed with her new hairstyle done up with perfection once again. She looked around, most likely hoping to catch a glimpse of Tristan, who was standing right next to me. Beth wore a different outfit that may have been a little tighter than the one she wore yesterday, which seemed to not bother Jordan in the least bit.

Once again, the grounds were packed with people, mostly small children squealing on the various rides that were already set in motion. We had one destination this time, with no plans of stopping to throw darts or shoot stacks of bottles with a cork gun. We headed straight to the fortuneteller's tent. I could see her from a distance, rocking in her wooden rocker while her gaze was fixed in our direction. My pulse quickened.

"So nice to see you again, my dear," her small, frail voice said as we approached. "I've been expecting you."

Expecting me? I looked at the others. They had the same dumbfounded look as I must have had. Why on earth would she expect me to return after the way I took off out of the tent yesterday? I felt Jordan grab my arm and inch me towards the entrance to the tent. When we entered, I noticed there were six old, wooden folding chairs placed inside.

"Sit," the woman said, entering behind us as she closed the tent flap. Several candles flickered, causing the light to dance off the tent walls. She made her way through the now crowded tent and took a seat across the table from us. We all sat, including Tristan.

"I—um—" I stuttered, not sure what to say.

"You are searching for answers," she said.

"Yes."

"Ah," she replied. A heavy blanket of silence filled the tent but she did not speak.

"The accident," Jordan said, breaking the silence.

"Ah—yes, the accident. A very tragic one indeed." She gazed through us as if she were seeing it take place behind us. Nobody said a word. She shook her head in astonishment at what she could see. Agitation swelled inside of me. How could she see what had happened to me when I still had no memories?

"Could you tell me—what happened to me?" I asked, barely more than a whisper.

"The sound," she began, still transfixed on an image we could not see, "metal, screaming, the smell of blood and burning flesh." My stomach sank as she described the noises she heard and the odors she smelled.

I could smell it now, too. I closed my eyes and heard the screaming, the screeching of metal, and then stillness. "Wake up," I heard him say, his voice angelic. I opened my eyes. We were back in the tent and I met his gaze. His eyes were full of sadness...for me. This was not helping. My body was shaking. Everyone was looking at me, including the old woman.

"You will make a long journey—not alone," she said as her eyes rested briefly on everyone around me. "The answers you seek will be at the end of your journey, as will there be peace."

This was not making sense at all. I was getting tired of these riddles; I needed definite answers.

"Tell me his name!" I yelled. My adrenaline was racing. I stood up, shaking. "I need to know his name!" I couldn't bear to go another night with him being yanked from my arms. Tears fell down my cheeks.

"You know his name, my dear," she said in a soft, soothing voice. My thoughts flew back to the names on the computer screen earlier this morning. Was it one of those names, the one who drowned or the ones in the car accident? I had thought, by chance, that he had possibly died in the same accident as me.

"My accident—did he die in my accident?"

Her face tilted to one side as she shook her head slowly. "No."

"Then tell me when! I need to know where to start looking!" Frustration and anger boiled inside me. She knew the answers, but she wouldn't give them to me. I looked at Tristan. He had a look of confusion on his face. I turned to Jordan. His eyes were narrowed, almost as if he were trying to see inside this crazy woman's mind.

Jess reached over and grabbed my hand; her hand was warm

and calm. "Will we all go with her?"

The old woman nodded. This was comforting. I would not make this journey alone.

"You must go now. There are plans you must make. He is running out of time." Her eyes were fixed on Tristan. Could she see him? I snapped back to look at her. She was definitely focused on him.

"You can see him," I said, disbelieving.

"I see only through your eyes," she replied. "But you must hurry. The fate of his soul rests with you and your friends."

It grew deathly quiet. The others stood after the fortuneteller rose to her feet. Jordan held open the tent flap as we all retreated back outside, all of us shielding our eyes from the sun. I looked back at the tent after Jordan let the flap fall back. The old woman did not emerge.

"I guess we're going to Paris!" Jordan chimed. "I've always wanted to see Paris," he said, grinning.

My mouth dropped. "How in the hell am I going to explain this to my parents?" I shot back at him. "Hey Mom, Dad, my friends and I—well—we're going to fly to Paris, you know, where I was nearly killed! Why? Because my spirit boyfriend is running out of time!" I was choking back tears again. I wasn't sure if it was more out of frustration or fear, but I assumed it was probably a combination of both.

Kari and Jess each wrapped an arm around me as they led me

over to a nearby picnic table. We sat in silence, all of us trying to soak up what the old woman had said. I had left the tent more confused than when I entered. I wanted to know a name, now all I know is that I'm taking a trip, with my friends. I had no idea where to start looking or what I was looking for. Tristan was running out of time. My head began to spin. He was running out of time with me. I was confident that was what the old woman meant. I think. Or, he was running out of time to cross over. Either way, he did not have much time. I looked for Tristan. He stood behind me a few feet, lost in thought.

"What?" I whispered to him.

"We have to go back," he said.

"Why? What are we looking for?"

"Your memories," he said. I watched him, confused until he spoke again. "If you go back, maybe you can remember what happened."

"How is that going to help you? Didn't you hear the crazy old woman? You were not in the accident I was in."

"There's a reason why I'm here with you, though," he said.

"I thought you were here because you love me," I said, hurt beginning to tear at my heart.

"I do love you. That's why we need to go back." He cupped his hands around my face, and I imagined I could feel the warmth of them on my skin. "This is tormenting you. If you could just remember, just fill in the gaps, I think it would help."

I turned back to look at the others. They were watching me, waiting for my next move. Jordan had commitments at home with his mother and sister. Jess, Kari, and Beth needed to return to school. How could any of them come to Paris with me? How could I ask any of them to turn their backs on their own obligations in search of answers for me, answers that we may not even find?

"Well?" Beth said.

"I can't ask you to come with me. You have your own things to do." I lowered my head.

Kari reached across the picnic table, laying her hand on mine. "We're going with you, right guys?" she said as she looked around at the others. They all nodded. "We can let school know we'll be leaving. Family emergency. It's college. You don't need a note from your parents."

I laughed a little. I had not experienced that kind of luxury yet, that kind of freedom. I looked at Jordan. How could I possibly pull him away from his little sister? His mom needed him as well.

"I'm in." He smiled.

"But—"

"Look, I said I was in. That's that. We're going to Paris; you, me, Jess, Kari, Beth, and the little ghost here."

I took a deep breath. All that was left for me to do was convince my parents. This I dreaded. We walked back to the cars. The others began making plans on what they would tell the professors at the college. We needed to decide on a time to leave.

"Passports!" Jordan stopped dead in his tracks. We all stopped to look at him. I had a passport; we had gotten mine several months before graduation. I hadn't thought about the others.

"We have passports," Jess said. "Spring break." And they broke out in giggles.

I had forgotten that they all three went to Cancun this last year. I had wanted to go, but my parents refused. They were probably afraid they'd see my face, or more, on some spring break video. We turned to Jordan.

"My grandparents live in Canada," he said, a grin creeping across his face.

We all had passports. I had enough money in my college fund to pay for everyone's ticket. When I mentioned this to them, they all refused. Jordan had been saving up, he said, for a special occasion like this. The others had their own college funds, student loans, and spending money. They didn't need mine. So maybe I wouldn't drain my bank account searching for answers I may not find.

****

We spent the rest of the day making plans. Since it was Sunday, the local travel agency was closed. I didn't want to use that travel agency anyway. I would rather make a trip to the city. News travels so fast in our small town. Jess, Kari, and Beth hoped to slip away from college without having to involve their parents. Jordan and I would obviously need a plan in place. His mom was a little more

260

lenient. Although she appreciated the help he provided, she was rather upset when he chose to take a year off in between high school and college. He planned to tell her that he wanted to travel a bit before he enrolled in school. The thought of enrolling in the local community college would probably thrill her enough to grant his wish to travel. Now it was just my getaway that we had to worry about. I couldn't say I was taking a trip with the others. Since Jess, Kari, and Beth's parents would know nothing of their trip, I didn't want to implicate them. My parents would never allow me to go anywhere with Jordan for an extended period of time.

Jordan came up with a brilliant idea. Of course, I would need Tiffany to go along with the plan. The others had not met Tiffany, but learned yesterday that she was the nurse in the psychiatric hospital, the one I had turned to when I was desperately looking for Tristan. I knew she would help. I planned to have Tiffany stop over several times during the week. By the end of the week, I would beg them to let me stay with Tiffany for a week, just to get out of the house for a while. She was a nurse after all; she would never let anything happen to me. All we needed was a plan to get away. If they found out where we had gone, that'd be something we would deal with later. The roommates would cover for Jess and the others. Jordan planned on saying he was going out of the country.

I felt excited and scared at the same time. Searching for answers would be much easier with all of my friends with me.

However, what happened once we found the answers scared the hell out of me. I wasn't ready to say good-bye to him. I never would be ready for that, but, in the back of my mind, I knew it was a possibility.

I dialed Tiffany's number and waited. On the fourth ring, Tiffany answered. I explained what had happened since I had last seen her and told her of our mission and where she fit in. She was ecstatic. She more than went along with the plan; she wanted involved in it as well. She had two weeks vacation time and, once again, reminded me that she had never seen Paris. I was happy to have her come along. All she needed to do now was put the charm on my parents.

By eight o'clock in the evening, the plans were in motion. I said good-bye to my friends. What wonderful, understanding friends I have.

Brandy Walsh

People will go to great lengths to be with the one they love, even if it means putting other people they love at risk.

Chapter 17

The Escape

Tiffany arrived at my house at six-thirty Monday evening. She stayed for supper and we watched a movie in the living room. Afterwards, we hung out in my room, where we talked until nearly eleven o'clock. She had to work the next day but planned to return after work. My parents were already beginning to like her. Tristan was also enjoying her company.

Jordan picked Tristan and me up on Tuesday. We drove to the city to meet Tiffany at the travel agency. We reserved the six seats we would need for the flights and returned home before my parents. Again, Tiffany showed up to hang out as if we were best friends. Actually, I was beginning to think of her as a best friend. She was fun to be around. She never forgot that Tristan was in the room and always included him in the conversation. Although she couldn't hear him, she knew I would repeat what he said.

By Wednesday, we would need to ask my parents about my extended stay. I couldn't just spring it on them Friday night. To my relief, Tiffany was a smooth talker.

"Wouldn't it be cool, Courtney, if you could come stay with me next week? I have the week off. We could go shopping—maybe hit a few museums. It really would be so much fun!" she exclaimed over supper.

I was just about ready to take a bite of my enchilada. I looked over at my parents to read their expressions. It was obvious, she had won them over. "Oh, can I?" I pleaded, knowing already that they would say yes.

Mom looked at Dad. "She does need to get out of the house for a bit before the snow starts falling."

My stomach did flips, and I could barely hold in the excitement.

I called Jordan later that evening to learn how well his plans went. He would be leaving in the wee hours of the morning on Saturday and planned to arrive at Tiffany's by 5:00 A.M. I called Jess after I hung up with Jordan. The three of them would leave after their last classes on Friday and meet us at Tiffany's. The plan was working wonderfully. My dreams, however, were terrifying me. Each night I would have a different dream, and each night Tristan was pulled from my arms. I didn't know what we would find in Paris, but it had to be better than losing Tristan every night.

Because our flight would be leaving at 7:00 A.M., Tiffany picked me up Friday evening, using the excuse that there was a new movie playing that she desperately wanted to see. My parents did not object. I wondered if they were secretly looking forward to a week of not stressing over their little girl. They deserved a break. I deserved answers. It was perfect. Yet, I still worried that something would go wrong. I would not feel totally comfortable until we were all seated on the plane.

****

266

As usual, Jordan arrived early, waking everyone in the apartment complex with his unusually loud car at four-thirty in the morning. We sat around Tiffany's kitchen table drinking coffee. I became very aware of my nerves when my cup shook uncontrollably in my hand.

Tristan whispered in my ear, "Courtney, are you okay?"

I turned and gave him a weak smile, afraid my voice would crack with fear. Instead of driving to the airport, we called two cabs to drop us off. We arrived fairly early, with plenty of time to work our way through the tight security at the airport. It was all happening so quick and smooth. There wasn't a flaw in the plan. I watched the others. My friends were excited about the trip and excited about going to Paris. Yet, Tristan seemed quiet and very reserved. I bit my lower lip, maybe too much, because it now felt tender. Once the flight was in the air, I relaxed...a little. I sat in the window seat, quietly watching the city disappear below us. Tristan could not sit with us; all of the surrounding seats were full. However, many times Tiffany would leave to use the restroom or stop to talk to other passengers, and Tristan would slip into her seat next to me. I wondered if she had mentioned her little plan of being absent from her seat to him before we left the house. She had always assumed he would listen if she spoke, like she did at the hospital during my stay.

Tristan and I sat quietly most of the time, me staring out the window, him staring at me. The ocean appeared far below; the blue was mesmerizing. I turned to look into his eyes; they had always reminded me of the ocean. I quickly turned back to the ocean and visions of him swarmed into my head. "Wake up," I could hear him say from a distance. I thought back to the accident. I could see him; I could hear him, as I drifted in and out of consciousness. He was definitely there when I had my accident. But why? Why was he there? I closed my eyes. I could smell the blood, my own maybe. Smoke, there was a lot of smoke. I could feel the heat; it was too close. The sound of screeching metal...people screaming...too much screaming. Why were so many people screaming? I tried to open my eyes. They wouldn't open and the pain flooded through my body. I could hear his voice, calm, caring. He was comforting me. Why? "Wake up," I could hear him say. What a beautiful voice he had. Then another voice, a much deeper, more frantic voice. "Courtney! Wake up!" My eyes flew open to see Jordan just inches from my face, shaking me. Fear was in his eyes. Jess, Kari, and Beth were leaning over the seats in front of me, concern also washed across their faces. Tiffany stood in the aisle, knowing that Tristan still sat beside me.

"What?" I said, startled by the attention. A flight attendant appeared next to Tiffany in the aisle and handed her a cold compress, which she laid across my forehead. It felt unbelievably cool, unbelievably good. I felt the sweat roll down beside my ear and realized I had been sweating profusely.

"Jeez, Court! You scared the hell out of us!" Jordan said with a shaky voice.

Tristan looked extremely worried. "What?" I whispered to him.

"You were screaming. What did you see?"

I thought for a minute while the others looked at me, waiting for an explanation for my terrifying behavior. The plane was silent except for the whispers from passengers.

"The accident," I replied. "But it wasn't a car accident. It was much worse." I looked back at Tristan, who still had concern in his beautiful eyes.

"How do you know?" Jordan asked.

"The people—" I said. "There were too many people, too many screams." I choked back a sob. I gazed out the window. I couldn't talk about it, not yet, with so many strangers hanging on every word. I didn't know how long I had drifted off. Yet, I knew, I couldn't fall asleep again, not closed in with a plane full of people. I prayed the flight would end soon.

After several minutes, the others settled back in their seats and the flight attendant disappeared down the aisle. I thought about the details of my dream as I stared out over the vast ocean. Yet, it wasn't a dream, it was a memory. If not a car accident, then what was it? What could cause so much horror? Tristan had been there…with me. I turned back to him. He was still watching me, probably worried I would fall asleep again. I studied his eyes, the same eyes that were there that day, urging me to wake up. The corners of his mouth turned up. That smile. I remember him smiling at me that day. I could feel the pain, but his smile calmed me...like a drug. I reached out to touch his face, unaware of the other passengers who may be watching. I reached for him as I did so many times in my dreams. He didn't disappear, but my fingers did not touch his skin.

"You were there," I whispered. "Tell me what you remember." I waited as he studied my face. He reached out and traced his fingers down my cheek. I tear fell from my eye. I lowered my eyes, wondering if he had been keeping his memories from me. And then he spoke, softly.

"You are so beautiful." He hesitated until I looked back up at him. "I thought you were dying. I was terrified for you; I couldn't leave you. I heard the others screaming, but I could only see you, covered in blood and screaming in pain. That is the first memory I have, seeing you—bleeding—dying." He stopped to read my expression. "When you looked back at me, relief filled me, it overwhelmed me, and I knew I could never leave you. You did not wake up again for so long. Doctors, nurses, your parents, all entered and left your hospital room without knowing I was there. I sat with you, by your bed, begging you to wake up, praying you would be okay. And you did wake. But I was worried how you would react to me, so I hid. The others couldn't see me, but I knew you did." His words were full of love, yet full of sorrow.

"Why, Tristan? Why did you want me to live? I could be with you; I could be like you."

He shook his head. "I didn't know the other people couldn't see me at first. There was a lot of commotion. It wasn't until I tried talking to the doctor, tried begging him to give me answers about your condition. That was when I realized he couldn't see me or hear me. But I would never want you to die."

I let his words soak in. He remembered nothing before seeing me…near death. And then, he only saw ME. I closed my eyes and envisioned him again that day. He was like an angel, a beautiful calming angel. His hair golden, his eyes were so gloriously blue. "An angel," I whispered.

The pilot's voice came across the speaker, announcing our decent to the Paris airport. I didn't want Tristan to leave my side, but I knew Tiffany would need to be in her seat with her seatbelt fastened. Tristan quickly rose and disappeared down the aisle before Tiffany appeared.

"Tiffany," I whispered when she was settled. I didn't know how to say it without sounding completely insane. She was watching me while I searched for the right words. I decided to just blurt it out. "Do you think Tristan could be an angel?" Her mouth dropped and her brow creased, but no words escaped. I needed to explain before the plane landed. "Did I ever describe him to you? Did I ever tell you what he *really* looks like?"

"Tell me again," she said, as if trying to soak in this new information.

"He has golden hair, beautiful golden hair. His eyes are so blue, a brilliant, heavenly blue." She continued to stare at me. "Tiffany—his voice, it's calming. He talked to me during my accident. His voice is beautiful." She was lost in thought. We were beginning to land. "He doesn't remember anything at all before the accident. He doesn't remember anyone around me during the accident. He only knew that he needed to stay with me." I waited. The plane touched down on the runway, yet Tiffany remained quiet. Everyone around us began unbuckling their seat belts and grabbing their carryon bags. I took hold of her arm as the plane emptied.

She shook her head. All she could say was, "I don't know."

I looked up as Tristan followed the remaining passengers down the aisle. *Could he be an angel? Could some people really see angels?*

We left the plane, grabbed our luggage, and boarded cabs that would take us to the hotel. Jessica, Kari, and Beth's cab stayed close behind. Jordan had asked the cab driver if he could sit up front. Tiffany, Tristan, and I sat in back. We remained quiet as Jordan carried on a conversation with the driver…in French. I was amazed at how well he could speak the language. I sat back in my seat and closed my eyes. My body felt drained from the plane ride.

"Why would an angel be running out of time?" she asked. "They have all the time in the world."

Tristan looked at me, and I quickly turned to stare out the window.

The cab dropped us off in front of the hotel. We grabbed our luggage and proceeded to the counter. Jordan did all the talking now that we knew he could speak French. I was so glad he was with us. I had only taken Spanish in high school and, honestly, could not speak it very well. Spanish was the only foreign language class our school offered, and I wondered where Jordan had picked up this beautiful language. I realized there was still a lot I did not know about Jordan, even though I thought I knew him pretty well.

We had only reserved two rooms in order to save money, each with two double beds. Beth, Kari, and Jordan would sleep in one room; Jordan would have a bed of his own. Tiffany, Jess, Tristan and I would have the other room. The rooms were connected with a door where we could enter each other's room without having to go out into the hallway.

Jordan and the others dropped their bags off in their room and came to ours. "So what's up with the angel comment in the cab?" Jordan asked as he sprawled across one of the empty beds. I looked at Tiffany. I wasn't sure I wanted to tell the others now, but it looked like he wouldn't let it slide. Tristan had sat in the leather desk chair, obviously eager to know as well.

"Okay, just don't laugh," I said. They all waited, and Jordan give me a scouts honor. "This whole thing has been a roller coaster ride." I turned to Tristan because, really, this was about him. "At first I thought you were just this amazing guy, someone I wanted to get to know. Then, when I couldn't feel you, couldn't touch you, I thought I was imagining you, even though you insisted I wasn't. Next, we realized you were a spirit, and I was already in love with you. I was content with that. On the plane, however, my imagination got the best of me. I started wondering—because you're so perfect, so angel like, that maybe you were an angel."

A smile formed on his lips. "What made you change your mind?" He said, with a laugh to his tone.

"Um—well, I haven't really but—Tiffany doesn't think an angel would run out of time and I guess angels probably don't wear blue jeans."

"Yeah, a jealous angel in blue jeans," Jordan said, laughing.

I threw a pillow at him, "You said you wouldn't laugh!"

"Sorry," he said, obviously holding back a roar of laughter.

"Well," Tristan said, still watching me. "I think it's sweet, you know, that you would think I was an angel."

"You're just—so perfect, though," I said, quietly. My face was feeling warm, obviously flushed red.

"I wouldn't go that far. Jordan has a point. I don't think there are too many jealous angels." He looked across the room at Jordan, rolled his eyes, and then looked back at me with his brilliant smile. "But I'm flattered you think I'm perfect."

I watched him get up and kneel in front of me. We stared into each other's eyes for several minutes, completely forgetting there were others in the room.

Kari cleared her throat. "Uh—hum—yeah, awkward moment," she said with a laugh. "Should we leave the room?"

My face flushed again.

"I think we should get busy and find out more about your accident, starting with the hospitals around here," Jess said as she looked over her list. The list was long with two dozen or more hospitals.

"Andrews—the doctor's name," I said, remembering the friendly doctor, "and Claire, that was my nurse."

"That helps," Jordan said. "There can't be too many doctors in Paris with the last name of Andrews."

I suddenly remembered Jordan's fluent French. "Where did you learn to speak French anyway?" I asked him.

"Yeah," Beth said. "It's quite sexy." We all laughed.

"I had always planned to vacation here someday. I thought, since it wasn't offered at school, I'd just teach myself. Plus, I love the art and everything here; why not learn the language too? Who knows? Maybe someday I'll move here."

We had decided, since Jordan could speak the language so well, we wouldn't split up. Sticking together with him doing the talking was bound to be faster than us all going different directions and getting us nowhere. Taking cabs everywhere, we decided, was also a little pricey. We were able to obtain a small van from a car rental business that the hotel recommended. I was hoping Jordan could drive in this country as well as he could speak their language.

We were losing daylight, and none of us had eaten since we got off the plane. We chose to find a fast-food restaurant and hit at least four hospitals before returning to the hotel.

****

Our first day ended without any luck. We couldn't find Dr. Andrews. We had met a nurse named Claire, but she was not the same bubbly nurse that cared for me. I didn't know what I expected to find on our first day in a city this size. Because only one of us knew the language, we managed to get lost three times (only because Jordan was sidetracked by the sites), and it seemed that everyone knew we were tourists. Jordan soaked up the attention. As a group, we must have looked ridiculous. He was the only guy, which anyone could actually see, with five girls.

Tomorrow we would leave the hotel early, visit the rest of the hospitals, and possibly stop at a library where we could sift through old newspapers. Our plan was to find out all we could about my accident, and also look for any information on Tristan. There had to be a reason why Tristan came to me that day. It was like looking for a needle in a haystack, only worse. It was more like looking for *something* in a haystack, and we didn't know what that something was.

We talked until eleven o'clock before deciding we were all exhausted. Jordan followed Kari and Beth to the other room but stopped, turned, and leaned against the doorway.

"Night, Jordan." I said, thinking that was what he was waiting for.

"Yeah, about that. Maybe Tristan should sleep in our room. Wouldn't want anything funny going on, if you know what I mean," he said in his most serious, almost parent-like tone. Pillows flew at him from all directions before he ducked out of the doorway and closed the door.

I waited after Tiffany and Jess had both showered before I carried my sweats and t-shirt to the bathroom. I soaked under the shower, feeling a little defeated, before I crawled into bed. Tristan sensed the reason for my silence.

"We'll find something tomorrow," he said, lying on his side while he examined my sober expression.

"What will we find, though? I don't even know what we're looking for," I whispered. He traced his fingers across my cheek and smiled. I closed my eyes, imagining his touch before I drifted off to sleep.

****

The dream began almost instantly. The place was crowded; too many people to walk comfortably. He kept a firm grasp on my hand, eager to get where we were going. I was being jostled around between total strangers. I tried to keep him in my sight, his beautiful blonde hair blowing in the breeze, but mostly I could only feel his hand, his fingers were locked with mine. It was just too crowded. I could feel his fingers start to slip as he hurried on, faster. It was hard not to trip because I couldn't even see my feet below me. I reached to grab his wrist, to tighten my grip on his hand. He was slipping away. Before my other hand could reach him, his grasp was gone. I pushed forward, constantly searching for him. Why were there so many people? Why wouldn't these people move out of my way? I tried to call his name, but nothing came. Terror overwhelmed me. "Don't leave me!" I screamed.

****

Brandy Walsh

A portrait painted of something truly exquisite begins as an image imprinted in someone's mind and gifted to the rest of the world to view.

Chapter 18

Missing Girl

Despite last night's dream, I still felt refreshed when the sun peeked its way around the edges of the motel curtains. Tiffany had already brewed a pot of coffee, and the aroma was wonderful in the small hotel room. I could tell that Tiffany's day did not start until she had at least one cup of coffee. She was chatting away, to no one in particular from what it seemed; until I realized her conversation was directed towards Tristan, who listened intently to what she was saying. I ran my fingers through my tangled hair and sat up before she noticed I was awake.

"Hey, Courtney!" she said in a cheery voice. "I was just talking to Tristan, although I'm not sure if he's even listening to me."

"He is," I said as I looked at Tristan sitting on the edge of the bed. She had been filling him in on the few serious relationships she had in high school and college and how they ended on sour notes. She laughed a little and sipped at her coffee before speaking again.

"You know, it's nice having a guy listen to you without having him interrupt you about cars and football," she said with a smile. "He's a keeper."

I looked at him, now wearing a big smile on his face.

"Just learning what I should and shouldn't be doing," he said to me.

Jess sat up in bed. "Dustin plays football. I don't mind when he talks about it," she said.

"Oh, that's different, if they actually play. But when they talk non-stop about their favorite teams and players, what plays they should have made, and spend a ton of money on football memorabilia, it gets obnoxious," Tiffany said with a laugh.

I could hear the others in the next room yelling at Jordan before he came barging through the door wearing a pair of boxers and nothing else.

"Jordan!" We yelled at him as he stood there, obviously unaware of how embarrassing his near nudity was. "Clothes!" I yelled.

"What? It's just like wearing shorts," he said with a smirk on his face. "It's not any different than if you were running around in your panties and a bra, it'd be just like you had on a bikini."

"That's what you were hoping for!" Jess exclaimed, before she threw another pillow in his direction. "Sorry to disappoint you."

We laughed as Kari and Beth pushed their way past Jordan and shoved him back into their room where he could dress alone. Beth and Kari both made use of our bathroom mirror to apply their makeup while I pulled my hair up into a ponytail. Once we were all dressed, Jess laid the list of hospitals out on the desk. Four were crossed off. This was going to be a very long day. We ate breakfast in the hotel and climbed back into the van. Jess shouted at Jordan to pay attention to the directions instead of the architecture.

We visited hospital after hospital and came up empty handed each time. I could read the discouragement in everyone's faces, especially when we failed to find Dr. Andrews at the last hospital on the list. We had skipped lunch, hoping that the next hospital on the list would be the one. Now it was close to supper and I could hear my own stomach rumble with hunger. We found a quiet little restaurant out of the way where we could talk about our next move.

The waiter arrived with the menus. He hesitated when he reached me. His face showed a hint of recognition before he quickly placed the menu in my hand and retreated through the swinging doors that led out of the dining area. I could hear him speaking to someone else in French before another person looked around the swinging doors. The others had obviously noticed the commotion as well.

"What do you think that was about?" I asked as we all stared in the direction of where the waiter had disappeared to.

"I don't know. It's like he recognized you," Tiffany said.

"I'll ask when he returns," Jordan said before he began looking over his menu. Several minutes passed before the waiter reappeared, a little shaken. Jordan spoke in French to him while the rest of us had no clue what he was saying. Jordan kept shaking his head but the waiter kept repeating the same phrase repeatedly. "Elle est une personne disparue!"

They seemed to be arguing.

"Non, elle n'est pas une personne disparue." Jordan shot back at the persistent waiter, clearly agitated now. "Son nom est Courtney. Elle vient d'Amérique."

"Oui, Courtney! Personne disparue!" The waiter's voice seemed panicked and twice as loud as it had been before. A woman appeared beside the waiter, and she also continued to argue with Jordan. I grabbed Jordan's hand, insisting he tell me what was being said.

He turned to face me while the waiter and woman continued to talk to one another. "They say you are missing."

"What?!" Panic overwhelmed me. It was only Tuesday. How could anyone report me missing already? I was in a different country on a different continent.

Jordan turned back to the clearly agitated waiter and the female. Once again, they carried on their conversation with Jordan; all three of them became very animated with their hands as they argued. Finally, Jordan rose, kicking his chair back where it fell over against the floor. "Let's go," he said as he gave the two a look of disgust. We followed him quickly out the door and climbed in the van. He turned the key in the ignition and sped away from the small restaurant as if he was being chased. I looked back behind us to see the two people standing in the doorway of the restaurant, but they were clearly not running after us.

"Slow down," I said, once I noticed how fast he was traveling. "What are we doing?"

"They insist that you are a missing person. The waiter said your picture was on flyers everywhere," he said as he shook his head and continued to drive.

"When? When was my face on flyers?"

"Several months ago. But that's not the point now. They want to call the police. We need to trade vehicles with the rental place."

I sank back into my seat and let this information soak in. I couldn't imagine why my face would have been on missing person flyers. I was in the hospital several months ago. My parents were with me. "Jordan—maybe we should go back and get some more information from them," I said, eager to know what this was all about.

Jordan snapped his head around with a look like I was insane. "Would you rather have to deal with the police, have them call your parents, and sort it all out that way?"

Definitely not, I thought to myself. I sat quietly as he drove us to the rental place. After dropping us off at the corner, he went in to return the van, which had been rented in his name. Once he returned, Tiffany walked into the rental place to rent a new vehicle, something that would seat us all. She picked us up in another van, and this time it was white. Instead of finding another place to eat, we drove through a drive-thru and carried our food back up to our rooms. We sat in silence for several minutes, with only the occasional slurp from our sodas.

"I had hoped," Beth began, as she was chewing on a mouthful

of fries, "that we would at least have the chance to eat some kind of French food. After all, we are in France."

Jordan tossed a fry across the room at her. "You are eating French food...French fries!" He laughed.

I looked at the clock beside the bed. It was nearing 9:00. Tristan sat on the edge of the bed with his head bent down into his hands. I remained quiet, only eating half of my sandwich and hardly touching my fries. My nerves were shot.

"It doesn't make sense," Tristan said softly. "Why would you be a missing person?" He looked up at me after he said this. I shook my head, not being able to come up with the answer to that same question I had already asked myself a million times. If I had been missing, wouldn't my parents have said something to me? I felt even more frustrated today than I had felt yesterday. Instead of finding answers, we were raising more questions.

"I suggest we go to the library tomorrow, since we didn't make it today," Jess said as she finished drinking her Coke.

"To look for what?" I asked. "We're not getting anywhere."

"Well—there must be something about this missing person thing in an old newspaper, right? Let's look through the newspapers to see what we can find. At least now we have something to search for."

Maybe she was right. I didn't see how this would help Tristan, though. I went to bed with a mixture of uneasiness and anxiety. The thought of my picture on a missing person's flyer was extremely disturbing. I wondered if I would need to keep a low profile the entire time we were here, always wondering if someone recognized me and if the police were a phone call away. I could hear Jess and Tiffany talking softly about things they would search for tomorrow when we arrived at the library. Obviously, the missing person's report was their number one priority. I wanted to look for information on Tristan. Maybe I would suggest visiting the graves of the names I had found in my search back home. If that didn't give us any leads, possibly visit their families. I hated the thought of showing up at someone's home asking to see their dead son's picture. What would I say when they asked "Why?"

"I'm in love with your son, who, by the way, is a ghost now." They would surely slam the door in my face. Not to mention, call the police.

Tristan was so quiet. He hadn't had much to say since we arrived in Paris. We were never alone anymore and I missed it terribly. I missed reading with him. I missed the movies we would watch together. I missed our walks in the park. I felt a sickening feeling settle in the pit of my stomach. What if I would never have those times with him again? What if, when we did find answers, I had to say good-bye? I was glad my friends were here, in Paris, because if I did lose him, I would hate the long, lonely flight home. I looked over at the bedside clock again. 11:11. I quietly made a wish. *Please let my only true love stay with me forever.*

Tristan lay down beside me on the queen size bed. Sadness

filled his eyes as he stared at me.

"Will you tell me what's bothering you?" I pleaded with him. "You've been so quiet."

He waited several minutes, maybe searching for the right words. "I'm worried about you, about what happened to you. I don't understand any of this—the missing person flyer, not being able to find the doctor or hospital. Courtney, I didn't recognize any of the hospitals we went to. I'm pretty sure I would remember the hospital. I didn't even recognize the airport we arrived at."

I thought about this for a while. I didn't recognize the airport either, but I was medicated when we boarded the plane. Everything was such a blur, including the hospital. There had to be an explanation. Obviously, there was more than one airport. Here he was, worrying about me...trying to answer questions about what happened to me, and I was worried about finding out who he was.

"This stuff doesn't really matter," I said to him. "I want to find out who you are. I need to know what your real name is." I waited a few minutes as he studied my face. "I keep trying to call to you in my dreams, but I can't ever say your name."

"Your accident is important, though," he said. "It's my first memory. It's where I saw you, where I feared that you would die. We have to find where the accident was."

That sick feeling returned to my stomach. I wasn't sure I wanted to see the accident site. The dream I had on the plane was so vivid, so real. I was sure he could sense my fear. I turned and lay on my back, staring up at the ceiling. He leaned over me, cupping one side of my face in his hand, caressing my cheek. I could feel a sensation run through my skin. I knew it was my own imagination feeling his touch, but I longed for it. I longed to have him touch me. He leaned down slowly to kiss my lips and I imagined the warmth of the kiss. I closed my eyes, exhausted from the day. I was more in love with him than ever. I tried to think about only him, how beautiful his hair was, how blue his eyes were.

"Talk to me," I said to him. "While I fall asleep, I want to hear your voice. Tell me again how you felt for me, how you feel for me now." He smiled and began.

He told me about how truly beautiful I was and how he wished he could feel my hair, my skin, my kisses. He insisted he could never leave me, regardless of what we learned in Paris. The last words I heard him say, before falling off to dream, were "I love you."

****

We sat beside a stream. Water ran over the shiny rocks that had been polished with age. "Promise me, Courtney," he said. "Promise me you'll never leave me. I've never met anyone like you. Your beauty, your laughter. You're so intelligent and mysterious. I could never be without you," he pulled me close, lifting my chin with his hand. His eyes were so beautiful; his face was so perfect. I loved being with him. I would give up anything, everything to be with him, to stay here with him, forever. He pressed his soft lips against mine. We lay back against the cool grass. "I will never leave you," I whispered. "I love you. I love you." I searched for his name. I sat up, looking down at him. His name! I needed to know his name! I reached for him, to hold onto him forever but he vanished before I could say his name.

****

I quickly sat up in bed. My heart was beating too fast. It was only a dream, just another dream. Tristan would still be with me. I turned to look at his beautiful face, to see him lying next to me, but he was gone. "Tristan!" I called out. Panic overwhelmed me. Had I lost him forever? I jumped out of the bed, running to the door to look down the hall. There was no one. "Tristan!" I yelled down the empty hallway. I barged through the door to Jordan's room. Beth and Kari bolted upright in bed.

"What's the matter, Courtney?" Kari said, obviously extremely startled from being woken so abruptly. "It's Tristan. He's gone." My voice cracked as I said this. I fell to the floor in the doorway. They both jumped from the bed to come to my side. "Jess! Tiffany!" Beth yelled. I heard the commotion around me. The others were talking, but I didn't care. He was gone, and it was all I could think about. The dream. He asked me to stay with him forever, but I didn't know his name.

"Courtney!" I could hear Jess call to me. "Courtney! Where's Jordan?" I looked up at her. I scanned the room but Jordan was nowhere. I turned back to look in our room but he wasn't there

290

either. "I don't know," I said, confused.

It was 5:00 A.M. according to the bedside clock. We couldn't imagine where Jordan would have taken off to so early in the morning. We began discussing all the possibilities. Tiffany insisted that Tristan must have followed Jordan somewhere. But, the dream left me terrified. The minutes passed. Beth left to check on the van, to see if Jordan had driven somewhere. When she returned, she confirmed that the van was gone. By 5:45, we heard the door open. Jordan walked through carrying a couple of bags while Tristan followed behind him.

"Tristan!" I ran to him, tears streaking down my face. "I was so worried!" I cried. "My dream, I thought you were gone. I was scared that I didn't get to say good-bye."

"Oh, Courtney. Please don't ever tell me good-bye," he said as he traced the tears running down my cheek.

Jordan dumped out the contents of one of the bags on the desk. "I had an idea," he said.

I turned on Jordan, who was now arranging the contents on the desk. "You could have told me about your idea before you left. You scared the hell out of me!" I screamed, before hitting him several times in the back.

He turned around suddenly. "Were you worried about me?" He said, smiling.

"Just tell us your idea," Jess said, clearly frustrated and obviously hoping to avoid me beating the crap out of him. He held up a sketchpad and several tubes of paint. I looked at him confused. Did he want me to describe my accident? What in the world did he plan on painting? I stared at him.

"You're going to describe him, Courtney. You're going to describe Tristan while I paint him," he said, smiling. I looked back at Tristan, who was also smiling now.

"Did you know—what he was up to?" I asked Tristan.

"Jordan came into the room about 4:30. He sat down in the chair while you, Jess, and Tiffany slept. He described what he wanted to do and said he was going to find an art store or something to get the supplies. He offered to have me ride along."

I looked back at Jordan. It was a brilliant idea, but why would he invite Tristan? He couldn't hear him or see him.

"How did you know he'd go with you?" I said to Jordan.

"I didn't. I just figured I should be nice. I mean, I do, sort of give him a lot of crap. I didn't think you'd wake up that soon."

I sank down on the edge of the bed. This is not how I wanted to wake up in the morning. I already felt drained. I wiped the tears off my face.

"Hey, Courtney, I'm sorry." Jordan sounded truly sincere. "Look! I brought us breakfast as he lifted another bag. Doughnuts anyone?" A small smile appeared on his face, obviously asking for forgiveness. "A peace offering?" We laughed as he laid the doughnuts on the desk before pulling out paper cups and orange juice from the bag. We relaxed and ate before Jordan settled into the desk chair, ready to create a masterpiece, according to him.

He sketched the curves of Tristan's face as I described them. The drawing came to life as he worked on the various features of his face. The others watched, fully engrossed in the transformation that was taking place on paper. He shaded where I told him to shade, he focused on the details of his eyes and the curve of his lips.

"It's beautiful," Tiffany said as she watched Jordan bring Tristan to life. "He's beautiful," she corrected herself.

"Oh, I'm not done yet," Jordan said, smiling. "Courtney's always talking about his hair, his eyes, his skin." He held up the tubes of paint. "Might as well put some color to him." Jordan began with the color of his skin, mixing different shades until I told him that it matched Tristan's skin tone. I was so excited that the others would soon see what I saw every day. I was amazed at how beautifully Jordan could paint. It took longer for Jordan to get the right shade for his eyes. The blue was such a heavenly blue. Finally, Tristan's eyes looked back at me from the painting. He painted his lips; they looked almost as tender as the lips I kissed in my dreams. His hair was a golden blonde. Jordan painted the waves in his hair perfectly; you could almost see every strand. He finished the shading of his cheekbones, around his lips, and lightening the bridge of his nose. Finally, Tristan's portrait was done. It was breathtaking. The others stared in disbelief.

"He does look like an angel," Tiffany whispered.

I turned to look at Tristan, who seemed a little embarrassed at the attention he was getting.

"Jordan," I said to him as he put his paintbrushes in water, "the portrait, it's perfect." He smiled a quick smile and returned to washing out the brushes. I could sense something was wrong, though. "You are an amazing artist, Jordan. What's wrong?"

He turned to face me, hesitating several minutes before he spoke. "I wish he could be more for you."

I was confused by this remark. I raised my eyebrow in question.

"I wish, Courtney, you could have everything a girl dreams of. You know, the wedding and all that. You and him would look really good together, if that's really what he looks like." He pointed at the finished painting. "Heck, if I was a girl, I'd be chasing after him too." He laughed as he said this last part.

"Thanks, Jordan. For making him real for everyone to see." He gave me a heartwarming hug, holding me tight against his chest. I walked back over to the painting again. The others were still staring at it, whispering to each other about how gorgeous my Tristan was. We would not be able to go somewhere to make prints until the paint dried. It was now 4:00 in the afternoon. We would wait to do that until tomorrow. Today we still had a few hours left to search through newspapers at the library. Everyone insisted we continue to investigate these missing person allegations. We left the painting to dry on the desk as we headed down to the van. The library was not hard to find. Although this was the first time we had left the hotel room, except for Jordan and Tristan, I still felt as if today had been the most productive day of all. I had a face I could finally show people, something I could show strangers. Maybe someone would recognize him. Maybe someone could give him a name.

What is one to do when a memory just slips away? How tight can you hang on to something that is fading, especially if there is nothing to hang on to?

Chapter 19

His Eyes

The library was exceptionally quiet. Several people were seated at tables reading books, studying, or flipping through pages of magazines. It was much larger than the library back home. There were only a few computers open for us to use; college students occupied the others. Beth, Kari, and Tiffany went in search of the archive of newspapers, while Jordan, Jess, and I settled in front of the remaining computers. I began searching for accidents during the months of May, June, and July in the local area. The accidents were numerous. I could tell this search would take days. I began searching major accidents, once again feeling frustrated. Tristan stood behind me, scanning each new web page for names he may recognize or something that would seem familiar. A few accidents involved several vehicles, one involved a semi. Nothing seemed very promising, though.

I could hear Jordan and Jess talking about something they had found before Jordan went to the librarian behind the counter, speaking to her in French. Again, I was amazed at how fluently he spoke French. He had obviously asked to print something before he carried a page back with him. Jess came over to where I sat.

"We found the missing person's report," she began. "It's strange, though. Jordan says you were missing on August 4th."

I had assumed my accident was in May, immediately after we

arrived in Paris. Jordan laid the paper he'd printed down in front of me; my picture stared back at me. The paper was in French. The only words I recognized on the paper were my name. Jordan read the rest, a description of me and the last time I had been seen.

"What does this mean?" I asked them. Neither could provide an explanation.

"This information helps us, though. Don't you see?" Jess said. "The accident must have happened in August, maybe around this date."

Well, it made sense. Surely I wouldn't have gone missing after the accident. My parents were there in the hospital with me. I turned to Tristan. "How many days do you remember waiting in the hospital with me? Before we flew back to the U.S?"

He shook his head. "I don't know. I wasn't keeping track of time. I just waited—for you to wake up."

Why hadn't I thought about this before? It still didn't explain why I couldn't remember the several months before I woke up in the hospital. I had still lost all memory from the time I was on the plane until the day I was in the hospital. Now I knew, though, I had not laid in that hospital bed for that long.

Tiffany, Kari, and Beth had returned empty handed from their tedious search through newspapers. We were anxious to begin searching for information in August. By nine o'clock, the missing person's report was still all we had.

Food was next on our agenda. We avoided restaurants, instead grabbing several pizzas to take back to the room. We discussed what we had so far. A missing person's report from August. This now told us we needed to focus on that month. We also had a portrait of Tristan, thanks to Jordan's extraordinary talent. The portrait was nearly dry; tomorrow we would take it somewhere to have it scanned and reprinted. We would make our own flyers if we needed. Maybe, if a waiter could recognize me from a flyer, someone may be able to tell us who Tristan is from a flyer.

Tristan promised to stay by my side all night, in case another dream startled me awake. I felt closer to my group of friends than I ever had. They were eager to help. They were concerned for my lack of memory, and terrified for me about what I may learn about the accident. They treated Tristan like more of a person, now that they knew exactly what he looked like.

"Now we have a face to go with your ghost," Jordan said, laughing, before he retreated back to his room.

Again, I asked Tristan to talk me to sleep. I dreaded falling asleep. I wanted to stay awake to listen to his voice all night. But sleep did win over, and I drifted off into the beginning of a peaceful dream.

****

The birds were singing. I sat on a wooden swing, a slab of wood attached to ropes that hung from a large tree limb. I could see the beautiful, large house in the distance. It was a massive brick structure that reminded me of castles I had seen in history books.

A slight breeze blew through the air, rustling the leaves above. I could feel his hands on my back each time I swung back to meet him. It was a wonderful feeling, reminding me of my childhood when my parents would push me on the park swing. Now the man of my dreams, the only man I had ever loved, and would ever love, was making me feel young again, free. I laughed as the swing took me higher. I could hear him behind me, telling me how beautiful I was. I closed my eyes and felt the breeze flow through my hair. Suddenly, I heard a horrible sound, metal against metal, people screaming out in agony. Excruciating pain ripped through my body, a torture I had never imagined before. I could taste the blood. My clothes clung to my skin, heavy. Every movement I forced my body to make sent another wave of agony through me. Let me die! Let this horror end!

****

I sat up in bed, sweat drenching my hair. My t-shirt was soaked with wetness. My entire body shook uncontrollably. I searched the room for Tristan and found him sitting at the desk, observing the portrait Jordan had created. "Tristan," I said softly. He turned and quickly came to my side.

"Are you okay? Another dream?" He asked, full of worry. I nodded and cried softly. He lay on the bed facing me for several hours, until we heard the others begin to wake. Jordan came in the room carrying more doughnuts and a huge smile on his face. He grabbed the curtains and pulled them open, quickly filling the room

300

with morning light. I studied Tristan's face, not wanting to move. I had only slept for a few hours, and I felt drained.

After looking into his eyes in the sunlight, I realized something was different, very different. His eyes, they were not as blue. I sat up with a jolt, rubbing my eyes to clear them of the night fog that must be clouding my vision. I leaned closer before I jumped from the bed to grab the portrait from the desk. The others seemed concerned with my frantic behavior. I ran back to his side, looking back and forth between his beautiful face and the face that Jordan had painted.

"What?" Tiffany asked.

"His eyes," I said, looking back at the others. "His eyes are not as blue." They looked at each other in confusion. "They're still blue but much lighter."

"Maybe you just need a nice hot shower," Jordan suggested. "Wake up a bit."

I agreed, hoping he was right. It didn't make sense. Yesterday Jordan had matched the color of his eyes nearly perfect. I stepped under the shower, letting the water run over my face for several minutes. *I'm just tired, just exhausted,* I told myself. The dream had startled me awake and I couldn't fall back asleep. Lack of sleep was playing tricks with my eyes, that was all.

After I had dressed, I spent time blow-drying my hair before returning to where the others were. They were all sitting there quiet, the kind of quiet that fills a room when the person who enters is the person you were just talking about. I sat next to Tristan on the edge of the bed, afraid to look into his eyes to confirm what I had seen before. "It may be the lighting," I heard Jordan say from across the room. I forced myself to study his eyes again. Still lighter.

"Maybe," I said, not believing it was the lighting at all.

"Look," Tiffany began, "why don't we find a place to make prints and ask around? Maybe someone will recognize his picture."

I was relieved to be doing something. The change in his eyes terrified me, and I needed something else to occupy my mind right now.

We found a business that could copy the portrait and produce about twenty prints. "Well?" Kari said. "Where do we begin?" I thought about this for a minute. Where *do* we begin?

"Let's start with restaurants, gyms, and museums," Jess said.

"Art galleries!" Jordan said excitedly. We all looked at him, knowing he would spend an entire day in one art gallery with us accomplishing absolutely nothing.

"What about clubs? You know, like dance clubs? We could go to several tonight and see if someone recognizes his picture." Beth added.

I shook my head. "He dances, but he doesn't seem like the type to go to dance clubs." I looked over at Tristan as I said this. He raised an eyebrow. "Well, you dance in my dreams, but it's just you and me," I added, blushing.

We decided to start with restaurants. After several hours with no luck and too many restaurants to count, we moved on to museums. After we had spent an hour in the first museum, we decided it was best to only speak to the front door man at as many places as we could. We grabbed lunch and proceeded with art galleries. Jordan could hardly stand it, not being able to enter each gallery, because we pulled him away as soon as the front door man shook his head at the picture.

"We need to come up with a better plan," Tiffany said as we climbed into the van. It was approaching late afternoon now and we were all beginning to feel exhaustion set in. "We know the accident was in August, probably sometime between August 4th and August 9th." She turned to me. "You went missing on August 4th." I nodded in agreement. "There's a million businesses in this place. We're only focusing on Tristan's picture. Maybe we need to ask if anyone remembers an accident at that time," she said. "If it was only a few months ago, people would surely remember something."

We all agreed. Although I was set on finding out his name, and not wanting to go through another night of losing him, she was right. Any information we could find at this point would be better than nothing. We looked through the list of hotels in the phone book and labeled them on the map. We followed Jordan into half a dozen hotels, waiting patiently while he asked if people remembered any accidents in the area the first week of August. It took longer than anticipated while people described car accidents and boating accidents they remembered reading about. Here we were, still looking for a needle in a haystack.

On our way back to the hotel, we stopped at various businesses along the way with Jordan asking the same questions. At a nearby grocery store that was located just a few blocks from where we were staying, Jordan ran inside to buy lunchmeat and bread. We waited in the van for nearly thirty minutes. Tristan mentioned that this was the grocery store they had stopped at just yesterday morning, the morning Jordan had painted Tristan's portrait. Finally, Jordan arrived carrying two sacks of groceries. He had a look of concentration on his face as he climbed into the driver's seat.

"Did anyone notice a computer at the hotel we're staying at?" he asked while he turned the key in the ignition.

"Yeah," Jess said, "in a small room next to the check-in desk." We stared at Jordan in confusion.

"I don't know if it's anything significant, but I want to research something when we get back," he said as he pulled onto the street where our hotel sat towering above the nearby businesses.

"What?" I asked. The anticipation was killing me. Had he found out information about Tristan? About my accident?

"There was an accident, according to the grocery clerk, but it wasn't in Paris." He turned to look at me when he said this.

My accident had to be in Paris. This is where my parents took me for graduation. Why wouldn't my accident have happened in Paris? I shook my head. No, it had to be in Paris.

Jordan parked the van and we followed him to the small computer room inside the front doors of the hotel that Jess had described. The room was barely big enough for all of us to stand, uncomfortably. Jordan loaded the search engine and typed four words. LONDON ENGLAND TRAIN ACCIDENT. My heartbeat increased as the information loaded on the screen. I scanned the page, and words jumped out of the screen at me. DEVASTATION. MASS CASUALITES. 187 PEOPLE PERISHED IN FATAL TRAIN DERAILMENT. HUNDREDS MORE INJURED. WORST TRAIN DERAILMENT IN LONDON'S HISTORY.

I heard gasps from my friends as pictures loaded on the screen. My head began to spin. I could hear the metal screeching along the track, the screams from hundreds of people, the crunching of train cars as they collided into one another. I began to feel faint, my body shaking, the room spinning.

When my eyes opened, everyone was leaning over me. I was back in the hotel room; sweat was clinging to my hair. I turned to see Tristan kneeling beside the bed; his face was filled with worry, confusion, and fear. "London?" I choked. Tiffany wiped the cool washcloth across my head. The others sighed in relief that I was okay, at least physically. Mentally, my head was full of confusion; questions, images I couldn't even imagine. I sat up to drink the glass of water that Kari offered me. I felt cold, most likely because my clothes were wet with sweat. Jordan pulled the desk chair up to face the bed and sat down. He concentrated on my face, his forehead knitted.

"Do you remember going to London?" he asked quietly. I shook my head. He waited before he spoke again. "There is a train that travels from here to London. Do you think it's possible that you were on that train—in London?"

A sickening feeling settled in my stomach. Why would I have been on a train in London? "I don't know," I said, looking back at him.

The others remained quiet as Jordan searched for words. "What does Tristan sound like? Does he have an accent?"

I looked at Tristan; worry was still settled on his face. I turned back to face Jordan. "Yes," I whispered, "an English accent." My heartbeat began to race again. Was this how Tristan died? In the same train accident that I may have possibly been in? No, it wasn't possible. The old fortuneteller said he wasn't in my accident.

"We have to go to London. We have to find the place of the accident," Jordan said. "Can you handle it?" he slowly asked.

I nodded. Jordan left to speak to the desk clerk about making reservations for the train. When he returned, we learned we would board the train that would take us to London at 7:00 A.M. the following morning. We talked for hours, and decided there was no use making assumptions until we were there to learn more facts.

We still weren't one hundred percent sure that I had been on that train, but the images I described made the possibility extremely likely.

It was near midnight when the others left to the adjoining room to get ready for bed. I lay in bed feeling anxious and terrified. We were close; I could feel it, close to finding out the truth. My parents had been keeping this secret from me, probably hoping I would never have to relive that horrible day. Probably hoping I would never remember the horror I had lived through, that so many others had not. Were they protecting me? Or were they hiding something from me? I was afraid to fall asleep, afraid my head would fill with the images of people dying in front of me. I looked over at the clock; my eyes were heavy with sleep. 1:30 A.M.

"You need to sleep," Tristan whispered to me, watching my eyelids grow heavy. I remembered those words he said. He had said them to me in the hospital after the accident. His voice was comforting, soothing. I tried to think only of him. I wanted to dream only of him. I had heard somewhere that you dream of the last thing you think about. I struggled to put the images of the accident to the back of my mind. I focused on his face, his silhouette next to me. *Dream only of Tristan*, I willed myself, *only of him*. I thought about the time we spent together at home. The hours we would stay up talking, laughing. I didn't have to ask him to talk me to sleep. He whispered how much he loved me. How beautiful I was. He talked about books we had read together and the children playing in the park back home. "No matter what, always remember I love you," he whispered. The clock read 2:30 before I drifted off to sleep.

Take this journey with me, even though I do not know where
it leads.

Help me to be strong, when I fall upon my knees.

Wipe away my tears, when the truth is just too much.

Don't fade away, my only true love.

Chapter 20

Accident Site

I awoke to the sound of people shuffling around me and the smell of coffee brewing. I opened my eyes to see the others packing up their suitcases. The time on the clock was 5:30 A.M. Tristan lay next to me, smiling. "No dreams?" he asked quietly.

I smiled back. "No nightmares," I said. I remembered dreaming of him. We were dancing alone in a dimly lit room. The dream must have lasted the entire time I slept. He had not disappeared. The image had not been replaced with the accident. Relief swept over me. I had made it through the night without losing him, yet I had only slept three hours.

The others had decided on checking out of the hotel. Our search had taken us to another country, although not far from where we were. There was no need to stay here; our answers awaited us in London. I climbed out of bed to gather my things.

Tiffany handed me a cup of coffee. "You look like you need this," she said, smiling. I sipped the cup of coffee as I brushed out my hair. Dark circles had settled under my eyes. The room was somber, everyone quietly anticipated the day ahead. The others were probably worried about how I would react to any information we learned today. I had to appear strong. I tried desperately to convince myself that I could handle anything, whatever that may be. I couldn't break down.

I grabbed my suitcase and followed the others out the door. I carried Tristan's portrait in my free hand, held close next to my chest. "No matter what," I could hear Tristan's voice in my head from last night, "always remember I love you." I smiled at him as we proceeded down the hallway to the front desk.

We stopped off at the rental place where they agreed to pick the van up at the train station. We would need to rent another vehicle once we were in London. They were very helpful, though, arranging for us to be picked up from the train station. We arrived at the station at 6:30. The hotel had reserved six seats for us.

As we boarded the train, I had half expected my emotions to react. However, I felt an unexpected sense of relief as I stepped aboard. One would have thought I would experience fear or shock from a suppressed memory. The others must have expected this too. They watched me carefully, always staying within inches. But why would I be feeling relief?

We settled into our seats, amazed at the beauty of the train cabin. My friends continued to glance at me often, relaxing as the train pulled away from the station, and I chatted on with them, un-phased. The scenery was extraordinary with views that took my breath away. I sat next to the window to watch the magnificent country side pass by with a blur. The train felt familiar as a sense of déjà vu sank over me. I wondered if I would know when we reached the place of the accident. I hadn't thought to ask Jordan exactly where on the tracks the train derailment had taken place. I looked down at Tristan's picture. Was I closer to losing him? My eyes searched the train car. He was standing at the far end of the car, looking out through a window on the opposite side. I turned towards the others. "Where was the accident?" I asked; my voice cracking as I spoke.

"It was near London," Jordan said. "We'll get off the train at the train station. It happened further out. I figured we'd drive to the site."

That was reassuring. I would rather be only with the company of my friends if I had to relive that day. I nodded before I rose from my seat to be with Tristan. There were several empty seats where he stood. Both of us decided to sit near each other.

"Are you okay?" he asked. "I'm really worried about you."

I still clung to his portrait. I looked down at it again to study the eyes that stared back at me. "I'm worried about you," I said softly.

He was quiet for a while. "Is it my eyes?" he said without looking at me.

"Yes." I hadn't told the others. His eyes were again lighter today, lighter than they were yesterday, much lighter than the day before. I had overheard the others talking. They wondered if his spirit was fading. Would there come a day when I wouldn't be able to see him, a day when he would be gone from me forever? The thought terrified me, more than the idea of visiting the accident site. Tristan was my life, and I couldn't bear to live without him.

We sat quietly as the train moved ahead. Eventually we came to a tunnel that took us under the channel between France and the United Kingdom. I wonder what went through my mind the first time I made this trip. Did the tunnel fascinate me? Right now, my only thoughts were about Tristan; would he be with me when we passed back through this tunnel to board the plane in Paris that would take me home?

I looked back out the window and noticed we were no longer in the tunnel. According to my watch, two hours had passed. We were approaching London. There was so much I wanted to tell Tristan, but I had let the hours drift by in silence. I didn't know what we would find. The old woman's words crept into my mind once again. *"He's running out of time."* Maybe the others were right. Maybe his spirit is fading. These last couple of hours had been the only time we had really been alone since we began this journey, and I had let them slip by. I should have told him how much I loved him. I fought back tears as the train slowed. "I love you, Tristan," I said softly.

"I know," he replied. "Don't say good-bye." I turned to look at him. He must have read my thoughts; either that or he was worried about the same things. Did he sense it was coming to an end?

The others approached us from behind once the train had pulled into the station. The station was crowded. People were waiting to board, while others were trying to get off. The rental company kept to their promise to pick us up. I turned back to watch the train pull away from the station. A sinking feeling came over me, as if my life was leaving with the train. I made my way to the back of the van where Tristan sat beside me. I realized I was unaware of our plans. Were we going to the accident site immediately? Would we check into a hotel first? I didn't care anymore. Suddenly I wasn't so anxious to find the answers, because I felt it was bringing me closer to the end, closer to good-bye. I held his portrait to my chest.

We parked in front of a beautiful grand hotel. I couldn't take my eyes off of it as we pulled our suitcases out and loaded them on a cart. It was still morning. There was a lot of daytime ahead of us. The foyer was magnificent, ceilings three stories high, chandeliers five foot in diameter. Once we reached our room, I realized how exhausted I really was. I collapsed on the bed. "I think I'll rest for just a few minutes," I said to the others.

"You look like you need it," Jordan said. They moved around the room quietly. Tristan sat against the headboard as I curled up next to him. I heard the door shut softly. I opened my eyes to see that everyone else had left the room. We were alone again. I could tell him everything I wanted to say on the train.

"Tristan," I whispered.

"Hmmm."

"Are you afraid?" I asked.

He hesitated. "I'm afraid of losing you," he replied slowly, his voice soft.

"Will you wait for me?" I asked as I studied the patterns on the bedspread. A heavy feeling settled in my chest.

"Forever."

I thought about this one word. After he was gone, how long would it be before I could see him again? It would feel like forever. My life would be empty. His portrait lay on the bed in front of me. This is what I would be left with, a portrait of an angel.

"I love you," I whispered.

"I love you—with all my heart," he whispered back.

I fought to stay awake. My body was drained from lack of sleep. Why did the old woman send us on this journey? I was losing him anyway. She said he was running out of time. I didn't want his spirit to be lost, to fade away to nothing. I wanted him to wait for me. I wouldn't say good-bye; I would see him again someday.

The door startled me awake as the others came in. How long had I drifted? I turned to the clock on the nightstand. It was now 2:17 P.M. The aroma of food filled the room, which triggered the growling in my stomach. "Where've you been?" I asked the others.

"We wanted to let you sleep awhile," Jess began, "you really looked bad."

"Thanks—I guess," I said laughing.

"We did some investigating," Jordan said, quite pleased with himself. "Want to hear what we found out?" he asked playfully. He didn't wait for me to respond. "Did you know you were reported missing here too?" I shook my head; this new information wasn't making sense. "And," he continued, "There is a Dr. Andrews here." His smile widened. "It was Beth's idea to look him up," he said as we all looked at Beth.

I thought about this new information. In fact, all the answers we were seeking were here, in London. We were so focused on the accident, I had forgotten about the doctor and Claire.

Tiffany came to sit beside me on the bed. "We think you should go to the accident site first," she said. "Maybe you will remember some crucial information. Afterwards, we will find which hospital Dr. Andrews is at, and talk to him and your nurse."

I nodded in agreement. It was already Thursday. On Saturday, we would need to board the plane in Paris to return home. We had today and tomorrow to help Tristan. Would it be enough time? We ate the food quickly. As we got up to leave, I grabbed the portrait from the bed and held it close.

The drive to the accident site took about forty-five minutes. As Jordan parked the van, I could tell immediately how devastating the accident must have been. Although the remnants of the broken train were obviously cleaned up immediately, you could see the destruction of the landscape it had left behind. A new track had been laid in the midst of what once had been an area full of trees. What remained now were huge ruts several feet deep, all vegetation was gone. There were several tree stumps, yet most of the trees were uprooted from the impact of the train. I could imagine the miles of broken train cars piled up in this one area.

The others watched me closely for any signs of recognition, any memories that would threaten to make me faint. Nothing. I walked across the bare ground, careful to watch my footing in the massive ruts; Tristan stayed close to my side.

"Anything?" Kari asked from somewhere behind me. I shook my head. Maybe this wasn't the accident I was in. Tristan moved ahead to the track, walking down the center. I sat down on the edge of an exceptionally large rut, my feet resting inside, as the others approached. I closed my eyes, trying to imagine the train car digging into the ground. I imagined I could hear the train in the distance. It was moving fast. What could have caused such an accident? I shuddered as the sound grew louder in my head, and I could feel the vibration in the ground.

"The train's passing through," Jordan said aloud.

I threw my eyes open. I had not been imagining the sound, it was real. Tristan! I could see him standing on the track still, the train approaching behind him. I pushed myself up and forced my way down through the rut and up the other side, digging my fingers into the dirt as I climbed. "Tristan!" I yelled as I ran towards the track. I could hear the others calling behind me. Images raced through my mind as I continued to run, losing my footing along the way. I felt a stabbing pain in my leg as I tried to stay upright. Suddenly Jordan grabbed me around the waist, my feet leaving the ground. I struggled against his grip, closing my eyes as I fought.

"No!" I screamed as Jordan and I fell back against the ground, him still holding me tightly around the waist. "No," I sobbed. "Julian, don't leave me!" I opened my eyes to see the train passing by, tears streaming down my face. My body slumped in defeat.

"Courtney," Jordan's voice was shaky, "who is Julian?"

I watched as the last of the train disappeared from view. The others had circled around us, out of breath and clearly shaken. Jordan's grip loosened, yet his arms still encircled my waist. He pulled me up to a sitting position and I could see the tracks in front of me, only a few feet away. And there he stood. Julian. His face was full of shock. He approached slowly, falling to his knees in front of me.

"Julian," I whispered. Jordan released his hold completely as him and the others let out a gasp. I studied his face. His eyes were now a light gray.

"Courtney," Jess said quietly, "I can see him."

I turned to look at her, seeing that her gaze was also focused on where he knelt. All of them were looking directly at him, their mouths open in disbelief. I turned back to him as he spoke.

"You called my name," he said softly.

Brandy Walsh

It is not by a name that I know love. It comes from the deepest feelings in my heart. It is not the love for the name I whisper from my lips, it is the love for the person who bears this name.

Chapter 21

Unexpected Visitors

Julian. I knew his name. I knew him. My body filled with excitement, not just because I knew his name, but because I knew him. I couldn't take my eyes off of him as tears rolled down my cheeks. Julian. He had been on the train. He had been there because we were in love.

We remained at the accident site. For the first half hour, we sat in silence. What did this all mean? When I finally looked over at Jordan, I could tell he was still clearly shaken by the incident. He must have sensed my eyes on him, because he turned back to face me.

"Damn it, Courtney!" he began, agitation dominating his shaky voice. "You scared the hell out of me!"

I lowered my head. I didn't know what I was thinking. I was so terrified the train would hit Julian, terrified that it would take him away from me forever.

"Why do you think we can see him now?" Beth asked, still staring at Julian.

We turned to Tiffany, hoping she had an explanation. She shook her head. "I really don't know," she said quietly. "Maybe it's because of Courtney, some connection of some kind."

We all sat there soaking this in while she continued. "Valerie once told me, back when I first told her about Courtney, you had to have an extremely strong connection in order to see an actual spirit."

"Why us, then?" Jess asked. "Why can we see him?"

"Maybe it's through *their* connection that we can see him, but it's *our* connection with her. We thought Courtney was going to die on those tracks, die to save him. If we're connected to her, then maybe, somehow, our connection to him grew stronger."

"He's not as colorful as the portrait Jordan had painted," Kari said. "And his voice sounds like it's coming from a long ways away."

I looked at her in confusion. "What do you mean?"

"Well—he sounds like he's talking through a tunnel, from a great distance—and he looks almost gray."

I turned back to Julian. His eyes looked a light gray, but the rest of him still looked much the same. Maybe his skin color was lighter, paler. They weren't seeing him as clearly as I was, but they could see him.

"So what's the connection then? Did you meet him on the train?" Jordan asked.

I closed my eyes. I could visualize him on the train, walking towards me down the center aisle. He was smiling at me, which left a butterfly feeling in my stomach. My chest swelled with joy, satisfaction...love.

I stared at Julian. "I loved him," I said to the others. "I was in love with you, even then," I said to him softly, reaching my hand out to his face. His smile widened. He still couldn't remember, but knowing I had loved him before the accident brought the smile back in his eyes.

"So, was he a ghost then?" Jordan asked, "When you were on the train?"

"I don't know," I said. "I don't think so."

"Well," Beth began, "if he wasn't a spirit on the train, he must have died in the accident."

I thought about this. One hundred eighty-seven people died on that train. What were we looking for? What answers were we seeking? If we could prove he was one of the people who had died, would his spirit rest? Would his spirit cross over, or would it continue to fade? He was still here. The blueness in his eyes was gone, but he was still here. One thing was for certain, we had not found the answers we needed yet.

"Courtney," Julian said, "I wish I could remember."

My heart ached for him. He had no memories; he just knew he had to stay with me. "Your spirit must have stayed with me because you knew you loved me," I said back to him.

Tiffany stood. "We need to find out his name, his surname. We'll go to where he's buried, go to his family, whatever it takes to find what we're looking for."

We were losing time.

"Where do we look?" Kari asked.

"I don't know, the library maybe? They must have all the

information on the crash. Surely there's a list of names of all the people who died," Tiffany replied.

We rose and made our way across the uneven ground back to the van. It was several miles back towards town before we reached a gas station. Jordan bought a city map and asked for directions to the nearest library. When we arrived at the library, we found the doors locked. It was already past 6:00 P.M. The library had closed for the evening. Our hotel was nearby; it was likely they had a public computer we could use.

As we approached the hotel, police cars lined the front. "What do you think is going on here?" Jordan asked. We climbed out of the van and began to make our way through the group of people.

"Officer," Tiffany said. "Can I ask what happened?"

He turned to face her. He held a picture in his hand as his eyes rested on me. "Miss," he said directly to me. "You need to come with us." Another officer gripped my arm.

"Wait!" Jordan yelled after them. "What's going on?"

They continued to guide me through the hotel doors, ignoring Jordan's question.

Once inside, realization hit me. There my parents stood talking to several more officers. My mother looked up, relief washing across her face. She ran to me, holding me so tightly it was difficult to breath. My father stood, his stare transfixed on my face. He looked angry, extremely angry.

"Your parents have been worried about you, miss," the officer said beside me. "You shouldn't go off flying to other countries without telling them where you were going."

Anger filled me. I wanted to yell at him, let him know that I was an adult. I turned to face him but all I could say was "I'm not a little girl."

His eyes softened a bit and he leaned down to whisper something in my ear. "No, but you're *their* little girl."

I watched as my father shook the officer's hands. The commotion in the hotel had died down as all but one officer had left. My friends stood back, waiting to see what my parents planned to do. My father had approached the front desk, reserved a room, and returned with a key card in his hand.

My mother turned to my friends, who still stood in shock. "I will be calling each one of your parents to let them know where you are and that you are safe, unless you would rather contact them and ease their minds," she said in a very stern voice. She turned to Tiffany, anger showing in her face. "We had trusted you with our daughter and you drag her to some other country?"

"I'm sorry, Mrs. Nacoal," Tiffany said.

"No, Mom!" I yelled. "I had them come with me. Otherwise I was coming alone."

She turned to me. It was obvious the relief she felt earlier had been replaced with anger. "We can talk about this in the room. We are leaving on the first flight out of here tomorrow."

I clutched the portrait I carried to my chest. I wasn't going to give up now. Julian needed help. I was tired of being treated like a kid, tired of them making all the decisions.

"What is that you're holding?" she asked. "And why are your clothes so dirty?"

I looked down at my jeans, the dirt still on the knees from where I had climbed through the ruts. My father reached for the portrait I held in my hands. They both looked at the portrait, shock on their faces.

"Mom, Dad, you know about him, don't you." I said with anger in my voice. "Why didn't you tell me?"

Mom shook her head, unable to form words.

"Let's talk about this in private," Dad said.

"No," I replied, maybe with too much defiance in my voice. "My friends came to help me search for answers. They're coming with me."

My father looked at them, and his shoulders relaxed in defeat. "Let's all go up to the room."

We followed him quietly, my mother with one arm still draped across my shoulders. Once we entered the room, my friends sat together on one of the queen size beds. Julian stood by the wall, his eyes never leaving mine. I could tell he wanted to be with me, to comfort me. My parents insisted I sit between them on the other bed.

I waited for them to begin, but I could tell my parents were not going to volunteer the information. "I was in love with him," I said, looking down at the portrait.

After a long silence, my father replied. "You were too young."

I turned to face my mom. "Why didn't you tell me about him?"

She shook her head before answering. "The doctor said it would be best to remember on your own. The accident was too traumatic."

"That was the accident!" I shot back at her. "You could have told me about Julian!" I felt betrayed. I had never yelled at my mother before, never…that I could remember.

"You wouldn't have been on that train if it wasn't for that boy," my father said angrily, pointing at the portrait I held in my hands. I looked at Julian who stood next to the wall. He didn't seem angry with them, not like I was. I fought back the tears.

"But I love him," I said in a weak voice.

"That's exactly what you said the night before we were to fly home. The next morning you were gone." He looked at my friends. "We had to file a missing person's report." Jordan nodded, letting him know that we had already learned about the missing person's report.

"You had college to attend, priorities. We couldn't let this Julian ruin your future," he said, justifying the actions they had taken.

"He was my future," I said.

"He's gone now," my mother replied, sounding more sympathetic than angry. "Why did you need to make the trip back

327

here?"

I looked at the others and back at Julian. I wasn't sure how to explain things. How could I tell them that his spirit remained? How could I tell them that he needed to find answers and that his spirit was fading?

"Mom," I looked into her eyes, praying she would believe me. "He's been with me all along." She looked at me in disbelief.

"That's absurd!" My father said.

"In the hospital—right after the accident. I told you someone had been in the room. Do you remember?" Dad just sat there, staring. "When I got home, I wanted you to meet him. You thought I was imagining him! And he was there, in the psychiatric hospital."

"You said there was someone named Tristan with you," Mom reminded me.

"He doesn't remember anything, not even his name, Mom. I gave him the name Tristan."

"My dog, Tinker, sensed him," Tiffany said. My father looked at her as if she was now the crazy one.

"Mine too," Jordan added, the others all nodding their heads.

"I am not going to fall for this kind of nonsense just because you all say some dog told you so!" my dad shot back at them.

"Dad, the old woman at the fairgrounds said he needed help, we were running out of time. She told us to go on this journey."

"So you flew to London because some old crazy woman told

328

you to?!" he yelled.

"Honey," Mom began calmly, "let's hear them out."

I took a deep breath. "We flew to Paris but we weren't finding any information. Jordan painted this picture by what I described to him." I held the picture out again.

My mom looked over at my father. "It is him, dear," she said.

"It's just a memory. She's imagining him. She has everyone fooled and now you're falling for this," he said to her.

"No, he is real," Jess pleaded. "We can see him now. When she ran towards the train we could see him."

"Ran towards the train?" Mom asked, worry in her voice now.

"We went to the accident site. He had walked up to the track but the train was coming. I panicked. Jordan caught me, but that's when I remembered his name. I thought I was losing him again." I looked back at Julian whose eyes stayed fixed on mine.

"They can't see me, can they?" he asked. I shook my head.

"Is he in the room, right now?" Mom whispered. I nodded.

"This is crazy!" my dad shouted as he stood up and began pacing back and forth. Mom was the only one showing any signs of believing us.

"Mom, please," I begged. "The old woman said he was running out of time. His eyes are fading, Mom."

"What does that mean?" she asked.

Tiffany tried to explain. "My friend Valerie believes that he is a lost soul. He is searching for something that would help him pass on. Until he finds it, he will remain here on earth. But, a spirit can only remain here for a short period of time until he starts to fade away. He must pass on or he will be lost forever."

Mom sat quietly as she thought about all that we had said. Dad still paced the room but said nothing.

"Mom, I love him. I want to see him again someday."

"Okay," she said. "He has no family, though." I looked at her, shocked.

"Mom, what all did I tell you about him?"

"He had been adopted. His father passed away five years ago, his mother passed away just two years ago. We thought he was too old for you," she said.

"How old?" I asked.

"He's twenty, at least he was twenty when he died."

"Mom, I'm nineteen, though," I reminded her.

"You were eighteen when you met him. And he lived here in London. He came to Paris every day at first, to see you. Then he rented a room at a local hotel. We thought it was innocent at first and, he lived in England, nothing for us to worry about. But then you would sneak off with him, to London. We refused to let you leave with him again. You left the night before we were to leave."

"My dreams, they were all memories?" I looked at Julian. "I did feel your touch, your kisses. We did dance," I said smiling at him. My father still had anger in his face.

"What is it that you need to do to help him?" Mom asked.

I shook my head.

"We were going to search the names of the people who had died," Beth said at a little more than a whisper. She had always been nervous around my parents.

"Mom, did I ever say his last name?" I asked hopefully.

Dad spoke up quickly. "No. If you did, we don't remember. We just wanted to forget about him. We wanted to get you back home so you could go to college."

"Would it be okay if we went down to the public computer to look?" Jordan asked.

Mom looked at Dad. "What could it hurt?" she asked him. Dad didn't reply, but he didn't object either. Mom followed us out into the hallway, leaving Dad to pace in the room by himself.

"Don't be gone long, Courtney. Your father is not happy about having to make this trip here," Mom said before she retreated back into the room.

When we arrived at the public computer, Jess loaded the search engine. She typed quickly.

LONDON TRAIN ACCIDENT; LIST OF DECEASED.

A list of articles popped up as she scanned through each one. Finally, she found a search that looked promising. An image of the train wreck appeared on the screen. I tried not to read the details, hoping to avoid another spell like last time.

"Here's a list," Jess said excited. "In memory of—they have pictures next to each name."

We all leaned in to watch closely as she slowly scrolled through the list. There were so many names. A lump formed in my throat as I fought back tears once again. All those people died in one day, in a matter of minutes. I could imagine the pain some had felt. I had hoped most had died quickly, too quickly to suffer. A tear fell as a child's picture came into view. More tears escaped my eyes. We were halfway through the list now. I scanned the faces, not reading the names. Soon, I thought, Julian's picture would be looking back at me. It would be a confirmation that I had lost my true love that day. My eyes stayed focused on the pictures as I thought about that fateful day. He was walking toward me, down the center aisle, when I heard the train wheels braking. He gripped the back of a seat to steady himself. The train lurched. I could hear metal. I could see the train cars outside the window; they were no longer on the track. I scanned the hectic car for Julian, no longer in the aisle. "Julian!" I called. "Julian! Don't leave me!" I yelled.

"Courtney," Julian whispered. I was resting against the wall. Julian knelt beside me.

I looked up at him. "I tried calling to you that day. You were in the aisle," I whispered. I looked at Jess. "Did you find his name?" I asked her.

She shook her head. "No, Courtney. His name is not there."

I sat up straighter. "It has to be," I said panicked. "Did you look at the pictures? Maybe Julian is his middle name!" I said frantically.

Jordan spoke this time. "Courtney—he's not on the list. We looked at the pictures. We read the names. He's not listed."

I couldn't understand why his name was not on the list. He had been there. He stayed with me; his spirit never left my side. I couldn't think clearly. We went out to the hotel lobby. Julian sat close beside me.

"Let's try to figure this out," Tiffany said. "We need to think of any explanation why his name is not listed." We sat quietly for a while.

"Maybe he was thrown from the train," Beth said. "Maybe he wasn't listed right away."

It seemed unlikely. Usually they wait to show the list of names after all people were accounted for. I shook my head.

"What if his body was never recovered?" Jess cautiously asked. "What if we need to find his body so he can cross over?"

"No," Jordan replied. "I'm sure they would have scoured that place with a fine toothed comb."

"Maybe he didn't die right away," Kari said.

I looked up at her. Could he have suffered, like me? Could he have clung to life for a short time? I had wished he had felt no pain.

"But Courtney said he was talking to her right after the accident. Right, Courtney?" Tiffany asked.

"Yes." I envisioned him in front of me. His heavenly blue eyes, his smile, his voice…so calm.

"Then his spirit had already left his body," Tiffany continued. "He must have died right away. His spirit has been with her ever since. It's the only plausible explanation."

"I thought the old carnival woman said he wasn't even in the same accident," Jordan added.

I tried to think back to that day in the fortuneteller's tent. What had she said? I looked around at the others who still wore expressions of confusion. "I asked if he died in the accident," I reminded the others.

"She said no," Jordan remembered. "She didn't say he wasn't in the accident, she said he hadn't died in the accident."

My heart began to beat rapidly. The others turned to look at Julian in shock. Obviously, they had the same realization as I did.

"Julian," I said softly. "You're alive."

Brandy Walsh

What does it mean to be alive? Is it just being able to breathe? To think? Or does being alive mean something more, something that has nothing to do with our physical body at all. Maybe being alive has more to do with our soul, deep within our soul.

Chapter 22

Hanging On

Jordan had returned from the front desk with a phone book. He frantically flipped through the pages searching for the list of hospitals. There were several. I listened to Tiffany as she struggled for explanations.

"If he is alive," she said, "his spirit must have left his body right away, but his heart kept beating."

"Is that possible?" Jordan asked, looking up quickly from the phonebook.

"I've heard of something like that," Kari said. "Out-of-body experiences."

My head was spinning. We were now talking as though he were alive...somewhere.

Jordan ripped the pages out of the phone book. "Let's go," he said, anxiously.

I thought about my parents up in the hotel room waiting for me to return. Dad would surely blow his top if he found out I had left again. But Julian was alive. Right now, Julian was all that mattered. I would just have to deal with Dad later.

I turned and gazed into Julian's eyes. They were very faint; his skin seemed even paler. I traced his face with my fingers. "If you're alive," I said, "why are your eyes fading?"

"Because he's running out of time! COME ON!" Jordan yelled

as he ran towards the door; we quickly ran after him until we reached the van.

Jordan drove as fast as he could.

"We don't know his last name yet," I said as Jordan screeched to a stop at the first hospital. We climbed out of the van and ran to the information desk inside. I was out of breath and my leg ached, but that wasn't going to stop me.

"Can I help you?" the woman behind the counter asked.

"Julian." I said to the nurse. "Do you have a Julian here? He was in the train accident in August," I said, between breaths.

"Oh, no we don't. All the patients from that accident have been released," she replied. "I don't recall any of them having the name Julian, though."

We thanked her and ran towards the door. "What if he's no longer at a hospital?" Jess asked. No one replied. We would just hope that he was.

The second hospital did not bring us any luck either. When we pulled up in front of the third hospital, I had a sense of déjà vu, like I had been here before, looking up at the same windows. It dawned on me that this was the hospital I had been taken too immediately after the accident.

"This is the place I stayed," I told the others. "This is where Dr. Andrews is at."

We ran inside to the counter.

"Is there a patient named Julian here?" I asked again, now for the third time.

The lady behind the counter looked up, clearly agitated. "We don't give out personal information here," she said sharply.

Tiffany stepped up to the counter. "May we speak to Dr. Andrews? Courtney, here, was one of his patients in August," Tiffany said in her most professional tone.

The woman picked up the phone and spoke softly into the handset. After she hung up, she looked up at Tiffany. "He'll be with you shortly," she said before she turned back to her computer screen. We waited in the waiting room for a few minutes before Dr. Andrews appeared through two large wooden doors.

"Oh, my!" he said, recognizing me at once. "You look wonderful!" His grin was contagious. Everyone smiled back at him.

"Thank you," I said. "Dr. Andrews, is there a patient here named Julian? He would have come in the same day as me."

He thought for a minute before shaking his head. "No. I don't believe we treated a Julian that day."

I sank back in the chair. Claire walked through the wooden doors wearing her bubbly smile as she had during my stay.

"Courtney!" she said, clearly excited to see me. She came over to sit next to me. "Have you been dancing again?" she whispered. "You talked in your sleep." I remembered in the hospital when she had mentioned me dancing, telling me I would be dancing again in no time. "Oh," she grabbed my arm, "did you ever find your angel?" she asked.

"Claire," the doctor interrupted. "Miss Courtney is looking for a patient named Julian. Would you mind calling the other hospitals to see if you could locate him?"

She jumped up. "Of course!" she said happily. She went behind the counter and began dialing numbers on the phone, clearly ignoring the other woman behind the counter.

Dr. Andrews asked me about my leg, how it was feeling, and if I had any pain when I walked.

"Only when I'm chasing after trains," I replied, remembering the sharp pain in my leg from earlier in the day.

He laughed aloud. "It's a miracle you have anything to do with trains," he said as he leaned down to examine the scar on my forehead, which I kept mostly hidden behind my bangs.

"You have recovered quite well. Remarkable, considering your injuries."

I turned to see if Claire was having any luck finding which hospital Julian was at. She laid the phone down on the receiver and returned from behind the counter.

"There's a Julian Scott at a nearby hospital. He's been in a coma for several months; the prognosis doesn't look good," she said as she handed me a small piece of paper. She had written down the name of the hospital with the address. Under that, the name Julian Scott was scrawled, age 20 written beside it. My heart began to beat frantically. I looked at Julian, and I could see the sorrow in his eyes. I thanked Claire and promised to write soon before we headed for the door. I could hear Claire talking to Tiffany, and I turned when she said Julian's name again.

"He has no family, no kin," she said. "The government has the decision whether to keep him alive. His estate will go to the government once he passes. It's only a matter of days now before they remove life support."

I turned away and went to the van. Julian was dying. There was no one there to insist he be kept alive. I sat quietly in the van; the only sound I could hear was my heart beating through my chest. Tiffany climbed into the seat next to me. She didn't say a word about the conversation she had with Claire. I could tell she was worried that we wouldn't make it in time.

We rode in silence as Jordan disobeyed every traffic law there was. Once we pulled into the hospital parking lot, I stopped as the others went inside.

Julian stood beside me; he reached to cup my face in his hands. "Courtney," he whispered. "It will be okay, no matter what." Tears rolled down my face.

When we entered the hospital, we could hear Jordan yelling at the woman behind the counter. "She needs to see him!" he yelled. "I'm sorry, sir," the woman repeated in a calm tone. "Only immediate family is allowed in intensive care."

I turned to face Julian. "You have to go," I said, "you have to go back to your body."

"I can't leave you," he said, shaking his head.

"Julian! If you don't, you will surely die," I cried. I sank to my knees. I could feel my friends wrap their arms around me.

Julian knelt down and stared into my eyes. "If I leave you here now and I don't wake up, I would never forgive myself. I don't want to hurt you like that. At least this way I can be with you until—" he stopped at the last word.

"If you don't go," I sobbed, "then this whole trip will be for nothing. We came to save you, not me. You are the one who is running out of time." I could see it in his eyes that he was scared to walk away.

The sliding doors to the front entrance opened and Mom walked through alone. My friends backed away as she knelt in front of me. "Honey, we need to talk," she said.

I rose and walked to the chairs, prepared to tell her I would not be returning with her to the hotel. I would never leave Julian's side and I didn't want to waste time arguing with her and Dad. She took the seat beside me.

"Mom," I began. "Julian needs me and—"

She interrupted me before I could continue any further. "Courtney, I went to the computer at the hotel looking for you and found that you had left. The desk clerk said you were searching for hospitals, so I called Dr. Andrews. He told me where you were heading and I took a cab straight here. Courtney, I didn't know. I didn't know he was still alive." I could see the tears pooling in her eyes.

"Mom, he is and I can't leave him."

"I know that now. We were only trying to protect you, to protect your future."

I lowered my head.

"Please try to understand. We didn't want you to make the same mistakes we had made."

I looked at her in shock. "You made mistakes?" She had never offered any information about their past, about how they met, about anything.

"We did—plenty. Your father and I met when I was just seventeen; he was twenty. We lived in Chicago. We were in love and my parents refused to let me see him. But we found ways. When I became pregnant, our parents refused to help; we had no choice but to leave. We had no money, no home. We told ourselves that love was enough. Your father took a job at a factory, and I took a job as a waitress at a diner. We moved into a little one room apartment where we shared a bathroom with all the other tenants. We saved what we could, hoping to move to a better place when the baby came." Her eyes looked distant as she thought back to her own teenage years. "We were like many young couples, excited about having a baby and getting deeper and deeper in debt. We never imagined something could go terribly wrong. There were complications; he was so small. He hung on for three days in the hospital before he died. It devastated us both. The medical bills had piled up and we needed to pay for a funeral. You remember the cemetery we went to in Chicago, don't you?" she asked.

I thought back to the weekend visit to Chicago, to the small headstone. I thought about how frustrated I was at the time, with my parents, and with this person I didn't even know. Now I felt guilty for being selfish, for not asking whose grave it was, for not being more sympathetic. I stood at my brother's grave and was angry with him. I couldn't imagine the pain my parents must have felt when their baby died.

"It took many years to move out of the one room apartment. We had to save to go to college. We had to work our way up from nothing, from less than nothing." She took my hand and squeezed it gently. "You have to understand why we were so protective of you. Can you understand?" she asked.

I thought about what she was saying. I would have never imagined their life had started off that way; and now, knowing everything, I did understand. "I do," I told her. Another tear rolled down my face. "Mom," I pleaded. "I love him."

"I know you do," she said as she pulled me into her arms.

"I don't want him to die," I cried into her shoulder.

"He's here now, everything will be fine."

"They won't let me go back there with him, Mom. He doesn't want to leave me because he's afraid he won't wake up."

"Courtney," she said, her voice cracking. "You can be with him." I looked up at her. She opened up her hand that held the diamond ring. "You and Julian married the morning you ran away.

You married in London," she hesitated, "just hours before the accident."

I held the ring in my hand and memories of Julian placing it on my finger came rushing back to me. She reached into her purse and pulled out an envelope, which she handed to me. There were dried bloody fingerprints on the white envelope. I reached inside and pulled out the marriage certificate. I was speechless. I struggled to find words.

"He is your husband," she said. "Go be with him." Tears ran down my face as I hugged her. After several minutes, she gently pushed me back, holding me at arms length. "Go," she said again. "Julian needs you."

I ran to the counter, showing the nurse my marriage license. Julian stayed close by my side as we followed the nurse down the hall.

"We're married," he said, grinning. I smiled up at him.

The nurse stopped in front of a wooden door, the name *Scott, Julian* in the name slot. She opened the door quietly, allowing me to enter. "I'm sorry," she said. "He's not doing very well. It's very sad."

I watched her turn and walk out, closing the door behind her. Julian's body lay motionless in the bed. His eyes closed, his face completely relaxed. A breathing machine pumped air into his lungs. The heart monitor kept a read-out beside his bed.

"Courtney," he said, standing beside me. "If I return to my

body and I don't make it—"

I cut him off. "Julian, you're going to live; you have to live. We're married," I said.

"Listen, Courtney, in case I don't, always remember I love you," he said.

"I love you, too. But, please don't say good-bye," I said to him. "Just wake up." I watched as his image was pulled towards his sleeping body and I was left standing alone. The room was deathly quiet except for the slow steady sound of the breathing machine. I walked to the side of the bed and lifted his hand gently. I stroked his arm. I didn't know what I expected, maybe for him to open his eyes immediately. But he didn't. After about an hour, I pulled a chair up next to his bed. Tears rolled down my face.

"Please wake up," I said. I heard the door open behind me and felt a heavy arm on my shoulder. I turned to look at my dad; his face was full of sorrow.

"I'm sorry, honey," he said. "I'm sorry I didn't believe you."

"It's okay, Dad," I said, choking back tears. Mom was standing next to him, gazing down at Julian's sleeping face. I was sure Mom had told Dad everything she had confessed to me. His face was softer, without a trace of anger in his eyes.

"The nurse allowed us to come in and check on you," Mom said. "I guess we're considered immediate family—you know, mother and father-in-law."

I smiled at her and looked back to Julian. I reached up and

brushed the blonde hair from Julian's forehead. The heart monitor beeped as I noticed the numbers increasing.

I stood, holding his hand tightly in mine. "Julian. Can you hear me?" I asked. I thought I could feel his hand move slightly, but maybe it was just my imagination. I kissed his cheek; the heart monitor once again increased in rhythm. I laid my head against his chest, listening to the sound of his heart. "The heart monitor is giving you away," I said softly, remembering what he had said to me when I laid in the hospital, pretending to sleep. I sat back in the chair, resting my head on the bed, still holding his hand in mine.

"Courtney," Dad said. "You need to eat. Your friends said you haven't eaten since 2:30."

"I'm okay, Dad," I replied, not lifting my head off the sheet. "I want to be here when he wakes up."

Mom kissed the top of my head before they left. I couldn't tell what time it was, but it was obviously late. It was dark when we arrived earlier.

After another hour or so, a nurse came in to check Julian's vitals. "I'm so glad to see he has someone with him now," she said softly. "He's been here all alone."

I smiled at her as she listened to the stethoscope.

"If I were to comment on his status," she said, "I would say he seems to be improving." She looked at the printout of the line graph. "We have never seen an improvement in his heartbeat. It's was always getting weaker." She looked back at me. "There was a point in time when we thought for certain that we were losing him. It lasted about a week. He barely had a heartbeat. His heart is the only thing we've had to go on, the only thing that was keeping him here. The machines have been doing everything else." She looked back down at the readout she held. "But, now, he seems to be getting stronger."

When the nurse left, I leaned closer to Julian. "Please don't leave me," I said. "I want to dance with you again. I want to swing, walk through the woods, to dangle my feet in the lake with you." I waited several minutes. "You promised me you would never leave me," I said. His heart beat increased and I smiled, resting my head back against the mattress.

It was morning when I awoke. My body ached from the position I had fallen asleep in. I lifted my head, imagining my face having creases imprinted from the sheet. I imagined him waking up, seeing me at my worst.

Another nurse came in and checked his vitals. There must have been a shift change; this was a nurse I didn't recognize. She hardly spoke, but I caught her smile as she listened to his heartbeat.

He looked peaceful. I thought about what I would say when he woke up. I would tell him how much he meant to me. I imagined him smiling at me, kissing me deeply. If he would just wake up. Fear settled in suddenly. What if he didn't remember me? What if he didn't remember anything? I tried to imagine what I would say to him then. *"Julian,"* I imagined. *"I'm the one who ran away with you, the one you married; I'm the one you love."* I realized I didn't know what to expect when he woke up, if he woke up.

Mom came through the door. "Your friends are still here, honey, in the waiting room."

I turned to look at her, astonished. "They didn't go back to the hotel? They've been here all night?"

She smiled. "They stayed the entire night. They're worried about you—and Julian."

I felt overwhelmed with joy and gratitude to have such wonderful friends, yet I felt guilty for not telling them to go back to get some sleep. I didn't want to leave his side, but I knew I needed to talk to them. I had so much to say to them, so much to be thankful for.

"Julian," I whispered as I leaned over him. "I'll be back soon." I kissed his cheek softly.

"I'll stay here with him," Mom said. "In case he wakes."

I thanked her as she settled in the chair beside his bed. I turned back to look at them before I slipped through the door. Mom had taken his hand. I hesitated briefly, long enough to hear her tell him he needed to wake up, to be a husband to her daughter. I smiled as a tear fell from my eye.

I found the others in the waiting room. Jordan was sprawled across several cushioned chairs. Beth was sitting on the floor in front of him. Kari and Jess were standing at the vending machine and Tiffany was sipping a cup of coffee at a small round table.

They ran to me and hugged me once they realized I was there.

"Oh, gosh you guys, I'm so sorry," I said, in between sobs. "I should have come out and told you to go back to the hotel."

"Are you kidding?" Tiffany said, shocked. "We wouldn't have left here even if you did tell us to."

Somehow, I knew she was telling the truth. They were probably just as worried about Julian as I was. We pulled chairs up to the small round table and sat down.

"How is he?" Jess asked as she grabbed my hand.

I shook my head. "I don't know. The nurse says she thinks he's improving." I looked into each of their eyes. "He hasn't woken up yet."

"I don't know what you're worried about," Jordan said. I looked at him, confused. A smile came to his lips. "The old woman said there was a man in your future, a man with the initials J.S." Realization hit me. She didn't mean Jordan, she meant Julian. Julian Scott.

"Yeah," Beth agreed. "And you would have a beautiful house and children."

I looked across the table at her, my heartbeat increasing. The old woman did say that. The old woman had been right about everything; I prayed she was right about this. I prayed we were not too late.

"We all decided that we would come to visit you every summer," Kari said.

I hadn't thought about what would happen when he did wake up. Would we return to Kansas? Get a small house in our small town? Would he even want to come to Kansas?

"What do you mean, visit me?" I asked.

Tiffany replied, "Don't you know? Julian's really rich, like filthy rich."

I shook my head.

"Yeah, some official came to speak to the doctor early this morning. The doctor told him that, in fact, there is an heir, a wife." She smiled at me. "He told the official that his wife had control over his estate and control over how long they could keep him on life-support." They were all smiling now. "The doctor told him that, from the looks of things, his wife would never let him go."

I sat quietly for several minutes, soaking this information in. The house in my dreams, could that have been his house? Would we remain in London? The thought excited and scared me at the same time. I could imagine building a life with him here; I could imagine children running in the enormous yard. But I would be so far from my friends, my dear friends who had made this journey with me. A lump crept into my throat and I bit my lip, fighting against more tears.

"Hey, Court," Jordan said, "we didn't mean to upset you."

I shook my head. "You didn't," I said sincerely. "I just hadn't thought about what would happen next. I hadn't thought about leaving all of you."

Jordan got a serious look on his face. "You ran off to marry the man, you nearly died, you were ready to commit suicide back home to be with him, not to mention, running towards a moving train to save him, and now you're worried about leaving us?" He laughed.

"You all mean so much to me," I said.

"Mrs. Scott?" A nurse asked as she stood in the doorway to the intensive care unit.

"Um—Courtney. She's talking to you," Jordan said. I turned, startled. I had never been called that, and it made me smile.

"Yes?" I replied.

"You need to follow me," she said.

Fear ran through me. Had something terrible happened? I jumped up to follow her through the doors.

Life.

Chapter 23

A Life Worth Living

As we approached the intensive care unit, I could see my mother standing in the hallway, clearly shaken. "Mom!" I yelled as I ran to her. "Is he okay? What happened?"

"Oh, Courtney. I was telling him he needed to wake up, he needed to take care of you!" she said frantically. Her body was shaking.

"Mom! Just tell me what's wrong!"

"I was just talking to him, but he began to choke. It was a horrible sound," she said.

I could see the fear in her eyes; I could hear the panic in her voice. I looked towards the door to his room as the doctor walked out. I couldn't find words. I searched his face for any confirmation that Julian was okay. My heart beat so loud I was sure everyone in the hall could hear it.

"Mrs. Scott," the doctor addressed me calmly. He reached out his hand to introduce himself. I slowly placed my hand in his, which felt cool against my sweating palms. "I'm Dr. Stewart," he said with a smile. "I've been caring for your husband for quite some time."

I smiled back weakly. Surely, he wouldn't be smiling at me if something terrible were happening. Yet, I still couldn't find any words to say.

"We've removed your husband's breathing tube. It appears—he wants to breathe on his own now," he said with a smile.

Relief washed over me. "Is he awake?" I asked as my voice cracked.

"Not yet, but I have a feeling it won't be long. We will be moving him to a private room soon. It appears, from how crowded our waiting room has been all night, there are a lot of people who would like to see him. When your husband was first brought in, back in August, we were dealing with a head wound and some superficial injuries. He has baffled our staff, though. He should have woken up, but it was like all the life had left him. He is improving, though, literally overnight." He patted my hand before he reached to shake my mother's hand.

I walked past them into the room. Julian lay peacefully. The heart machine still monitored his heartbeat, but the breathing tube had been removed. He was breathing on his own. I approached his bedside, brushing his hair aside before I kissed his forehead. I was inches from his face, remembering the softness of his lips in my dreams. The breathing tube was gone. I leaned down to softly kiss his lips. I could feel the warmth of his breath.

I hadn't heard the nurse enter. "We're going to move him now," she said, smiling. I stepped back as others came into the room.

"What room?" I asked.

"Room 421," she replied.

I gathered up my purse and started for the door.

"Mrs. Scott?" she said as I reached the doorway. I turned to look at her.

"His belongings are in the closet, if you wouldn't mind taking them, that is."

"Of course." I walked over and opened the closet door. A hospital bag hung from the hook inside.

"His clothes, they were soaked in blood," she said as they turned his bed towards the door. "We threw them out. Everything else is there; his wallet, his pictures, shoes, everything is there in the bag."

"Thank you," I said, as they maneuvered his bed through the doorway. I reached in the bag and pulled out several pictures; all of them were of him and me. We were truly in love, happy. His smile brightened every picture. And I looked so happy, so in love. *I am so in love*, I thought. I could never be without him. I placed the pictures back in the bag and half walked, half ran back to the waiting room where my friends stood, anxiously waiting.

"They're moving him," I said as I entered the room, out of breath. "To a private room."

"Did he wake up?" Jess asked.

"No, not yet, but he is breathing on his own." I smiled at them, tears of joy streaming down my cheeks.

"Oh, Courtney, that's wonderful!" Jess said, hugging me.

"He's in room 421. I want you all to come up, if you want."

"Of course!" Tiffany said. The others looked just as anxious as she did.

We boarded the elevator to the fourth floor. It would be good for him to know they were all there, when he woke up. I prayed that he would remember. Mom had followed the hospital staff up, and she was waiting at the doorway again.

"He's whispering your name," she said to me, quietly. I entered the room, and the others followed behind me.

"Julian," I said softly, "everyone is here." I took his hand in mine.

"Courtney," he whispered, his voice raspy from the breathing tube. My heart skipped a beat at the sound of my name. His eyes moved behind his eyelids and I could feel his fingers tighten around mine.

"I'm here. I'm right here," I said. I watched his eyes slowly open; the brilliant blue reminded me of the ocean again. Tears rolled down my cheeks. He was awake. Memories came flooding back of us professing our love for one another, stepping on the train together, saying "I do". My one true love had awoken. He was not a figment of my imagination, not a lost spirit, he was real. My angel was real. I had shed so many tears on this journey, but the tears that fell from my eyes were full of joy and there wasn't anything I could do to keep them from flowing.

"My wife," he said, as he tried to smile. I leaned across him, my heart beating frantically. My chest swelled with happiness. He remembered. I kissed his lips again. He reached to cup my face in his hands as he had done so many times in my dreams, in my memories. I could feel the warmth of his hands now. He traced a tear down my cheek. "Don't ever say good-bye," he said. I shook my head, tears still streaming down my face. He turned to look at everyone in the room, and his smile widened with recognition.

"Jordan," he said.

"Glad to see you alive," Jordan said with a smile.

"You kissed my wife," he reminded him, smiling back.

"Yeah, about that—sorry," he said.

"It's okay," he tried to laugh. "It was worth it seeing her slap you." Jordan's tan face turned a deep shade of red at the memory.

I looked at Jess, Kari, Tiffany, and Beth. They all had tears in their eyes.

We sat in the hospital room, going over the last several months. He remembered it all. He also remembered the day we met in Paris. He described how beautiful he thought I was. I was sure I was blushing. After several hours, Mom and Dad entered the room. Dad hugged me tightly. He turned to Julian and hesitated before he reached out his hand to shake his.

"Mr. Nacoal," Julian said as he shook Dad's hand. "I suppose it's too late to ask for your daughter's hand in marriage."

I looked up at Dad.

"Well now," he said thoughtfully. "I had always hoped to give my little girl a beautiful wedding, to walk her down the aisle." He looked at Julian for a minute. "Just because you two are already married, doesn't mean the wedding can't take place," he added, smiling at us both.

I stood up and gave my dad a big hug, and he squeezed me tightly in return.

"I suppose we'll be returning home without you this time," he said quietly in my ear.

"Dad, I'll come home to visit soon."

He stroked the back of my hair. "We'll pay for a room at the hotel for as long as you need."

"Mr. Nacoal. If it's possible, I wish you both could stay a while. My place sits just a little ways outside of town. Our place, that is," he added as he took my hand. I looked at Julian. "There's a great deal I would like to discuss with you." I raised my eyebrows in question. "I was hoping to invest in some land, possibly build a nice little home in this quiet little town in Kansas. I find it to be a very friendly place," he said with a smile. "We could have two homes, don't you think?" he said to me, smiling. "We could stay in Kansas while you attend college. I was thinking of enrolling myself."

Dad's face beamed with delight. The thought of his little girl living nearby *and* going to college clearly impressed him.

The nurse opened the door and leaned in. "Mr. Scott, you have some more visitors." She held the door open wide as a well-dressed man and a beautiful brunette woman entered.

"Joseph! Abigail!" Julian exclaimed. Their faces lit up.

"Julian, it's so good to see you doing well—finally. They would not let us in to see you before today. They called a short time ago, and told us you were awake," Joseph said.

"Mr. and Mrs. Nacoal, this is Joseph and Abigail Stanford. They are my friends. They helped to raise me, in fact. They take care of my place; cooking, cleaning, and gardening."

I stood as recognition flooded me. I had met them, several times. Abigail was a wonderful cook and Joseph had always been so kind.

"Miss Courtney!" Abigail said as she took my hands in hers, clearly happy to see me once again.

"Will you be able to stay a bit longer, then?" Julian asked my parents.

"We wouldn't want to impose," Mom said in her most polite tone.

"My in-laws at my home, it's far from imposing. I beg you to stay. If you would feel more comfortable, there is also a guest home on the property as well."

I looked at Mom who seemed very intrigued by the idea. "Dad, stay. Won't you?" I said in the sweetest, childish tone I could muster. This was surely how Kari batted her eyes at her parents to get what she wanted.

"I guess we could, for another week maybe. I'll call the office," he said as he looked over at Mom and smiled.

"Wonderful!" Julian exclaimed. "Joseph and Abigail can show you the way; give you a tour of the place."

I could just imagine the looks on my parent's faces when they pulled up in front of the grand stone home.

"We'll stop back later," Dad said, before he turned to kiss me on the forehead. Mom gave me a hug good-bye and they followed Joseph and Abigail out into the hall. My friends and I were the only ones remaining in the room with Julian now. I relaxed back into the chair next to the bed.

"So," Beth said. "I just can't believe you two are married! I thought, out of all of us, you'd be the last one to get married, Courtney."

"And kids too! You've never even had a pet," Jordan added.

"Wait a minute!" I stopped them. "Julian and I haven't even talked about kids yet!"

"Didn't have to. The old woman predicted it," Jordan shot back as a satisfied grin appeared on his face.

"We'll wait until we're both out of college," Julian said, squeezing my hand. I let out a sigh of relief. "And then, I hope we have a beautiful little girl who looks exactly like her mother."

I imagined a small, blonde headed child gripping her daddy's hand while he showed her the beautiful flowers in the garden.

"Or a handsome little boy with brilliant blue eyes just like his father—who we'll name Tristan," I said, as I leaned over to kiss him.

Julian

August 4 (Three months earlier)

The streets looked much different at 3:00 A.M. The cab drove along in the quietness; the headlights cut through the darkness, leaving me to think only of her and what we were about to do. Her parents didn't approve of our relationship, which left us with no choice.

I thought back to the very first day she came into my life. I watched her from a distance as she carefully studied every painting, and although Jacque could paint a beautiful picture, nothing compared to her. The art exhibit was crowded, and her parents were never far from her. I didn't have enough nerve to approach, but Jacque, being the outgoing friend *and* the artist on display, took it upon himself to embarrass me. He called my name from across the gallery, and suddenly, the only sound I could hear was my own heartbeat thumping loudly against the walls of my chest. Her blonde hair fell in ringlets around her face as she turned to look my way. I could feel my palms begin to get clammy and I knew I had only two choices; make my way to the front door and possibly regret this moment for the rest of my life or follow Jacque's lead and introduce myself. The closer I came, the more beautiful she was. Her blue eyes sparkled like the sky on a cloudless summer day and her warm smile caused my heart to skip.

Jacque introduced her as Courtney, from Kansas. When I took

her hand, her skin was soft as velvet.

"It's nice to meet you, Courtney from Kansas," I said as I held her hand longer than one normally would.

"Hello," she said, her cheeks blushing a bit.

"How long have you been in Paris?"

"My parents and I just arrived yesterday," she replied as she looked, spotted them, then turned back to me quickly.

"Are you enjoying it so far?" I asked.

"Yes, it's better than I expected," she said with a smile.

Jacque had already disappeared into the crowd, and the only two people left on Earth were her and I. We talked about the paintings, how the colors flowed so well together. We talked about her life in Kansas and mine in London. I asked if I could see her again.

Her parents and she were going to the Rodin Museum the following day. I waited from the minute the doors opened until she arrived. Every day we found a way to see each other; every day we fell deeper in love.

But her parents didn't like the idea that I was around. They didn't like the idea that I had checked into a nearby hotel so I could see her as much as possible. The tension and animosity was growing between her and her parents, and I hated that I was the cause of it. I just couldn't stay away from her. She was on my mind every minute of every day, and I couldn't wait until each morning when we would see each other again. We began spending all day together, even secretly taking the tunnel train to London to my home. Joseph and Abigail fell in love with her immediately, reassuring me that my mum would have loved her as well.

****

The cab pulled up in front of the sleeping condo. I searched through the darkness from the backseat for any sign of her, fearing that her parents had caught her trying to leave. We hadn't planned on what we would do in that situation. Should I have the driver leave if she didn't come out? Should I approach the door and ultimately deal with the consequences? Should I just wait for her, hoping she would still find a way to escape the hold they had on her? I knew I couldn't leave. They were to fly back home to Kansas at daybreak. Although it wasn't the best plan, it was the only one we could think of in this short amount of time. Her father made it quite clear from the beginning that we would not be able to see each other once she returned to the states. We were both devastated. Life wasn't worth living if we couldn't be together.

There was a movement by the front bushes, and I strained my eyes in the darkness, my heart beat more rapidly. Excitement and fear grew inside, simultaneously. Fear of something or someone stealing her away from me, and excitement that, quite possibly, we would get away with this and remain together forever.

I opened the cab door, and when the dome light blazed brightly, I slipped from the cab quickly.

"Julian," she whispered from the darkness.

I made my way across the front lawn, and took her into my arms, holding her as close to me as I could, breathing in her scent, and thanking God he had brought her into my life.

"I'm nervous," she said with her head buried into my chest.

"It's not too late to turn back," I reassured her. "I'll wait for you, however long it takes."

"I don't want to turn back," she said, looking up at me. "I want to be with you forever."

"I promise, we'll always be together," I said before kissing her softly. "Nothing will take you away from me; nothing." I traced the outline of her face with my finger, cupped her face in my hands, and kissed her again.

"It's 3:33," she whispered, "we should go now."

I laughed quietly at her superstition. She believed her wishes would come true if she wished on the time when all the numbers were the same on the clock. I loved these things about her; I loved everything about her. After grabbing her two luggage bags, I followed her to the cab, where she slid into the back seat quietly. I handed her the suitcases because putting them in the trunk would surely wake her sleeping parents.

We held each other tightly, thankful we had cleared this first obstacle. She insisted our plan would work, she wished on it several times, at 11:11, at 1:11, and at 2:22. When the cab dropped us off at the train station, we sat close to the building, blending in with the wall, until passengers began to arrive.

We boarded the first train that took us under the channel. Nobody stopped us, no one questioned us. I knew her parents would have awoken already, most likely frantically searching for her and quite possibly in a panic about what they should do. They planned on boarding the plane by 9:00 A.M. We both knew they would come looking for her. If we could just get to London, everything would be fine.

As the train made its way from the tunnel, the bright sunlight flooded through the window, illuminating her perfect skin and making her blonde hair sparkle. I could see the nervousness in her eyes, her beautiful eyes.

"Are you okay?" I asked.

"More than okay," she said, smiling. She snuggled into my side where I held her until the train pulled to a stop at the station. We would need to board another train to take us to the small village near my home, but we had one thing to do before we continued on.

After taking a cab to the register's office, I gripped her hand tightly in mine. We had been planning this for a month, since her father said "under no circumstances would we continue our relationship." I could feel my mother's ring on her finger. When she said "I do," my body flooded with emotions, all wonderful emotions, of course. She was now my wife and even her father couldn't force her to leave.

I hated that things had to be this way, that we were doing this to her parents. We were soul mates, though. We were meant to be together forever. Even Joseph and Abigail said, "a love like yours is rare, cherish it always."

We stood outside the train station, waiting, hoping things would continue to go so smoothly. I held my wife close to me as the crowd outside grew and the next train pulled to a stop.

"Julian," Courtney said as she sifted through her luggage bag and withdrew a hat. "There are officers looking our way."

I scanned the crowd and noticed several officers approaching. "Let's board," I said quickly. With her hand in mine, I worked my way through the crowd. What could they do, really? She was eighteen. Yet, the adrenaline built, the blood running hot through my veins. I didn't want them taking her away from me, so far away. I knew her parents would come to the house eventually, but there we could sit down and talk. She believed, once we were married and back at the house, she could reason with them; we could both reason with them. They would see that I could provide for her.

The crowd was thick. I could feel her hand slipping through mine, but I could see the doors of the train, the one opening we needed to get to. "We're almost there," I said to her. Once we reached the door, a man stopped me before I could climb on board.

"Sir," he said, "are you traveling with a young lady by the name of Courtney Nacoal?" I looked back at Courtney who had pulled the cap further over her eyes.

"Ma'am," he said to Courtney, "Is your name Courtney Nacoal?" I gripped her hand tighter.

"No," she replied quickly. "My last name is Scott."

He studied her for a minute. "Sorry to bother you both; you may board," he said, before he released his arm to allow us to pass. We made our way to our seats and both let out a long sigh of relief. I watched out the window as the officers randomly stopped unsuspecting passengers before they boarded the train. I didn't feel at ease until the train pulled away from the station. Courtney's head rested against my shoulder, and I could tell, when her body relaxed, that she had fallen asleep. I breathed in the scent of her hair, listened to the rhythm of her steady breathing, and imagined myself waking up with her every morning for the rest of my life. She looked so peaceful, so beautiful.

It would be another hour before we would reach the next stop; Joseph and Abigail were probably already there waiting for us. Although my body was telling me I needed to sleep, I couldn't let myself drift off. I watched the doors, prepared to shield her from any other officers that made their way onto the train. As the minutes passed, I knew I needed something with caffeine to keep myself awake.

After gently moving her head, I slid from the seat quietly and made my way towards the front of the coach where I hoped to find a cola of some kind. I looked back once, at the beauty that was still fast asleep where I had left her, before I reached the doorway.

A slight jolt in the train made me stop. I had traveled this train hundreds of times and never felt the train jerk like this. Less than a second had passed before another jolt threw me into the doorway. After regaining my footage, I turned to look at Courtney again, now awake and eyes wide with fear.

"Julian!" she called, her hands gripping tightly to the seat in front of her.

I steadied myself with the seats as I began to make my way back to her. Another jolt threw me forward several feet before the train car began rocking, and the sound of metal against the track drowned out the screams of the frightened passengers. My heart raced as the car moved violently, throwing me from side to side. I could no longer see her, and I began crawling over luggage that littered the aisle. Smoke filled the cabin, and screams rang in my ears. But I had to get to her, to keep her safe.

"Courtney!" I yelled.

"Julian," she answered in a weak voice.

I could see blood trickling down her forehead, and I grabbed her hand, pulling her closer so I could wrap my body around her. "It's going to be okay," I said as I held her tight against my chest. I could feel an intense heat from the flames, could hear the screams of the passengers. I lowered my head to hers and closed my eyes.

"I love you," she said as she gripped me tighter.

"I love you, too, more than life itself," I said to her.

In her hand was our marriage certificate; in my arms was the only person I could ever love. The blood from the gash in her head soaked her blonde hair. "It's almost over, I'll be able to get you some help soon," I said.

She looked up at me, her eyes wide and her cheeks were stained with tears. "Don't leave me," she said.

"I promise, I will never leave you," I replied, knowing this may be the last minutes we had left together.

I could feel the train car lift off the ground as I held her as tight as I could. The smoke was thick and robbing us of air, the screams grew louder, and I felt the train car slam into another car. And then... blackness.